SINFUL LITTLE LIES

BLACKWOOD UNIVERSITY #2

S.J. RYDER

Cover Design by S.J. Ryder

Formatting by S.J. Ryder

AUTHOR'S NOTE

Please keep in mind that this story is a *DARK* romance and it is a complete work of fiction. S.J. Ryder does not condone any of the events that happen throughout the book. The main characters in this book go through traumatic events, which can be found on the Trigger and Content Warning page. Please read all Trigger and Content Warnings before proceeding for the best experience. Your mental health is important and comes first.

Sinful Little Lies is a standalone dark romance book within an interconnected series. Each book will take place in the same universe. There are no cliffhangers and there is a guaranteed happily ever after.

I hope you enjoy the ride,

S.J. Ryder

TRIGGER / CONTENT WARNINGS

Sinful Little Lies is book two of an interconnected-standalone series that includes dark and sexual elements. If you have any trigger warnings, please read through the entirety of the warnings before you read Sinful Little Lies. A full list of triggers is provided below. Consider this a **blanket trigger**, in case there's anything missing from the list.

Anal, Breath Play, Cannibalism, Domestic Abuse, Domestic Violence, Forced Contraception, Forced Drugging, Forced Orgasms, Graphic Murder, Graphic Torture, Graphic Violence, Grief, Infertility, Mention of Parent(s) Leaving, Psuedo-Necrophilia, Racism, Rape (Not between MCs), Suicidal Ideation

DICKTIONARY

Here is the Sinful Little Lies Dicktionary, in case you're wanting to skip, (or skip to), the spicy chapters:

Chapter 3
Chapter 17
Chapter 22
Chapter 24
Chapter 27
Chapter 28
Chapter 32
Chapter 33
Chapter 37
Chapter 43

PLAYLIST

Everywhere I Go - Hollywood Undead
Two Dope Boyz (In A Cadillac) - Outkast
Smoke Two Joints - Sublime
American Horror Show - Snow Wife
The Feels - Labrinth
34+35 - Ariana Grande
Needles - System of a Down
Seduce - Russ, Tamae, Capella Grey
Dragula - Rob Zombie
Die For - Maggie Lindemann
Blood On My Hands - The Used
Good Times - Styles P
Dirty Thoughts - Chloe Adams
Wet Dream - Snow Wife
Soft - Motionless in White
Sweat - Haiden Henderson
I Only Have Eyes For You - The Flamingos
Sex & Palo Santo - Jutes
The Way - Kehlani feat. Chance the Rapper
Drywall - Paris Paloma

Mary Jane - Rick James
Killing in the Name Of - Rage Against the Machine
We Do This Shit - MODSUN feat. DeJLoaf
Rabbit Hole - Qveen Herby
Naked - Amelia Moore
Hold Yuh - Gyptian
Let Em' Know - Bryson Tiller
Wanted - Kehlani
UGOMDN - chlothegod
All The Time - Jeremih, Lil Wayne, Natasha Mosley
Hrs & Hrs - Muni Long
Who's Ya Daddy? - Necro
P*$$Y Fairy (OTW) - Jhené Aiko
Why'd You Only Call Me When You're High? - Arctic Monkeys
Bed Chem - Sabrina Carpenter
About Damn Time - Lizzo
Gangsta - Kehlani
Supernatural - Ariana Grande
Amber - 311

To the jokers, smokers, and midnight tokers who want an intimidating goofball to shower them with love and affection,
May I present to you, Grimm Griswold.

PROLOGUE

Verena - Sophomore Year

THUNDER CRACKS across the sky as lightning rips it open, the blinding light providing a glimpse of the concrete road before me. The way the clouds split and break above me is a faultless imitation of the way my heart fractures in my chest. The rain pelts down, stinging my skin and threatening to drown me with every drop. My bruised and battered flesh aches underneath the onslaught of rainfall as my feet slam into the pavement.

Mascara runs into my eyes and along my cheeks. Whether it's because of the tears streaming down my face or the rain, I don't know. Probably both. My lungs burn as I struggle to breathe. I need to find shelter before someone sees me and questions my current state.

I run like my life depends on it. In some ways, it does.

Using the sleeve of my soaked shirt, I wipe my eyes, trying to clear my vision, as my legs continue carrying me as fast as they can. My ankle rolls on a crack in the pavement and the sharp pain causes my body to fall forward.

"Ow! Fuck!" My voice is hoarse as I whisper-shout, landing on the cement. Bringing my bottom lip between my teeth, I bite down as hard as I can to keep from crying out. I refuse to show weakness right now, to myself or anyone else who happens to be roaming the streets at this hour.

The dry skin splits, and blood coats my tongue, but the pain is nothing compared to the fresh black and blue blanketing my right eye. The impact of the fall only heightens the soreness in my body. Feeling defeated, I stay there for a moment, hands flat against the ground, pebbles digging into my palms and knees. Closing my eyes, I inhale a large breath, desperate for air. My body shakes with effort as I try to calm my racing heart, but it's no use. My heart rattles against my ribcage the same way the thunder shakes the sky.

The adrenaline coursing through my veins is pumping strong. I'm stuck in flight mode. I might have gotten away tonight, but my body knows that it won't last long. I'll be looking that familiar danger in the face soon enough. I hope next time it chooses to fight instead of running away, avoiding the problem yet again. I can't stay, but where will I go?

Exhaling the air from my trembling lips, I push myself up off the ground.

BOOM!

Another crack of thunder shakes the sky, lightning illuminating the ground for me once again. I see traces of blood from where my skin split open on the unforgiving ground. Taking a step forward, I hiss as the pain shoots through my ankle and causes me to stumble in my step. Time is a luxury I don't have right now. Safety, either.

Run.

Ignore the pain.

Don't look back.

I scan the empty streets for signs to point me in the right direction. But between the darkness of the night, my swollen eye, and now my bad ankle, I'm fucking lost. Usually, a night like this would bring me comfort and security. The pitter-patter of rain against my window is almost hypnotic in the way it can calm me and bring serenity to my mind. But currently, despair and survival are the only things I feel.

Instead of the window, it falls against my skin, reminding me of my desperation to get out of the rain and find shelter.

My throbbing ankle threatens to slow me down, but I relent, pushing myself until I come across familiar street signs and buildings. My housing unit isn't far from here, but it would be impossible to sneak in without alerting the girls of my presence. They can't see me like this. They'll ask too many questions.

Covering my face, I hobble past my front door and walk for about another five minutes until my feet are dragging. My breathing is labored, my eyelids heavy, I'm getting weaker and need to rest. But if I stay out here in the piss-pouring rain, in the middle of December no less, my injuries will worsen.

Hypothermia is *not* on my bucket list.

Coming to a stop, I stand at the massive house in front of me. Through my blurry vision, I stare ahead, knowing that I might be making the wrong decision, but the promise of safety beyond the large double doors is too tempting to walk away from. Blinking away the rain, I close the distance between myself and the imposing structure.

Hoping and praying that he's home, I take the remaining strength in my body and pound my fist against the front door.

Within seconds, it flies open, and I'm face to face with Elijah. He doesn't acknowledge me or my condition, thank fuck. Instead, he immediately calls for the man I'm looking for.

He turns the corner and comes into view of the front door. He freezes in his steps as his jaw drops. The look in his eyes starts with confusion, makes its way to anger, and finally settles at concern.

"V, who did this to you?"

1

GRIMM

THOSE BROWN EYES that are usually filled with light stare up at me with such helplessness that my heart cracks a little. The sight of it, paired with V standing here, has my brain short-circuiting. Verena never comes knocking on my door.

"What are you doing here?" I ask, my heart pounding erratically in my chest. Seeing her typically stirs this reaction, but seeing her like *this*, bruised, bloodied, and scared, makes it pound harder.

"I didn't know where else to go, I couldn't go home." She whispers, her eyes never leaving mine. Pain and despair shine through, and I understand how delicate the situation is. I try not to panic, both at her proximity to me and because of her current state. One has my dick threatening to harden in my pants, while the other has me seeing red.

Fully opening the door, I grab the sleeve of her shirt, pulling her inside. I push the door shut and gently lace our fingers together. We make our way upstairs to my room, and I tell her to wait by the door while I rummage through my drawers, looking for clothes that may be small enough to fit her.

Finally landing on some sweats and a t-shirt, I nod my head towards my bathroom and give her my clothing. "Go ahead and change in there. I'm going downstairs to grab some water. Do you need anything else?"

Verena shakes her head no, stepping into the bathroom and closing the door behind her. Taking off downstairs, I swing by the kitchen and get our water. Opening the pantry, I grab crackers in case V decides she's hungry. I don't know what she needs, and I don't think she's too sure of it, either. The best thing for me to do is be there for her in any way I can, and I will.

I'd do anything for her.

Trailing back upstairs, thoughts pass through my head wondering what brought her to my doorstep. *Is she in trouble, or is she going to forget about this tomorrow and expect me to do the same?*

Not going to happen.

Unfortunately, everything Verena does is permanently etched into my brain. We met in middle school, and she's been my purpose for living every day since. This California girl arrived in Devil's Lake and completely stole my heart.

Granted, she hated me and always did her best to steer clear of me. A few years after Emmett and I became friends, her family moved down the block from us. I spent months chasing after her. She never gave me the time of day. In her eyes, I was another young boy with no control over his heart or his dick, and she didn't want any part of that.

My mind wanders to a memory I've held close for so long. It was when I ran into her at a house party. She was a freshman in high school, and I, a sophomore. I knew which guys were cool and which were creeps, and the creeps were eyeing her. She was fresh meat in the depths of the jungle, and when the fresh meat is wearing a blood-red, skin-tight two-piece, it attracts predators from a mile away.

I pulled her into a game of spin the bottle that was happening in the living room, and when it was my turn to go, guess who the bottle landed on? Being the hopeless romantic that I am, I surely thought it was fate. Verena, on the other hand, did not.

She laughed it off saying, "I am *not* kissing you!" She shoved me playfully, but I caught her wrist, and our eyes met. Her breath hitched, and I pulled her body closer to mine. Our eyes never broke contact, and it felt as if we were the only two people in the room.

"Are you guys gonna kiss or what? Let's go!" A whiny voice shouted from across the room. I dropped her wrist and cupped her face, brought her lips to meet mine, and gave her a simple, soft peck. When I pulled back, her face of dissatisfaction told me everything I needed to know.

She wanted more.

Everyone did. There was the beginning of hooting and hollering from douchebag athletes, encouraging us to give them a show. It was anticlimactic. It was safe. I don't know why I didn't take what I wanted and devour her whole when I had the chance. It was absolute hell, giving myself a taste of ambrosia, knowing I'd live the rest of my days without relishing in the heavenly flavor of her lips.

But it showed me something. Eventually, she would be mine. Major trust the process vibes, but I'm trusting it nonetheless.

Besides, she's currently cuffed up with some asshole, Leo. Can't wait for her to ditch that stupid fuck. She's too good for him. He's a complete douche, and I wouldn't be surprised if she came here because the dickwad broke her heart.

Is he the culprit behind her appearance? I wouldn't mind breaking his skull if he was.

V kept her distance after that night at the party. She never had many friends and didn't care about having a social life. Verena had a younger sister, Veronica, who she referred to as Ronnie, and that was enough for her. They were attached at the hip. Two peas in a pod, always giggling and whispering secrets back and forth to each other. It was a breath of fresh air compared to the reality I've known with my own siblings. Seven of us in total, and I hate every single one of them.

In her junior year of high school, Ronnie passed away of cancer, and Verena changed after that. Her chocolate brown hair was dyed to an inky, midnight black. Her shoulder-length curls were stretched and straightened, cascading down her spine. The usually bright wardrobe transformed into edgy and gothic, and her features were accentuated with the darkest liners and shadows possible.

To an outsider, she changed overnight. But I saw her slowly falling apart from afar.

Bringing myself back to the present moment, I feel my growing hard-on make an appearance, and I maneuver the drinks in my hand, freeing one to cover up my excitement towards her presence and the reminder of our moment that prematurely ended.

I sigh and climb the stairs back up to my room. Opening the door, I spot Verena on the small black loveseat next to my window. Apparently, she found my weed because she's taking a hit from my bowl, and when her eyes meet mine, she freezes.

I chuckle, "Make yourself at home. Please." Little does she know how serious I really am. She gives me a small smile and takes a hit, visibly calming down with the inhalation.

Desperate to know the truth behind her visit, I sit and waste no time trying to get answers to my questions.

"So, where were you tonight? At home? Out with some friends?" I ask, hoping her answer has nothing to do with her douchebag boyfriend.

"I was with Leo." She replies after a few moments of hesitation, barely loud enough for me to hear.

My jaw flexes. Was he the one who did this to her? There's no way she would be honest with me, but I need to know the truth. Black and blue bruising appears around her right eye and it seems to have swollen since she arrived. My shirt hangs off of her, baring her neck to me. Ligature marks are forming on her neck.

I try to bite my tongue and figure out the best way to approach this, but the words are rolling out of my mouth before I get the chance to reel them back in. "Did he do this to you? What happened? You can tell me, V. I'm only here to help you. To protect you."

Her eyes widen, and she shakes her head. Clearing her throat, she chuckles and says, "No. No, of course not. He'd never. I tripped. Hit my face on the doorknob. I'm such a klutz."

A fucking doorknob?

"Verena, do you think I'm fucking stupid?" I ask her, my expression deathly serious.

Her jaw drops in shock, and she fumbles over her words. "I- Uh- Grimm you-" She lets out a huff. "I fell. I'm okay. I just drank a little bit too much and got emotional over Ronnie. I'm okay, Grimm. I just miss my sister."

Bringing my hands to my face, I drag them down and shake my head. "You're a bad liar, you know? You really need to work on your facial expressions matching the words that leave your lips. I hear you saying he's innocent, but your eyes are screaming for help and for someone to see through the bullshit. I *am* that someone, Verena. So I'm going to ask you again. If you lie to me, I'll know. Was it Leo who hurt you? Did he leave these marks all over you?"

A tear falls down her face, and she nods her head softly. I'm up and rushing to her side, her arms instantly wrapping around my neck. The scent of cocoa butter and blackberries clouds my senses, and it is all-consuming. My arms envelop her waist, pulling our bodies flush against one another. The feel of her body against mine is unbearable. If I wasn't so concerned for her safety, I'd let my hard-on make a quick appearance.

But this has to end now. Both my hard-on and her relationship.

"You need to leave him, Verena. Let me help you. I can kick his ass. I can kill him. Say the word and I'll do it for you." I beg.

Her head shakes profusely, "No Grimm, please don't. Don't do anything. Leo has this sick and twisted side to him. He's batshit crazy and I do not, under *any* circumstances, want you getting involved with him. Over me, no less."

"He's batshit? Verena, I'm fucking psychotic," I argue. "Absolutely unhinged and certifiably deranged. I do not need safekeeping. I'm here to protect you, not the other way around."

She untangles herself from me and wipes the tears from her face. I bring my hands to her chin and cup her cheeks gently. "I know you've grown used to the darkness. I have too. But you are not safe with Leo and you know it. Go back to him and I will make sure he ends up six feet under." I promise. Kissing her nose, I release her.

Standing, I walk over to my nightstand and grab a pre-roll. I sit back down next to Verena and spark it. We pass the joint until we're high and sleepy, blissful silence filling the room.

Setting the roach in the ashtray, I lean back, letting my head rest on the couch. Her head finds my shoulder and they connect like two perfect puzzle pieces. Made to fit each other and only each other. Shortly after, her breathing evens out, telling me she's fallen asleep. I look down at her, resting and at peace, and feel that twinge in my chest telling me to claim her.

My missing puzzle piece.

My V.

One day, she'll be mine.

2

VERENA

I DON'T UNDERSTAND his need to protect me. We're acquaintances, that's it.

But if that were the case, I wouldn't have come knocking at his door in the middle of the night—*nice one, Rena*.

I'll admit, Grimm is fucking gorgeous. Seeing him round that corner without a shirt practically impregnated me. There's just something about him being muscular and tattooed to the fucking balls–I'm just assuming–that does it for me. He towers over everyone, standing tall at 6'6". Dark, long curls fall to his shoulders and frame that godly jawline of his perfectly. His eyes resemble the color of freshly brewed black coffee. My fucking favorite.

He's the complete opposite of Leo, in more ways than one. Ashy blonde hair, green-eyed Leo. That's who I should be with right now. Sighing, I sit on his couch and wait for Grimm to return with my water. On an inhale, his smell envelops me, sandalwood and sage, clouding my senses.

Examining Grimm's space, I spot his bowl and a grinder. "Oh, thank fuck," I whisper to myself while reaching over to the side table holding my favorite playthings. After dumping the ash into a garbage can, I twist open the grinder and begin to pack a fresh bowl. I take my first hit as the door swings open and Grimm fills its frame.

"Make yourself at home. Please." He says, chuckling. A hint of a smirk creeps across his full lips and grants me access to see those profound dimples and perfect pearly whites.

I gulp, my throat feeling drier than when I was screaming for my life earlier tonight. Reaching for the water, Grimm begins to shoot out questions. I assumed he wouldn't pry, but I guess it's reasonable enough for him to ask what's going on.

I don't want to lie to him, but he can't know the truth. In an attempt to change the subject, I mention Ronnie. Typically, everyone ends the conversation as soon as I bring her name up. No one wants to talk about the little girl who died at such a young age and never got to experience life, because what else is there to say?

Nothing. At least for them. They didn't know her like I did. Having a six-year age difference did zilch to put us on opposing sides. We knew each other better than anyone else. Based on the look he gives me, I should've known better than to try and lie my way out of it with Grimm. He's a people watcher. Studies their body language, their emotions, and facial expressions. He's always been that way, knowing just how to seduce and intimidate everyone with his charm and mysterious nature.

Grimm looks scary on the outside, but underneath all of that muscle and ink, is a big, goofy golden retriever. In our younger years, he was rambunctious and careless. Always running away from the trouble he had caused with Emmett, pranking the neighborhood kids and their parents. It wasn't until I came to Blackwood that I learned of his kind-hearted nature. Somehow he was at every party, that infectious smile plastered on his face, with friends in every crowd, and a line of girls following him, waiting for their turn to get his attention. He thrives on that shit, I swear.

He was always around. Not watching me, but watching *out* for me. I noticed it once at a high school party many years ago. As soon as I walked in, Grimm was pulling me into a game of spin the bottle, making some sort of claim on me. Of course, his bottle spin landed on me and we shared a kiss. One small peck that most likely meant nothing to him, but changed the way I saw him forever. It changed the way outsiders looked at me too. Boys avoided me like the plague after seeing us together. Girls envied me over a boy who wasn't mine to begin with.

The knight-in-shining-armor act doesn't make sense to me. Besides that one night at the party, Grimm and I have barely spoken full sentences to each other. We acknowledge one another with head nods and small smiles so why did I feel the need to run to him and why does he feel obligated to save me?

Where does the need to protect me come from? I couldn't tell ya. But holy shit, does it feel good to be held by him, listened to, and promised that he'd do anything I asked if it granted me protection.

Admittedly, I've thought about what Grimm and I would've been like in another life. Another life where Leo and I didn't exist. Another life where I wasn't so wrecked over losing Ronnie. Another life where I wasn't weak, where I wasn't Verena Losado.

I've stayed up late one too many times, fantasizing about what it'd feel like to be underneath him, his breath fanning my skin and his fingertips tracing along my collarbone. I've dreamt about following each line of every tattoo on his body with my tongue and satiating the hunger that's made a home within me.

I clear my throat, focusing on the present moment. Fantasies are just that. Unrealistic and fleeting. My reality is Leo and we're just going through a rough patch…again. Tonight was just another misunderstanding and I need to sleep it off. The last thing I want is for Grimm to poke around my relationship with Leo and try to be my savior.

We share a joint in silence and it's the most peace I've felt in months. I'm too buzzed to even think about leaving at this point, so my plan is to curl up on this couch and sneak out first thing in the morning while Grimm is asleep. But to my surprise, he doesn't leave my side. Putting out the joint, he drops his head back onto the couch and closes his eyes. The heaviness of my head is too much for me to carry and it connects with his shoulder. His arm snakes around my waist, pulling me in closer.

I shut my eyes, but I'm unable to fully relax because I'm too preoccupied thinking about everything Grimm said tonight and where it's coming from. Is he looking out for me as a long-time friend? Or is it something more?

The most important questions are, where do I go from here? How do I ensure my safety and my freedom?

Tomorrow's another day, and my pestering thoughts are just going to have to wait until then. Tonight, I'm basking in the scent of sandalwood, sage, and bud.

Tonight I'm safe with Grimm.

3

GRIMM

MY FISTS clench and unclench as I walk along campus. It's been a few weeks since that night Verena came to me, looking for help. Seeing the empty couch that next morning buried an ache in my heart that I haven't been able to dig up. Knowing that fucker hurt her, I've been filled with nothing but rage. The need to pummel someone's face grows stronger by the day. I want to see blood spilling, seeping, and soaking into the ground beneath my feet.

Verena deserves so much better. I'd give her heaven and hell if I could. She doesn't understand how truly captivating she is. How is that possible? Only the devil knows. She doesn't shine like the sun. She's not flashy, nor does she demand attention. Instead, she resembles the moon. Quiet, and soft, but she illuminates the darkness around her without even trying.

I've watched her from afar for such a long time, I know her like the back of my hand. This is my chance to prove to her that I'm worthy of even a modicum of her love. I'll be damned if I don't take it.

Pulling out a pre-roll from my back pocket, I spark it and inhale. Letting the weed do its job and put my mind at ease, even if it's only for a little while. After a few hits, I'm feeling nice and turn around to make my way back to the house.

Muffled screams make their way to my ears, stopping me in my tracks. I'm certain that's what they are because of the many times I've pulled the same noises from people. It's debatably one of my favorite sounds. Right next to the sound of assholes choking on their own blood. The thought gives me a rush and my cock jerks beneath my zipper.

Who are we having fun with tonight?

My eyes narrow as I take in the scene in front of me. A girl is being pinned to the side of the darkened house. The guy stands against her, pushing himself into her. His hand covers her mouth as the other one holds her wrists above her head. The tears streaming down her face and the sounds she's emitting tell me it's anything but pleasurable.

"Hey!" I shout as I stalk towards the couple. The man jumps away from her, attempting to shove himself back inside his pants. He tries to snatch the woman by her wrist and run. My height gives me the advantage of reaching him in just a few steps. I near him and grip him by the neck before yanking him back.

I'm vaguely aware of the teary-eyed woman looking at me like I'm her savior and providing me a soft thank you before running into the darkness of the night. But all my focus is on the asshole I've just tossed to the ground. He's a scrawny fuck and easily flies to the concrete. I could probably squash him like a fucking bug if I wanted to. Unfortunately for him, I do.

I *really* fucking do.

He tries to scramble from the ground, but before he can, I'm straddling him. Gripping his hair, I shove his head against the hard asphalt. His skull drops against the concrete with a thud and a scream rips from his throat. Usually, I love these sounds. Cherish them. But I'm outside where anyone can spot me, and I need him to shut the fuck up.

Whipping my pocket knife out of my back pocket, I grip his face and force out his tongue. With a stronghold on the muscle, I press the tip of the blade into the middle of his tongue and apply pressure. The muscle is thick but easily splits under the sharp metal. I chuck his tongue into the darkness, satisfied with the lack of noise he's able to produce.

Lifting his head once more, I slam it back to the ground. I repeat the action until I hear his skull crack and splinter, and his screams fade. Dropping his bloodied head from my grasp, I let it fall to the ground with a thud. My fists clench and unclench at my sides while I stare at him. If I stop now, he'll probably still live.

He doesn't deserve to live. Not for forcing himself on that girl. The image of Verena bruised and bloody, standing at my doorstep, comes to the forefront of my mind. My nostrils flare.

Clench. Unclench.

Fuck it.

I rear my fist back and slam it forward. The sound of cartilage splitting mixes with the crunching of bones beneath my bloody fists. The satisfaction it brings makes me do it again.

And again.

And again.

My knuckles split against his exposed bone and blood sprays up at me, coating my hands and arms. I slam my fist into his face again before dropping my arms to my sides. My chest rises in heavy pants as I stare down at the pile of flesh and bone in front of me. Because that's all that's left. He's unrecognizable and I'm pretty sure I've broken every bone in his face.

I can't stop the psychotic laugh that bubbles up my throat. I stand up and feel pressure against my zipper. "Fuck," I chuckle while adjusting myself. Watching the life leave his eyes went straight to my dick.

What I'd give to whip him out right now and take care of myself here, but I can't risk being seen and his body needs to be discarded. Whipping out my phone, I shoot a quick message telling the Brotherhood's cleanup crew there's an issue that needs their attention and provide them with the address. The best thing about being in the Red Skull Brotherhood would hands down be the ability to get my hands dirty and having someone ready to clean that shit up.

Once I have confirmation that the cleaning crew is on their way, I turn around and head home, whistling. It was a great release, but it won't hold me off for long. Soon, I'll be itching for another kill. A sinister smile creeps across my face as I wonder who will be the next? I wish it could be that fucking prick, Leo, but not yet. I'm taking my time with him.

Until then, anyone else will suffice.

BACK HOME AND in my room, I undress and step into the shower. The hot water runs down my face and body, cleansing the devious act I performed on my night stroll.

My cock twitches thinking about that asshole's bones cracking and splitting, his blood seeping into the ground. I close my eyes and imagine the wetness of the water is the warm liquid leaking out of his cold, pale body.

Wrapping my hand around my shaft, I slowly pump my hand. Nothing gets me turned on like the smell of fresh blood. The only things that could make this moment perfect would be my little monster here with me and if the corpse was Leo instead of whatever dipwad I killed tonight. Blowing out a sigh, my erection grows when Verena's body forms like a holographic image, next to the deceased piece of shit.

She looks up at me then down at the blood, not showing any semblance of fear. Her hands dive into the ruby river and spread it over every inch of displayed skin. She locks eyes with me and crawls on all fours, stopping right when she's at my feet. Her bloody fingers grab my erection and pump my length until I'm hard and thick in her hand.

"How does that feel, Grimm?" She purrs, and I'm putty in her hands. Nodding, I attempt to respond but at that moment she takes me into her mouth, her warm lips wrapping around the tip of my cock. My head falls back as I get closer and closer to my release.

"Oh, shit. Yes, V. Fuck, clean it up for me, baby." I whisper. Grabbing the sides of her head, I lace my fingers through her silky, onyx

hair and push my cock deep into her mouth, hitting the back of her throat. My pace quickens and her blood-covered hands run down my thighs, her long nails gently scratching my skin, talk about a fucking sensory overload.

My balls tighten and spots line my vision. A shiver skirts down my spine and my release spurts out of the tip of my cock. Curses slip from my lips as I snap out of my daydream and reality fades back in.

My heart aches knowing that she's at home or with Leo, and she's hurting. Thoughts run through my mind at one hundred miles per hour and questions of Verena's state, whether or not she's safe, causing the slight relief I grasped to slip away.

Washing myself off, I turn off the water. I dry and dress, then roll up a blunt and smoke it till it's nothing but a nub. The night ahead of me will be a long one. I will come up with a plan and make sure Leo is never able to touch her again. It may take some time, but I'm taking what's mine and there's no stopping me.

4

VERENA

Ten Months Later

"UGH, NO! IT'S ALL WRONG." I huff, throwing my paintbrush on the ground. The first week of my junior year and I already feel like I'm losing my mind.

Why did the introductory assignment for a contemporary art class have to be so frustrating?

Create a piece that shows your personality and passion. The piece must represent who you are as an individual and exhibit at least four principles of art.

I know it's not *actually* that difficult, but every bit of my individuality went out the window after Ronnie died. It's strange, you'd think I would've just grown into something different, but you would be so fucking wrong. Ronnie passed, and I didn't know who I was anymore. I second-guessed everything I did, from the clothing I wore to the air I breathed.

Grief is a bitch and it can choke on the fattest fucking cock there is.

Picking my brush up, I sit up straight and plaster a disingenuous smile on my face. Fake it until you make it, right?

Wrong. So wrong. This painting can't be saved. It's muddy and sad and miserable.

On second thought, this would represent me as an individual and I'm debating on turning in this absolute pile of shit.

"I give up!" I exclaim, admitting defeat and carrying my brushes and paints to clean and store them away. Turning back, my eyes catch one last glance at the monstrosity I created. They roll so hard at the sight, I swear they almost get stuck.

Storming out of the art studio and into the fresh, dewy air, I take three deep breaths before heading out. My phone pings and I reach for it, hoping it's someone, anyone who's willing to provide me with an escape from my unfortunate reality.

ASPEN

Hey babe, RSB party tonight. You in, right?

ME

Abso-fucking-lutely. I was just praying for a stress reliever. Are you...God?

ASPEN

More like Persephone but less Queen of the Underworld. That's your realm. I'm leaning more towards the Goddess of Spring.

ME

Makes total sense. I'll see you back at the house in a bit for pregaming.

ASPEN

Yes ma'am!

OPENING THE FRONT DOOR, I'm met with loud music. No one notices as I close the front door and sneak into my room. I just need a moment to myself before having to put on the mask of Miss Carefree.

It doesn't take long for the patter of footsteps to follow my movements and a familiar voice to speak through the door. "I heard you come in!" Aspen sings as she lightly taps on my door. Fuck. My estimation skills are way off. I thought I had at least two minutes before she noticed I was home. It hadn't even been thirty seconds!

"Hey, I'm hopping in the shower so I'll come find you when I'm ready," I respond, hoping to get her off my tail for just a few more minutes.

"Oh, how perfect! I was just going to suggest a little hotbox sesh before the other girls get home?!" She asks brightly, and how can I say no to that? Aspen is not a stoner. She is not a smoker, toker, or pothead of any kind. Unless it's a special occasion. I'm sure the first RSB house party of the school year equates to a special occasion in her mind.

But I'm afraid she'll see my bruises and ask questions I don't feel like answering. But I never turn her down to smoke, so if I do that now, she'll ask questions, anyway. I need to be smart about this.

"Yeah, I'll roll one up. Meet me in the bathroom in five minutes." I say, making my way to my nightstand. Within a couple of minutes, a new joint is rolled and I'm undressed by the shower. Turning on the water, I step in while it's still cold and call Aspen.

The cold water sends jolts throughout my body, sparking a second wave of energy in me. Goosebumps break out on my skin from head to toe, and it feels as if my muscles go numb. I take choppy deep breaths, trying to calm my racing heart from the slight shock it just went through.

My art project is draining me and things are still a bit rough with Leo. Stress and contusions have taken over my life and cold showers have been proven to help with both, so let's put this bitch to the test.

Aspen and I pass the joint back and forth a couple of times. With each pass, I'm careful to use the same non-bruised arm, mindful not to alarm her of my situation. Shortly after, Aspen taps out, and leaves the bathroom. Smoking the rest of the joint, I put it out in the mini ashtray on the ledge of the shower. Yes, I have an ashtray in the shower. Can't smoke in public areas and the shower isn't all that bad or uncommon. Moving on.

Rinsing my hair once more, I turn off the shower and peek outside the curtain, double-checking that Aspen is gone. I snatch the black towel from the counter, wrapping it around myself before dashing back to my room.

I lock the door, quickly dry my body, and throw on the first outfit I find in my closet. Thank fuck for matching sets, because they make my life a whole lot easier.

It's one of my favorites, a velvety two-piece, pants, and a tank top with a mesh long-sleeve underneath. I slip on my beloved chunky black platform boots. The mesh paired with the tattoos that litter my arms make it harder for my bruises to grab the attention of my peers

Aspen's music booms throughout the house and I feel the vibrations from my room. The blunt helped to calm my nerves and I know she'll be calling me over soon to start drinking. Softly singing along to the music, I sort through my mostly silver accessories, looking for the perfect pieces to match my outfit. Earrings decorate the edge of my ears from diamond studs to miniature weed leaves and simple hoops.

An hour later I emerge from my room, my inky hair is straightened and my makeup is smokey and dark. I look so fucking good, but I wish I felt better. About myself. About my life.

Sighing, I put on yet another fake smile, and walk out into the kitchen area where Aspen is dancing and mixing drinks. "I'm just finishing up our drinks!" She squeals, adding a pineapple wedge to the rim of the glass.

I raise my eyebrows, impressed with her presentation, "Fancy! Thank you!" Her feet lightly pad out of the kitchen and I guzzle down the drink.

"I'm going to get ready with Blair, but we shouldn't be too long. Leave in an hour or so?" She asks, disappearing down the hallway.

"Yep! Sounds good. I'll be here." I say and gulp down the rest of my beverage. The buzz of mixed vices is euphoric and makes life bearable. If only feeling this good was an option all the time.

ANOTHER HOUR PASSES and the girls, including Lorelei, our fourth roommate, finally make their grand entrance into the kitchen. Dressed and ready to go, we take back another shot and get ready to head out.

It's not a long walk to the party, about fifteen minutes later we're rounding the corner, the vibrations of the music shaking the whole block. Blair, our newest roommate, questions who lives here and Lorelei gets her tits in a twist over her lack of knowledge. To be fair, she's been here for a fucking week. I wasn't exactly excited for a new roommate either, but hell, she's quiet and keeps to herself, mostly.

A small pang thumps through my chest as I realize I wasn't as welcoming as I could've been. Should've been. All because of my personal problems that she most certainly was not the cause of.

Be better, V. Don't turn into him.

We enter the house and Aspen and Blair head to the kitchen for more drinks, while Lorelei trails off to go find her prey of the night. I do my best to blend in with the walls, hoping to be noticed by one person and one person only. Stealing glances around the room, I bob my head and sway to the music to not look too awkward. I spot a couple of fellow art students and we discuss the latest project.

That's when I feel *him*.

The hairs on the back of my neck stand tall and goosebumps trail down my arms.

My eyes scan the living area as I try to locate him. And when I do, I wish I didn't.

Grimm. This is his house after all, so I fully anticipated him being here. What I didn't anticipate was seeing a replica of *me* hanging on his arm. Black hair, dark eyes accentuated by thick black liner, the details are there, down to the olive skin tone. I also didn't anticipate the jealousy that shot into my chest when I saw them together, either.

Well then, I guess I'll be ending my night early.

Heading towards the door, I look back for a split second and his eyes catch mine. My feet stop dead in their tracks and I'm unable to move or speak, completely trapped by the hold of his gaze on mine. It feels like everyone else fades away for a moment as we stare at each other. Using the entirety of my strength, I pull my eyes from his and continue weaving through the crowd when a strong hand catches hold of my arm.

Turning around, I see those deep, rich chocolate eyes staring back at me. Eyes that I'm instantly hypnotized by. A beautifully straight smile stretches across his lips, causing dimples to form on either side of his expression. My thighs clench at the sight and I gulp, attempting to regain at least an ounce of my composure.

Damn, he is beautiful.

"Hey V, how was your summer?" He asks. His gravelly voice is like a defibrillator, shocking my heart and sending electric currents throughout my body, reviving me. "I haven't seen you around much. I've been missing you."

Did I hear that right? He misses me?

"It was alright. I've just been working a lot." I respond, unsure of how much detail to provide. That wasn't true. Leo didn't want me working. In his words, he has the means to take care of us, so I don't have to lift a finger. Instead, I spent the majority of time inside his apartment reading, writing, and painting.

Don't get me wrong, I love having so much time to focus on my craft, but at what cost? The inability to be a functioning member of society? It's not ideal, but I know Leo loves me and wants to support me. His way of going about things isn't as gentle as your average person, but no one is perfect and if you love someone, you need to work through those bumps together.

The last year replays through my mind in an instant and a single thought it left within the blackness follows:

How many bumps and bruises do I have to withstand until I'm truly happy with him?

An awkward silence passes between Grimm and I before he speaks. "You look like you could use a distraction. We can ditch these losers and head upstairs. We'll get high off our asses and no one will even notice we're gone."

His hand is still gripping my arm as he tugs me towards the staircase. "I don't know. What about your…friend?" I ask, trying to not be obvious, but it's obvious I'm definitely probing.

His smile seems to grow at my words and for a moment, I wonder if my jealousy was loud and clear. "I don't even know her name. Won't be seeing her again." Grimm chuckles ascending the staircase. He slides his hand to my palm and interlaces our fingers as he guides me to his room.

The ping of my phone draws my attention and when I open the message, my heart sinks.

LEO

Trip got cut short. I'll be back tomorrow afternoon.

My buzz is starting to wear off, causing the reality of life to seep back in, so a distraction of any kind sounds perfect.

5

GRIMM

SHE'S HERE.

I haven't seen her at a party in months. After that night in my room a while back, I hadn't seen or heard from her much. A head nod here, a small wave there. But none of it was enough.

She is here now and I have another chance to be with her. If I didn't already completely fuck it up and turn her off.

Now she's got the wrong fucking idea, seeing me with my arm draped around this girl. I was only with her because I saw a resemblance to Verena, but seeing her right here in front of me, I realize I'm a fucking idiot.

No one comes close to Verena. She's an absolute goddess. Her long, dark hair flows down her back and I can't help but wonder what it would feel like wrapped around my fist. Her big, brown eyes bore into mine and I'd fucking kill someone, myself included, just to change the look on her face.

Our eyes clash before she looks at the girl under my arm and pulls her gaze away. What feels like hours, passes by before she moves again. Towards the front door.

Shit.

She begins to storm out of the house and I stride through the crowded living space to catch up to her. When I do, it doesn't take long for me to convince her to come up and smoke with me.

So far, so good.

V MAKES herself at home on the couch we cuddled on all those months ago. My spine stiffens as I remember I haven't touched it since she left that next morning. Afraid it would lose the blackberry scent that lingered on her skin.

Clearing my throat, I sit at my desk and begin rolling a joint when Verena breaks the silence. "You can still roll that, but can we hit the bong too? That shit looks wild," she asks, giggling and pointing at the four-foot bong collecting dust on my top shelf. Nodding, I finish rolling and tuck the joint behind my ear.

"As you wish." I agree, reaching for the bong and bringing it to the bathroom to fill it with water.

Walking back into the room and towards the couch, I hold up the four-footer and present it to her. "Alright. All clean, the bowl is packed. Anything else you need from me, pretty girl?"

Fuck. *Pretty girl?*

It just slipped out. Being in her presence feels right. Saying it felt right. I clear my throat and continue speaking before she can think about it too much. "Need me to help you light it?"

She nods and positions herself behind the bong, ready to inhale. I light the bowl and pull the piece out when she gives me a thumbs up, telling me she's ready to take the hit.

Inhaling and exhaling, she makes it look so easy. The beauty that radiates from her still shines, but it has been dimmed.

By who or what? That's the million dollar question. One I would do fucking anything to have answered. Something about her is different. She's definitely lost some weight and her face looks more sunken and hollow. Maybe no one else notices her dire need for help, but I'm not like everyone else. I see right through her placating facade.

I see her darkness.

I see her rage.

I see her.

My mind flashes with images of Verena standing over a dead body. We're covered in blood, standing over someone we've killed together. I feel my heart pounding in my chest as she turns to me, blood coating her clothing and skin. She looks like the goddess of death. Destructive and so fucking beautiful. She walks towards me, cupping my cheek, and smearing the blood on my face. Pulling me closer to her, she whispers in my ear, the most heavenly words ever spoken.

"Fuck me, Grimm. Use me until every inch of our bodies has been bathed in their blood."

Verena's coughing snaps me out of my fantasy and immediately, my hand moves to cover the erection tenting my pants. I turn around and fix my situation as I'm walking to grab the grinder. Dumping out the ash, I repack the bowl and hand the lighter to V. "Would you be able to assist me?" I ask, my voice hoarse. Keeping my cool has proven to be way more fucking difficult than it should be.

She nods softly, a smirk appears on her face, but falls as quickly as it arrived. Just a glimmer of that beautiful smile makes my heart pound. The sound fills my ears and I'm afraid it's loud enough for her to hear it.

Fucking hell, Grimm. Relax.

"That was nice, thank you. I feel good," she announces, taking a seat on the couch after my hit of the bong. I hope this means she doesn't want to go back to the party. "Do you mind if we stay up here a little while longer?"

Fuck, yes.

"Yeah, no problem. Same old party happens every weekend. It's not every day that I get to see Verena Losado in the flesh. Only happens once a year as of late." I joke, sounding more spiteful than intended.

Verena's eyes widen slightly, like she's caught off guard. I shake my head as I start to apologize. "I'm sorry V, I didn't mean for it to come out like tha-"

She's holding out her hand, telling me to stop. That smirk creeps onto her face yet again, and she chuckles. "I guess I deserved that one. I'm sorry I've been MIA. This last year threw a lot at me and work was piling up. I've been picking up more shifts recently." She explains, her eyes shifting around the room. Is she…lying?

She sounds like she's been genuinely busy, so I'd like to give her the benefit of the doubt but something isn't right, here. In reality, I'm hoping that means she's been too busy for her boyfriend, too.

I want to ask her about Leo. Are they still together? Has he hurt her since that night? Would she be honest with me if I asked her? Probably not. Sighing, I push the questions to the back of my mind. Unless she brings him up, I need to respect her relationship. No matter how much I want to fucking pummel him for ever hurting a hair on her head in the first place.

Walking over to the couch, I take a seat and her intoxicating scent wafts all around me. That familiar smell of blackberry and cocoa butter fills my senses. My cock jerks in my jeans, wanting to bury itself deep inside of her, never washing her scent off of my skin.

Reaching over, she plucks the joint from behind my ear. If her fucking scent didn't get enough of a reaction out of me, the spark of electricity that flows through me when her fingertips graze my skin surely will. If I wasn't buzzed from the weed filtering through my bloodstream, I would be well beyond fucked from the sheer high she's capable of giving me from a single touch.

My hard-on is making a great, big appearance right now and there is no stopping him this time. It physically hurts to restrain him from stealing the spotlight and ruining my moment, but I think of things like my siblings, my dog, and the fact that Verena is still with her douchebag boyfriend.

That last one calms the little man down with no problem.

Verena holds the joint out to me. "You rolled it, you light it," she says. I stand and bow, emphasizing once again that I will do anything for her, no matter how big or small.

"As you wish."

She giggles at me; the sound making my heart thrash against my chest as it wraps around and squeezes every fucking fiber of my being. She may think I'm joking, but I'm not.

Slipping the joint out of her fingers, I spark it and inhale. We pass the joint back and forth, making small talk. We share what classes we're taking this semester and what our schedules are like. Eventually, we tap out and she stands. She disappears into the bathroom and my heart sinks, knowing the end of our time has come.

Just when she emerges, I reluctantly stand, ready to walk her back downstairs to the party. Instead of heading towards the door, Verena pads over to my bed and flops down on her back. Keeping her gaze fixed on the ceiling, she pats the spot next to her, gesturing for me to join her.

She wants me to lie next to her.

On my bed.

Little guy, please remain calm.

"Have you ever wondered how much life would suck if we had to be sober all the time? Always having to face reality with a clear mind?" She laughs and lets out a heavy sigh. "I could never."

"What reality can't you face sober?" I question, wanting a glimpse into her life, even if it's just a sliver.

She turns her head and looks at me. "You know what I'm talking about. Don't make me say it." Her head moves back to face the ceiling.

My heart aches with the confirmation that Leo is still hurting her. I want to kill him. I *will* kill him. As I'm about to respond, she continues. "I'm pretty sure he would kill me if he knew I was here, but I think there's a part of me that hopes he actually follows through with it and puts me out of my misery..." She pauses for a moment, chewing on her lip before continuing, "I'm sorry. We're supposed to be at a party having fun and I'm holding you hostage upstairs with my sob stories. Let's go back dow-"

"No." I insist, cutting her off.

Verena questions, picking her head up but I cut her off once again. "No? What do you mea-"

"Are you serious, Verena? Did you hear what the fuck you just said? You think I can go and party after you just told me you have a secret death wish just to escape your relationship? I told you once and I'll tell you again. I'll remind you every fucking day if I have to. I will kill him myself, with my bare hands, if you ask me to. The only reason I haven't already is because I don't want you to fucking hate me." I spill out, truth lacing my every word. "He could be dead by the end of the night and the brotherhood would have him cleaned up come sunrise. Say the word, and I'll kill every man on this earth if it makes you feel safer."

Verena lays down and reaches her hand out to me. The second her fingers touch mine, my dick twitches and presses against my zipper. She slowly interlaces our fingers and I'm immediately shifting to prevent my instant hard-on from being exposed.

Fuck, I need to gain some self-control around this woman.

"Thank you for always being here, Grimm. Thank you for not pressuring me to report Leo. Thank you for respecting my decision. Thank you for being a true friend." A sharp pang shoots through my heart at the mention of friendship, but I ignore it. Now is not the time. She begins humming the Golden Girls theme song and I palm my face, making her break into a fit of giggles.

Oh little monster, the things I'd do for you.

I let a smile stretch across my face. Today, I'm a friend but soon, I'll be so much more. I will be the air she breathes and as well as her reason to smile. I will bend and mold myself into whoever she needs me to be, whatever she needs me to do, as long as I can call her mine.

Squeezing her hand, I turn my head and look deep into her eyes, so she knows just how serious I am about her.

"Always. I'll always be here, V."

Always.

6

GRIMM

TWO WEEKS. Fourteen days. Three hundred and thirty-six hours. Twenty thousand, one hundred and sixty minutes.

That's how long it's been since I've seen Verena. She has been radio silent and practically MIA, once again. Every time I think we're getting somewhere, she shuts down and disappears.

This semester, I enrolled in a writing class with the hopes of landing in the same lecture room as her. Unfortunately for me, my luck fucking sucks and the class Verena is in was full, so now I'm in the class after hers. The only writing that I've done so far has been her name, with little hearts around it like a fucking middle schooler.

Verena leaves the classroom every day with a somber look, clutching her books for dear life. The other day, I watched her as she scurried to her next class. Lifting her arm, she tucked a piece of hair behind her ear and the black bell-sleeve slid down, exposing her bruised wrist. Before anyone else managed to notice, she brought her arm back down to her side, pulling on her sleeve for good measure.

At that moment, I realized she doesn't wear dark colors and long layers as a fashion statement. She dresses that way to blend into the background, to hide. Everything is a facade. One big spooky

Halloween mask that's two seconds away from sliding off of her face, revealing the pain that lives underneath it.

The reality of her relationship with Leo tugs at my heartstrings. My mind races with possibilities of what he would do to her if she tried to leave.

I know she needs help. *She* knows she needs help.

Why won't she let me fucking help her? How many times will she knock on my door, bruised and bloodied, with tears streaming down her face before she realizes she's playing with her life?

I refuse to standby and watch Leo suck the life out of V. I'll drain his blood and let her bathe in it, if it means a chance to save her soul, her spirit, her life.

The devil suppressed in me, itches to break free and indulge in some much needed playtime. But I can't, not yet. I need to be cool, at least until Verena gives me the okay to slice Leo into a million tiny fucking pieces.

I'm fucking stressed. I just want my girl safe.

I walk to my nightstand and open the top drawer. Grabbing a pre-roll, I put the tip between my lips, light it up, and inhale.

A few pulls later, I'm feeling pretty good. Puffing my cheeks, I blow out the smoke from my lungs and watch as the hazy cloud floats from my lips, into the surrounding space. The smoke swirls in the air and, for a moment, I swear it crafts the image of Verena's beautiful face.

Maybe I'm just stoned as fuck. My chest shakes as I laugh at the fact I got so high, I started seeing her face in the vapor. Shaking my head, I put out the joint, cutting myself off for now.

Verena's laugh replays in my mind, the sound so angelic and soothing. A smirk creeps across my lips and my dick twitches.

The perfect image of V is ruined by the most recent image I have of her, with black and blue covering her olive skin. My erection immediately softens and instead, my vision turns red.

An idea pops into my head before I can stop it, a huge grin spreading across my face. I'm a fucking genius. I'm up and on my feet, quickly heading to Eli's room to use his printer. He's the only one in this house who finds use of it because of school and whatever weird techy shit he does in his free time.

I don't bother knocking as I swing the door open. My eyes catch on the screens he's sitting in front of and before I can tell what he's looking at, they all go black as they power down. My gaze goes to his as he stares at me with narrowed eyes. I don't let Eli's sour mood bother me, though. I have something too fun planned to let anything kill my vibe.

"Wuddup, baby? Can I use your printer?" I ask while already making my way over to the machine and hooking my phone up to its bluetooth.

"You should learn how to knock, Grimm." He greets me.

"Yeah, yeah. Next time. Sorry, didn't mean to interrupt your super fun cyber-nerd activities," I quip. He doesn't respond, and that's fine by me. The noise of the printer working out the picture is music to my ears.

I tap my foot impatiently as I watch the picture print out. The smug face of Leo slowly inches out of the machine. Disgust turns in my stomach and I clench my teeth while snatching out the paper. The ugly fuck staring back at me makes my blood boil and I can't wait to watch the life drain from his eyes.

My mood sours quickly with the stupid fuck's face in my hands. It takes everything inside of me to not crumple it up in my fist. Without a word, I turn on my heel and stride out of his room, back to mine.

Making my way over to my desk, I grab a thumbtack from the drawer. Taking the tack, I slap Leo's printed face to my wall and stick it through the paper, nailing him to the wall. Stepping back, I tilt my head and wonder in which way I want to live out my fantasy of taking Leo's life.

As I look around the room, my eyes land on the discarded pile of darts, and I smile.

I reach for the red sharpie and start drawing a bullseye on top of his face. Satisfied with my target, I head over to my pile of darts and pick them up. Walking back in line with Leo's ugly ass face, I rear back my arm and swing it forward; the dart embedding into his face and my wall.

I feel some of the tension leave my body as I look at the dart sticking out of his left eye, so I do it again. I toss the darts at his face until I've run out, and a laugh bubbles up in my chest at the sight. Walking forward, I pull them from his photo and laugh harder when I see all the holes littering his face.

"This is so much fun, Leo. Don't you think so?" I ask his photo while walking back to my spot. Pulling my arm back, I go to throw another dart when my phone vibrates inside of my pocket. I drop all the items in my hands and reach for it, hoping it's V who just sent that text.

Looking down at the screen, I suck my teeth and roll my eyes. Nope. Not V. My heart sinks in my stomach and the previous joy I had from puncturing holes into Leo's face diminishes as I look at the text from Lorelei.

AVOID AT ALL COSTS

Hey Grimm, it's been a while… I was wondering if you were busy? Wanna link up tonight? 😉

Gross.

Shivers run through my body, and it feels like a thousand little bugs are running across my skin. My thumbs fly across my keyboard as I respond, hoping I come across as clear as can be.

ME

No thanks, I'm good. Getting a new number, you can delete this one.

It seems sufficient enough. If it were me, I would get the message. I go to her contact and block her number for good measure before tossing my phone onto my bed. Picking up the dart I dropped, I toss it at Leo's face.

It embeds itself into the center of my drawn target, making a sad smile lift my lips.

"Bullseye."

7

VERENA

BALANCING the bags of groceries in my arms, I push the key forward and unlock the apartment door. Walking inside, I kick it shut with my foot before heading toward the kitchen and setting down the grocery bags filled with ingredients.

I start unloading the refrigerated items into Leo's fridge to keep cool until I need them. I move around the kitchen with ease, as I have a hundred times before. His apartment is off campus in a neighboring city, the large windows offering a welcoming view. Walking over to the windows, I stare out at the surrounding busy city. There's a mix of professionals and artists and I hope to make a name for myself among that crowd one day.

Leo says I should focus on a career that'd be more practical than art or writing. Easy to say when he comes from a line of established doctors and physicians. I come from two stuck up wanna-be's who do everything in their power to blend in. Born and raised in Aguadilla, you'd think my parents would show more appreciation and acknowledgement towards our culture. But since they both landed corporate jobs, every ounce of our Puerto Rican heritage has slowly chipped away.

As much as I would love to work a boringly stable job it's just not going to happen. That's not me. It's the same argument I've had with my parents for years. The most irritating thing about Leo, he's like them in more ways than one. Sometimes it feels like he's my third fucking parent.

I'll be moving in here after I graduate. I hope I can find a job nearby, like Leo has mentioned. He's twenty-five and even though I'm only twenty-two, he's constantly reminding me that I should be looking for a job close to "home" since he's made my choice for me.

The thought makes me feel uneasy, but I shove it down. I always thought my first place after college would be my own. We've been together for a while, but that didn't mean we had to live together yet, right?

I mentioned the possibility of getting my own apartment for a while, and Leo immediately shut it down. He wouldn't hear of it. He said there was no reason for me to not be under the same roof as him, yet live in the same town. The only reason he *allows* it now is because I'm on campus, in a house full of girls.

Why wouldn't he trust me to live on my own? The thought swirls in my mind and the reality of the situation is, I've questioned our relationship more times than I can remember. His loyalty has been faulty and I've lost count of the amount of times that pictures of naked women just happen to slip into his phone. But tonight, I don't want to do that. Tonight, I want to relight the spark that was there when we first met.

Not wanting to let my intrusive thoughts ruin my good mood, I head back to the kitchen and start setting up everything I need to make arroz con pollo y tostones. I've been craving the dish for days and when Leo told me to come over tonight, I knew it'd be the perfect opportunity to make it.

THE RICE IS SIMMERING, and the chicken is baked to perfection. The tostones are cut and ready to be fried. I grab a frying pan and place it on the stove, then pour the oil into the middle. Once there's enough, I turn the dial on the stove to low. As I wait for the oil to heat, I grab the salt and an unopened bottle of wine.

The door slams and Leo walks in. I feel the energy in the room change from tranquil to cynical. Just by the way the door was slammed shut, I know I've wound up in the crossfire of a war I had no part in. He rounds the corner and my heart picks up speed, knowing that I'm in a delicate situation and this could go one of two ways.

Bad or very bad, depending on if I respond accordingly. Air gets stuck in my throat as he chucks his keys to the counter and tosses his bag down. He doesn't say anything as he makes his way over to the island behind me.

I turn around and offer him a small smile, but when he sees it, his lip curls in disgust. "Are you not going to ask me what's wrong? You're just going to smile at me like I'm not visibly upset?" he spits and my heart stutters in rhythm.

"I-I'm sorry. Are you okay? What happened?" I stumble out my words while trying to keep the tostones from burning.

A scoff is my response as he shakes his head. "No, Verena. Clearly, I am not okay. I was fucking busy and the ER was overflowing. Ingrid screwed up the charts of three different patients. And-" His nose scrunches as he takes an audible inhale of air, "-what the fuck are you cooking? It smells like absolute shit."

"It's tostones," I say softly, not wanting to somehow piss him off more. "I have some arroz con pollo ready for us, too."

His eyes look up from the food to meet my own. The anger and disdain in his eyes trigger the hairs on the back of my neck to rise. "You're in America, Verena. Speak. Fucking. English," he spits at me, his tone laced with venom.

I swear I feel a part of my heart crack and splinter with every word he says. Not only is he disrespecting my culture, a part of who I am, but he knows how his comments affect me. I've made this meal for him before too, and he liked it, might I add, but I can't say that. I look down at the meal in front of me as I continue to prepare it.

"It's tostones. What else does it look like?" I say back, my voice coming out harder than I intended. I freeze. My eyes snap up to meet him and the look has my lungs seizing. My brain begs me to get the hell out of this house before things get worse, but I can't. My limbs are frozen in place as I stare back at him.

"What the fuck did you just say?" he sneers.

"I- I just meant that I've explained what it is before. I make this dish more than a few times a year for us and we've been together for three years. I'm sorry, I didn't mean to upset you," I reason with him. I don't know when I became such a weak bitch, but I don't want to be on the receiving end of his anger right now, or ever again, for that matter.

"Huh," he responds. "Excuse me for not remembering how many times a year you make your shitty meals. Most of the time, I'm ordering us dinners from high-end restaurants, where the food smells as good as it tastes. I'm not eating that shit. Toss it."

I scoff and turn to face the stove when his hand shoots out and locks around my wrist. The force of his grip has me clenching my teeth together to keep from crying out. "Let me go, Leo. You're hurting me," I beg, while trying to pull my arm back from him.

He yanks me roughly, and my hand slams into the hot pan filled with oil. The bottom of the pan and the popping oil touch my skin, making me scream out in pain while trying to yank my hand out.

"Fuck! Let go!" I shriek, tears spilling from my eyes at the burning pain covering my hand. He grips the back of my neck and shoves my face toward the hot pan. The heat licks at my skin and I squeeze my eyes shut, trying to pull my face back.

"Yell at me again, Verena. I'll shove your fucking face inside this pan the next time you decide to talk to me with that fucking smartass tone. Watch your goddamn mouth." He shoves me closer to draw his words home and popping oil catches on my cheek, making me wince.

He releases me and steps back while I immediately fall to the kitchen floor, cradling my burned hand to my chest. I peer up at him as he stands above me and fear wraps around my heart. "Your cooking fucking sucks. You're nothing more than a pretty face and a hot body. Don't think you can get fucking smart with me, Verena." He picks up the pan, still filled with oil and tostones, and tosses it across the kitchen.

I turn my head to keep it from splattering against my face. The pot clatters to the ground and I flinch at the loud noise of it. "Clean this nasty shit up," he demands before leaving the room. I sit there for a few moments, trying to calm my erratic heart.

The shower turns on and only then do I attempt to move from my spot on the kitchen floor. The normalcy of the routine is the only thing giving me comfort. I allow myself from now until then to sit here and feel sorry for myself. To cry and feel the pain.

I bring my good hand to my eyes and swipe away my tears. Taking a big inhale of air, I exhale and push myself up from the ground. With the food left on the counter, I grab a plate and set it in the microwave for when he comes back.

A voice in my head whispers, clearly on Leo's side.

He was just angry. He had a long day at work. Leo's days are filled with trying to save lives, V. You need to cut him some slack.

But there's another voice that combats it, unable to let Leo and his actions off the hook that easily.

Is it your fault he had a long day or that patient charts were fucked up? No. Was it your fault when he came home last week and forgot to pick up his dry cleaning? It damn sure was not, but you let him take it out on you, nonetheless. These situations are adding up, V. They've been festering inside of your heart and soul. Soon you'll snap. Break the pattern. Break the cycle. Don't let him break you.

Taking a few deep breaths, I grab the cleaning supplies and clean up the mess of my hard work. I head to the spare bathroom to grab the first aid kit I keep under the sink. I'm running low on supplies and I don't understand. I just bought this kit last month. Every new kit that I buy seems to dwindle down faster and faster.

The right side of my brain speaks: *Maybe I should start buying them in bulk.*

Then the left: *Or you should stop letting him hurt you. Tell someone. Get help.*

Sighing, I take out the burn cream and the gauze. With everything done, I can tend to the aching pain pulsing over my hand. Unfortunately, there isn't enough gauze and antibiotics in the world to heal the lacerations marking my heart.

8

VERENA

I'M *awoken by a knocking at the front door. Opening it, I'm met with a broad muscular frame holding a bouquet of blood-red flowers.*

His arm extends and I notice every muscle, vein, and…tattoo? His arm is littered with them. I step back, surveying his other arm and neck. All covered in ink. "For you," he says and his full lips stretch into the most annoyingly perfect smirk. Dimples appear on both sides of his smile and my core instantly clenches. I take the flowers and offer a small thank you, turning to display them in the living room. The man follows me inside and I question it, but not because I'm scared. Because I'm curious.

When I turn to face him, he's sitting on the couch with that devilish smirk on his lips. I can make out dark eyes and matching curls that frame his face. His tongue glides over his lips, wetting them before breaking into another panty-dropping grin. "Come sit. Let's watch a movie," he says, patting the seat directly next to him. The voice is warm, familiar.

But it couldn't be. Could it? "Grimm?" I whisper, anxious to see if he'll respond.

His head turns on a swivel. "Yeah, babe." My mouth drops and my

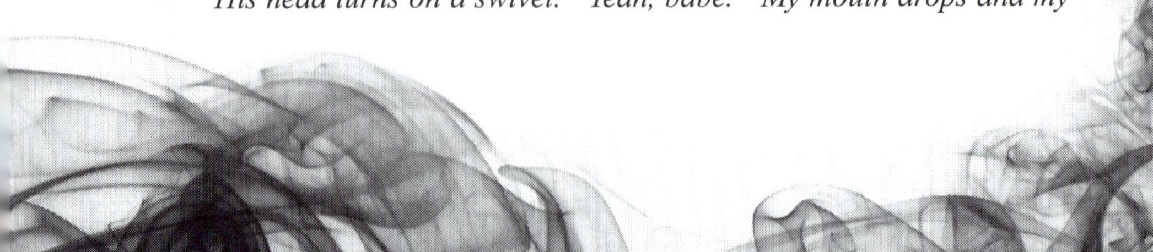

hand swings up to cover it. Babe? Did I die? Where's my handbook for the recently deceased?

Padding over to the couch, I snuggle in next to Grimm, but I'm still weary of his presence. He wraps his arm around me and pulls me in close, the smells of sandalwood and marijuana filling my senses. His finger traced circles on my shoulder, traveled in towards my collarbone, and down the slope of my breast.

I feel my nipples harden through the tiny camisole I had worn to bed last night. His fingertips brush over them and my legs squeeze together, attempting to appease the ache in my core just a smidge. Grimm's hand trails back up my shoulder, grabbing the strap and letting it fall. The other strap follows shortly after and before we've turned on the television, he's nibbling at my neck.

Those soft lips and lingering kisses make my head spin. I'm dizzy off of a few innocent kisses; something must be wrong with me. But being in his arms, feeling his skin on mine, it's just right. This is where I'm supposed to be.

His hands slowly trail down my chest and he hooks a finger in as he pulls it down, my chest spilling out of the top. Grimm massages my breast and pulls at my taut nipple. His voice sounds like smooth whiskey, the heat of his breath intoxicating and sexy.

A pound on the door breaks us out of our intimate moment. Clearing my throat, I fix my cami as Grimm stands to open the door. Before I can see who is on the other side, three gunshots ring aloud. I cover my ears and drop to the ground. What the fuck is going on?!

Grimm's body falls with a heavy thud and I look up to see Leo standing in the doorway. "You thought you could escape me, baby? You're not going anywhere. You'll be with me until the day you die. Until the day I say you've had enough. Until I fucking say so, you are here, with me. Got it, you fucking slut?" With that, his hand rears back and comes towards me at full force, making contact with my face. My face heats from the sting of the smack and I fall back into something wet. Looking down, a sticky sea of red has formed around me and my head whips toward the front door to see Grimm's lifeless body, two holes through him. His forehead and his chest.

A loud sob racks through my body and turns into a scream.

Sitting up in bed, the scream continues as I realize it was all just a dream. Taking slow breaths, I regain my composure. “It was just a fucking nightmare. Thank God it was just a nightmare.” Placing my hand over my heart, I sit in bed and wait for the excruciating pulse to slow.

It's been a few days since Leo and I had an argument. As the days go on, I’m more and more set in my decision to leave him, but how the fuck can I pull that off? The burns littering my hand are still there, but slightly less visible than they were the other night, but present enough to reinforce my choice to leave Leo in the dust and focus on bettering myself. Nonetheless, I'm thankful for the style change I had after Ronnie’s death. Otherwise, everyone would be able to see the marks marring my skin.

And *that* is something I wouldn’t be able to handle. There’d be no lying my way out of this mess.

Despite the fact I’ve grown rather creative over the years at covering up Leo’s abuse, I can’t keep it up forever. I know that.

Leo and I met here at Blackwood. He was a senior and I thought I was the coolest little bitch on the planet for catching the eyes of someone older. But I had to give it to him, Leo put on an Oscar-worthy performance the first year of our relationship. Fancy dinners, lavish vacations, he was never humbled a day in his life and it showed. It didn’t matter to me that he had money, but he chose to spend it on me. He gave me his attention and his time. Something my parents never cared to do.

Even when the money started flowing in, it was spent on a new house, new cars, and cancer treatments. Oh yeah, and a fucking mommy-makeover.

Leo saw my vulnerability fairly easily and took advantage of it. If only I was smart enough to see it back then.

One day, he changed. It was that simple. I don’t know what set him off. I don’t know exactly what I said or did to lose his love. Even with years to think about it, I’m no closer to understanding it than I was on day one.

What I'm unsure of is why I continue to do it. Why do I let him get away with causing me so much physical, mental, and emotional pain?

What the fuck is wrong with me?

I don't know what is being covered in my classes anymore. I sit in the lectures, my mind wandering to a place where pain is forbidden and peace is worshiped.

My art has been affected by the downfall of our relationship. My writing is pretty much non-existent because all of my creativity is being used to make excuses for Leo's actions. These used to be my outlets when things got tough. They were an escape. A peaceful escape where I only needed to depend on myself to fill my canvas or the piece of paper in front of me.

My mental health is taking a turn for the worse and I feel my artistic side slowly slipping with it. I'm so tired of fighting this feeling on my own, but there's nowhere for me to go.

You could go to him. You know you can. He wouldn't deny you. Not like mom and dad will.

I could never run back to California and tell my parents about Leo. I'd just be met with a big, fat, "I told you so." They were so against my choices of coming to Blackwood, to major in the arts, they would find a way to blame everything that's happened on me. For so long, they had pushed me to study business at Stanford and move back to California with them, but it wasn't where my heart was. I was grateful for the distance. Grateful for the chance to express my individuality. Grateful to be able to focus on the things that mattered to me. Art, writing, keeping Ronnie's memory alive, experiencing life for myself and not being someone's accessory or plaything.

Look where the fuck I ended up anyway. Maybe they were right.

Every single night of my senior year of high school, I would pray to whoever would listen and ask them to change the way my parents saw me. They've never appreciated my talents and they sure as hell do not appreciate self-expression. All my mother cares about is preserving her looks, and my father only cares about how much money his businesses bring home.

You'd think cosmetic surgery would be put on the back burner, especially when her ten-year-old was teetering on the brink of death. But there she was, getting her third nose job just two days before Ronnie took her last breath.

The only good thing about my home life was Ronnie. Ronnie was sweet and funny and charismatic. She cared so much about others, which wasn't a common trait that was acquired in our family. She was a vibrant energy with an infectious smile and a big heart. She was my world. Her days in the hospital consisted of her reading endless novels about love and fluffy romances that gave her the happily ever after she yearned for. Living vicariously through those characters gave her strength, hope, simple happiness. When she wasn't reading, she was writing her own happy endings.

So many girls always wish for a big sister to show them the way. They dream of having someone older, cooler, more experienced to walk them through life. A built-in best friend who swaps secrets with you at night after your parents go to sleep. One that covers for you when you sneak out and holds you close after your first heartbreak. A sister who *wants* to share her clothes with you. A sister who wants to share her *time* with you.

I never dreamed of those things because I had Ronnie. I had a little sister with such a fire in her heart. She took care of me. She held my hand through backstabbing friendships and lying teenage boys. Ronnie was my rock.

Whenever I think about her, I try to reminisce on all the good stuff. The late nights filled with gossip and movies, tanning by the pool, and creating a million inside jokes with each other. It was always me and Ronnie. Two sisters against the world.

A few days before her last, we were having a movie marathon, playing card games, and relishing in our time together. Ronnie had leaned on my shoulder and sighed.

"What's up?" I asked, as I turned my head to place a peck on her forehead.

Another sigh, and then, "That movie we watched yesterday. The opening line was, "Bad things happen to good people," and it has been on my mind since the moment I heard it. It's true. I'm only ten and look at me." She covers her face and a small sob follows.

I wrapped my arms around her and spoke lowly in her ear, "I do look at you. Everyday I admire your bravery and strength at such a young age. Everyday I think to myself of how scared you must be, but how well you hide it because you want to seem strong to those around you. You've brought so much light to everyone's lives in the ten short years you've been here."

Ronnie clings to me, "But what about Mom and Dad? I'm nothing but an extra bill."

Rage filled my heart as she spoke, "Ronnie, no. You are amazing. If they can't see that, it is there loss. You have me. I have you. We have each other. It will be us against the world. We'll have our own place, just us, and we can fill every wall from top to bottom with your art. Our favorite movies and shows will run on repeat and we'll stay up late eating garbage and gossiping about the losers we're so done with and the cuties we're moving on to."

Ronnie's smile made a slight reappearance. She shook her head, accepting all that I could give her were promises that were destined to be left unfulfilled.

The sad thing is, I'm pretty sure I believed it more than she did.

She was too good for us. For our family, for this earth. Seeing her deteriorate did a number on me. I was destroyed after her passing and vowed to never let happiness sneak its way into my life. Maybe it's why I find it so hard to leave Leo. I don't want to find my own happiness because it feels unfair. Ronnie should have gotten her happily ever after, too. If that was unattainable in her lifetime, why do I deserve one?

Short answer, I don't.

Besides Ronnie, the only other people I've been able to lean on are Aspen and Lorelei. Granted, Lorelei is a lot like my parents. Her main focus has always been herself and her grades. I know she's under a lot of pressure to prove herself to her parents and compete with her siblings' achievements, but gosh, would it kill her to genuinely care about someone else for five minutes?

Aspen, on the other hand, she's quite possibly the most caring and nurturing soul to exist. She reminds me of Ronnie and I know it's the reason I was drawn to her on the first day of our freshman year at Blackwood.

We have a new roommate this year, Blair. Let's just say I wasn't excited when we were notified that another student would be moving in. Mainly because I didn't want Aspen to spend less time with me, but Blair has been nothing but a sweetheart.

I know I can tell them pretty much anything without fear or judgement, but I don't want to place unnecessary worry in their hearts. A part of me feels like they wouldn't be able to handle the darkness I've succumbed to, and I wouldn't want to put any of them in Leo's violent path of destruction. If anything were to happen to them because of something I said, I would never forgive myself.

There may be one other person I can trust wholeheartedly with my situation. One person strong enough to handle the reality of what I'm going through. One man who possibly knows me better than most and has told me plenty of times that he'd be there to help me, save me.

I've pushed him away more times than I can count, afraid of getting too close. Afraid of blowing my cover. Afraid of realizing sooner that Leo isn't who I should be with.

The least I can do is try and hope for the best.

9

GRIMM

BALANCING the spoon between my teeth while my hands are filled with the snacks for my movie night for one, I walk towards my room. My phone vibrates in my pocket and I adjust the mountain of snacks to fish it out. My dad's contact flashes on my screen. I'm really not in the mood to talk to him, especially when I know he's just going to bug me to come home for family dinner.

Letting his call go to voicemail, I begin heading up to my room, but my feet abruptly stop in their tracks as I pass the door and a knock sounds against the wood.

Grumbling behind the spoon in my mouth, I walk over to the door and try to open it with the hundreds of items in my arms. By the time I get the lock flipped and the door opening, sweat lines my forehead. I could've set down my snacks, but it took me forever to get everything perfectly stacked in my arms and I'm a one trip kind of guy.

When my eyes look out the door to see who it is, my mouth opens and the spoon clatters to the ground as my pile of snacks drop to my feet.

"V?" I say, "What's up? What are you doing here? Is everything okay?" She doesn't respond, rather she pushes past me and rushes straight up the stairs and into my room. My heart was already thrashing wildly in my chest at the sight of her, but her nonresponse makes it pound harder.

My eyes bounce to the pile of goodies on the floor, to my favorite snack of all walking to my room, debating on if I should pick them up first. Coming to the conclusion that Verena usually shows up when she's drowning in her relationship, I leave the snacks behind and rush after her.

The bedroom door is left open and when I step inside, she's in her usual spot. The couch in the corner. Closing the door behind me, I walk over to my bedside table and pluck out a pre-roll. Sparking it up, I take a few hits and sit on the side of my bed, across from the couch and her. "Hello to you too, V. What the fuck's going on?" I question, concern wrapping around every word. I hand her the joint and she takes a couple of hits, her body relaxing the tiniest bit.

She stays silent for a moment before handing it back, her legs bouncing between as she wrings her fingers in her lap. A white bandage is wrapped around her palm. What happened there? Her eyes close and I watch her chest rise as she takes a big inhale of air. When she lets it go, her eyes spring open to meet mine, and she begins to speak.

"He's hurting me Grimm. I know you know and I know you see it, but I've never said it outright to anyone. I can't do it anymore. It feels like I'm suffocating. Every day, I wake up close to tears, questioning why I couldn't just die in my sleep," Verena says, reaching for the joint.

Extending my arm, I hold it out, and she takes a long pull. Exhaling, she continues. "He burned me the other night. Usually after an argument he-"

Immediately, my vision blackens. "Verena, stop. What the fuck do you mean he burned you? How? Tell me, now."

"I was making dinner. Earlier in the day, I was craving tostones, so I made them for us. He had a bad day at work and was angry when he came home. He started spewing all of these horrible insults at me. He said I shouldn't speak Spanish because we live in America; he said the food smelled disgusting and he refused to eat it. My feelings were hurt, and I lashed out. Maybe I shouldn't have, but I was so angry. I love my culture. I love who I am. Is it such a fucking shame I want my partner to be proud of it and embrace it, too?" She stops, her breathing ragged.

Taking another hit, a tear drips down her face and my body reacts without a second thought. My finger reaches her cheek, catching the tear. Our eyes lock and for a moment, there's no one else. Hopefully she came here because she wants my help and she's not going to leave my heart empty and aching.

Eyeing the wrap on her hand, everything clicks. Pointing to it, I ask, "Is that where he burned you, V?" She's silent but when her eyes lock with mine, I see the truth pouring out of them. "I will help you, but I need you to tell me everything." I promise her.

"The tostones were still cooking. He grabbed my wrist and forced it into the pan. The oil so was fucking hot, and I tried to rip my arm away from him, but he's stronger than me. He threw the pan and the oil; the tostones flew everywhere, then ordered for me to clean it all up. He's always breaking plates and glasses, leaving marks on me, but never has he gone to that extreme. "

She looks up at me, nervous for what my reaction will be. With every new confession leaving her mouth, my fists clench tighter and my vision turns darker. I knew it. I knew it this whole fucking time, and I didn't kill him.

It's just as much my fault as it is Leo's and now I'll do everything I can to make it up to her.

"I'm scared, Grimm. I'm scared that if I stay, it'll get worse. The more I think about it, the more I realize that I don't want to die just to escape him. There has to be something I can do to be free of him without living in fear and uncertainty for the rest of my life." Verena confesses.

"What's his address, V?" I ask, trying to keep my voice steady despite the fury thrumming through my veins.

"W-What? No, Grimm. He's crazy and I don't want him to hurt you, too." I can't stop the laugh that bubbles up in my throat and fills the room. He's crazy? Does my little monster even know the person she's sitting across from?

"What you need to understand is that I'm crazier. Now either you'll give me the goddamn address or Eli will," I demand.

"Grimm, you are my only chance at freedom, but there's a difference between you helping me get out of this shit and putting yourself in Leo's line of hellfire." She speaks softly and her voice cracks.

Her only chance at freedom? As shocked as I am to hear the words come from her mouth, I can't argue with them. Damn, right. I'm her best bet at getting away from Leo for good. If only she'd just fucking let me help.

I sigh while looking at her, "Verena, that's the point. That's what I'm trying to do. Let me help you. Please, for five minutes, stop being so fucking stubborn and let me *help* you. You cannot expect me to sit back and watch when I know he's hurting you the way he is."

The frustration overtakes me. The joint went out, but she didn't put it down, so I pluck it from between Verena's fingers and light it up again, pacing. After a few pulls, I turn to face her. The question that burns through my mind every night rises to the surface once again, and I know it may be now or never. I'm so fucking thankful she chooses to come to me time and time again, but if she doesn't let me take care of Leo now, who knows what will happen to her?

Taking a deep breath, I ask, "If you're going to continuously interfere, why do you keep coming to me for help?"

Her lip wobbles and another tear trails down her cheek, dropping onto the couch and soaking into the cushion. Finally, she answers, "Where else would I go, Grimm?"

10

GRIMM

HER WORDS SEND a tsunami of feelings through my chest. Instead of letting her see that, though, I give her a nod.

The moment is fucking interrupted by Mr. Blackwood himself. Emmett wouldn't call if it wasn't important, but why the hell did his little issue have to interfere with my time with V. I remind myself that if he's calling me, it's serious.

I clear my throat and speak, not alerting him of my annoyance at his shitty timing. "What's up?"

He says he's got Braxton fucking Willingham and needs me to help him move his body. All I'm saying is, if he waited until after he died to cut him up and didn't let me in on the fun while the dickhead was still breathing, I'm going to fuck him up for cutting my time short with Verena.

Emmett asks me for a pumpkin carving kit and some chloroform.

Good. Braxton is alive. I can still have some fun tonight.

"Alright. I'll see you in ten." I say before ending the call.

Turning to face Verena, I see her frown deepen. "I have to go help Emmett with something and I'm not sure how long it'll take. Might be an hour or two, so stay here." I tell her.

Placing her hand in mine and lacing our fingers together, she repeats herself. "Where else would I go?" And if that doesn't make my dick stand at attention…

Quickly, I untangle our fingers and gather everything Emmett asked for and more… just in case… I toss the bag over my shoulder and turn back to Verena before heading out. "You're welcome to change into anything you'd find comfortable and lay in my bed. Mi Netflix es tu Netflix," I say with a small nod.

She flashes a soft smile and I feel myself melting *and hardening*. I have to get the fuck out of here.

I meet Emmett behind Verena's place. Will I ever be able to go anywhere that I don't associate with her?

What the douchebag did to piss Emmett off, I haven't got a clue. Maybe it has something to do with Emmett's newest little obsession, Blair. I've caught him gawking over her more times than he'll ever care to admit.

WE ARRIVE at the cemetery and since I've gone long enough without my questions being answered, I ask, "So, what did Braxton do?"

"He touched what's mine," he says with a sneer, his eyes wild like a feral animal.

I shove down the string of questions that build on my tongue. I don't want this fucker to kill me for questioning him. I've got a couple of inches on Emmett, but that doesn't mean shit. My psycho-radar still goes haywire every time he's near.

We come up to the Red Skull Brotherhood entrance and lift the crest to gain access, then carry him to a secluded room towards the back of the underground tunnels. Emmett directs me to set him by the chains on the wall and we sit him upright, binding his hands and neck.

Emmett wakes Braxton up and, even though I don't really know what's going on, I'm excited. I want to see blood spill.

Emmett shows a side of himself I've never seen before. Of course,

I've seen him kill on brotherhood missions, but that's about it. There must be something about this new chick that's turned him into this crazed murderer.

Can I judge? No, I've got a deep love for all things torture and gore. However, I will admit I'm a bit shocked at what's happening in front of me right now.

Emmett whips out the pumpkin carving kit and goes to town on Braxton. He stabs Braxton in the thigh, slices his hands off, and fucking cuts his eyes out of their sockets. But he doesn't stop there.

Braxton won't quit his annoying ass screaming, so Emmett stuffs his fucking hand in his mouth and duck tapes that shit shut. I am in complete and utter awe.

After scooping Braxton's eyes out, he removes the tape, rips his hand out and replaces it with his goddamn eyeballs.

It was genius.

Hiding my boner this entire time has been killing me. I am being edged like a motherfucker tonight and it is absolute torture. My frustrations need to be released ASAP.

I know just the thing to help me.

"Can I cut his head off?" I ask, barely able to contain my excitement.

"You know he's dead, right?" Emmett responds.

"Yeah, but I want to cut his head off." I insist.

He chuckles and shakes his head. "Go for it, Grimm. I'm heading out."

Adjusting himself, I see the hard-on he's also sporting and for a minute, I'm unsure if simply killing Braxton had that effect on him or if it was because he dedicated the kill to Blair.

Either way, we're one and the same and that's why I chose that crazy motherfucker to be my best friend.

My phone vibrates in my back pocket and I really hope it's not my dad trying to reach me again. Pulling it out, I see it's two texts from Verena and my dick twitches.

VERENA

Almost done? Just had to watch Gerald's Game all by myself! Boo.

VERENA

Also, these snacks may or may not be gone by the time you get back and a couple of prerolls ran out of your drawer and lit themselves on fire. I only did my due diligence by smoking them to put out the fire. You're welcome!

A cheesy grin spreads on my face, and I reply quickly. I see Emmett side-eyeing me, and I'm not grinding a single gear he owns tonight.

ME

They're all yours. I've got a different snack in mind. Hope you enjoyed. Be back soon.

I wait and listen as Emmett's steps retreat. I dig into my backpack for a sharpie. Opening the cap, I tilt my head and look at Braxton's carved face. A laugh bursts out of me at the sight of him. I gotta hand it to him. Emmett's one creative fucker. I love when his artistic side shines through.

Taking the marker, I start to write a word on his forehead. When the name, "Leo", in red sharpie is reflected back at me, a sigh of contentment leaves my lips. I've been itching to spill some blood recently and with everything that's been happening between him and Verena, the urge has only intensified.

Stepping back over to my bag, I pull a knife out and twirl it between my fingers while staring down at Braxton's carved face. Looking down at the masterpiece Emmett made, thoughts of how I plan to take care of Leo fill my mind. One by one, I carve the three letters into Braxton's forehead; with the blood dripping down his face, the smell causes my dick to push itself against my zipper, begging to be set free.

I want to plan something special. Something that gives my little monster the revenge that she deserves. I want her to be a part of it, too. I've always seen the darkness buried deep inside of V.

I noticed it before she changed her hair and clothes to match the pit of her soul. I know when I end Leo, when I make him scream and beg for his worthless life, she'll want to be there.

My cock throbs at the idea of V covered in blood and taking the final stab into Leo's worthless heart. At being the one who ends his life. Regardless, there is nothing I wouldn't do for her.

If she asked for the world, I would burn every inch of this planet and rebuild it to showcase all of her desires from the ash. There's not a single person I wouldn't kill, a single thing I wouldn't do, for my Verena.

With the thought of her thrumming through my veins and the need to please her even stronger, I go into my bag and dig around for the clay wire cutters. They're a little different from the typical version. Stronger and thicker wire attaches to two handles. I modified them to meet my needs and they always get the job done.

Lifting the wire and lining it up with his neck, I began to saw diagonally through the skin. Blood gushes out as the muscles and tendons split and give way to the wire. My eyes catch on the sight of Leo's name carved in his forehead and I saw faster.

Blood sprays out when I nick the artery and makes my grip loosen on the handle, but I keep going. By the time I get to the opposite side from which I've started and his head has dropped to the side, hanging on by a thin piece of skin left, I finish sawing through.

His head falls to the floor with a wet thud by my feet. His sunken holes for eyes stare up at me and the blood is splattered along the name in sharpie. Not wanting to see it anymore, I bring my foot back and kick it forward, sending his head across the room.

The head lands perfectly between two of the torchlights on the wall, making me bark out a laugh while throwing my hands in the air. "Goal, motherfucker!" I shout into the empty room, my laughter echoing off the walls. That was fucking awesome.

Reaching down, I adjust my hard cock. The blood on my fingers wipes off on my pants and I twitch against my zipper in response. The thrill of killing, of the blood on my hands, mixed with the knowledge that my little monster is at my house, in my bed, because she came to *me,* has me rock fucking solid.

I need to head back. Now. Before I use the blood coating my hands as lube to jerk off to thoughts of the vixen in my bed. I make quick work of packing up all the tools Emmett and I used before throwing my bag on my back and making my way back home.

GENTLY, I turn the knob of the front door and tiptoe inside the foyer. I slip off my shoes and climb the stairs to my room, hoping V is fast asleep. It's late and I really don't want to explain why I'm covered in blood right now.

I open the door and peek my head in. The light from the television shines on her face and a pang hits my chest. She looks angelic, relaxed.

To think she's so fucking stubborn when she's awake is the biggest contradictory known to mankind. But now that I know the severity of her situation, it makes sense why she keeps her guard up and her circle small.

Her worries and anxieties show on her face like a tell-all documentary. She thinks she does a good job of hiding them, but I can read her like a book. But when she's asleep, my precious little lady looks nothing but peaceful. My mind floods with questions of why that is.

Does she always look this delicate when she's sleeping? Is she sleeping this good because she's under my covers, surrounded by my scent?

Slipping into the room, I close the door behind me gently and beeline to the bathroom. I undress and stuff the bloody clothes and shoes into a trash bag. A nice shower is what I need to calm down my mind and the raging boner that hasn't subsided in the slightest.

I finish my shower and dress, then slide into the bed next to her. I urge my dick to not spring up and ruin this moment. Her sweet scent of blackberry and cocoa butter fills my nostrils as I inhale. Her back is to me, so I take the risk of leaning down and placing a soft kiss on the top of her head.

My lips press against her hair and my heart thrashes in my chest. The touch is innocent, yet my throbbing cock begs to differ. Forcing myself to remove my lips from her head, I lay down on my side and face her back.

I reach down to adjust myself so I can try to find sleep when the bed moves and my eyes shoot upward to look at V as she rolls over and scoots closer to me. She pulls her body into mine, nestling her head under my jaw and curling herself around me. It doesn't matter how hard I try to stop it; my cock jerks and I'm sure I cum a little in my pants at the fact she just willingly--even if it was unconsciously–snuggled into me.

Not wanting to wake her up in the horror that she'll realize she's cuddling me and back away or worse, fucking leave again, I stay still. I don't move a muscle regardless of the pain in my shoulder with my arm halfway to my aching dick. I just close my eyes as my heart threatens to burst through my chest and fall asleep with her warmth wrapped around me and a soft smile on my face.

11

VERENA

A FEW DAYS have passed and I've successfully dodged all of Leo's calls and texts. I haven't spoken to him and as much as I want to keep it that way; I know he'll come looking for me sooner or later.

The idea of whether or not I should leave him has been tossed around in my head since the abuse started. But lately, it's been on my mind more frequently. Logically, I know I should. And part of me wants to, but a larger part of me is scared.

Scared of his reaction. Of what he'll do to me in retaliation.

Do I really want to find out?

Will I *survive* if I try to leave him? Will I survive if I *stay?*

If death is the only way out, then hopefully once I'm six feet under, I can finally rest in fucking peace.

Sighing, I get out of bed and head to the kitchen to make some coffee. My phone pings and I open it, checking the notification that just came through.

Oh, fuck. My period is late.

He cannot know that my period is late. Leo doesn't want kids. He loves nothing more than to be selfish with his possessions, especially his money. Where he used to dish it out on fancy dinners and wines,

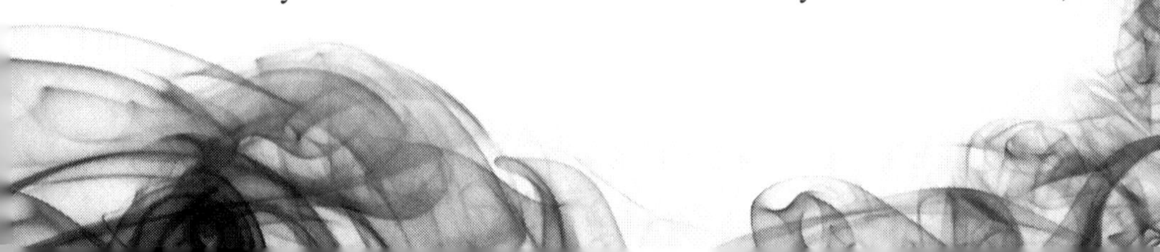

now I can't even ask him for so much as an extra twenty dollars for groceries. Spending his hard earned check on useless shit is his specialty; he'd win a gold medal in that Olympic category. And after everything that he's put me through, having his babies is not something that's on my bucket list.

Clicking on the notification, the app opens up to show me that I am not one or two days late, but five. *Five* fucking days.

The room starts spinning and my vision blurs slightly. I grab onto the doorframe to steady myself, and bile rises in my throat. Grabbing the small trash can by the door, I hover over it and release the contents of last night's dinner into it, the putrid smell filling the room.

I dart to my bathroom and rinse out my mouth, then dig in the cabinets underneath the sink. "Fuck. Where is it?! I saw it here just last week!" I whisper-scream, careful not to wake up the other girls. I rummage through haircare products and makeup just to come up empty.

"Fuck!" I hiss under my breath, afraid of what this may mean for my future.

It's the asscrack of dawn and no stores are open yet, not to mention the trek to the store and back would make me late for class. A lightbulb goes off in my head and I'm racing to grab my slippers, keys, and phone. I always keep an extra test at Leo's apartment. It's hidden in the guest bathroom, stored in the first-aid kit. Checking the time, I know he's at the halfway point of his shift and should be at work for a few more hours. The good thing about knowing his schedule, I can avoid running into him at a time like this.

TWISTING the key into the lock, I quietly enter Leo's place. Out of habit, I remove my shoes and make a beeline towards the guest bathroom.

Whipping open the cabinet doors, I spot the first-aid kit and swipe it from its place. I dump out the contents and reach for the pink box as soon as my eyes find it. Ripping open the box, I sit and begin to pee on the stick.

Popping the cap back on, I lean over and place the test on the sink. I remain seated for a minute, my leg bouncing at a quickened pace. I glance over at the test to see if the results are in, even though it's only been about twenty seconds. When I see that there is in fact no result yet, I rub my sweaty palms down over my pants while blowing out a puff of air.

A few minutes pass by and my patience is wearing thin. I reach for the test and close my eyes, afraid of seeing a positive sign on the little screen in front of me. After taking a deep breath and saying a silent prayer to whoever's listening, I slowly open one eye and see the bright blue horizontal line.

Negative. I'm not pregnant. Thank fucking God. Letting out a sigh of relief, I place the test back on the sink and run my hands through my hair, repeating the phrase to myself until my heart rate slows. *I'm not pregnant. The test is negative.*

I've been under a lot of stress recently, so it makes sense as to why I'm a few days late and continuing to worry about it won't help my situation. I turn on the cold water and splash my face in hopes of settling my nerves. Reaching over to grab a towel to dry my face, I stiffen when I hear the front door close.

He's not supposed to be home for at least another four hours. How am I supposed to get out of here without him seeing me? Crouching down, I scramble to put away the contents of the first-aid kit. Shoving the kit back into place, I stand and turn. The sight I'm met with has me freezing in place.

"I thought I heard someone in here. Where have you been?" Leo questions, stretching his neck to see what I'm doing. "Is that a first-aid kit? Did something happen? What's going on, babe? Where have you been?" He asks again.

I need an excuse. Quick.

"Uh, we ran out of tampons and my period should be coming soon, so I came to grab some." I reply nervously.

He steps into the doorframe and surveys the bathroom, his eyes landing on the pregnancy test box, then shifting to the test on the counter. His eyes meet mine again and I see the usual anger I know all too well within them. How could I miss the fucking box. I'm so stupid. He knows I'm lying.

Fuck.

Leo leans down, his face inches from mine. His breath fans my face and a lump forms in my throat.

"You mean to tell me that you disappear on me for fucking days with no explanation and you come back for *tampons*?" he says, his voice gravelly. "Verena, one day you will be my wife and I will not tolerate being lied to. Don't even think about lying your way out of this. Tell me now. Where were you and why is there a pregnancy test on my sink?"

Sighing, I reply with the same answer as always, hoping my lies will help me once more. "I'm sorry baby, this semester has been kicking my ass. I needed a few days to catch up on my assignments. My creativity has been slacking and my art is suffering the consequences. The stress affected my period, so I just wanted to rule out a pregnancy." Little does he know, he's the sole reason for my stress and anxiety.

He turns on his heel and storms out of the room. My brows furrow in confusion, but I sigh a breath of relief. Turning around, I pick up the box and test, disposing of them. Leo rushes into the bathroom and grabs my arm, spinning me towards him and pinning me to the wall. "Leo, what the hell?" I ask in surprise, my eyes widening when he roughly grabs a hold of my face.

"Well, I'm not taking any fucking chances. You disappeared for days. Who knows what or *who* you were doing. I can see it all over your face. You're fucking lying. Open up and swallow, bitch," Leo sneers.

His grip on my face tightens as he attempts to force my lips apart.

Once there's an opening, a pill is dropped in my mouth and his hands are on me. The right hand wraps around my throat while his other hand covers my mouth and nose. "I want to feel you swallow it. You will not breathe and you will not leave, until you do."

My adrenaline is pumping, and my nerves are shot. Giving in, I reluctantly swallow the emergency contraceptive pill. Only when he feels the pill slide down my throat does he remove his hand from my face, but his grip around my neck tightens.

"Never fucking lie to me again. Should there be a next time, I won't extend such kindness and grace, Verena." With that, he releases my neck and rears his hand back. Leo musters up all of his strength and sends his fist flying straight into my stomach.

Once.

Twice.

Three fucking times.

Grabbing the back of my neck, he pulls me to the sink and slams my face onto the counter. My head throbs in pain and I yelp, pushing against his hand to put space between my body and the counter. He's too strong, and he sends me straight into the marble a second time. Bending down, he growls in my ear, "You are mine. You do as I say and stay in your fucking place. You don't want to find out what will happen if you choose otherwise."

Tears form in my eyes because I know what's coming next. It isn't enough for him just to hurt me. He needs to piss on his territory like a fucking dog. He releases my neck and shoves down my pajama shorts. I hear the scuffle of his scrubs being pushed down, and he slams into me without warning.

"Leo, please no," I cry, unable to handle his brutal force any longer. My voice is faint, but it needs to be heard. "Please, I'm sorry, Leo. It won't happen again!"

His fists wrap around my hair, pulling up my torso until I can see his reflection in the mirror. He grunts and groans, a wicked smile spreading across his lips. "Damn right, it won't. Try that shit again and I will fucking kill you." With one final thrust, he releases inside of me.

Tucking himself back into his scrubs, I slowly push off the counter and begin to walk away. He snatches my wrist, bringing his face just inches from mine. His finger traces my cheek and jawline. "I love you, Verena. I just want us to be happy. I want the best for you, and that's me."

Isn't it funny how the ones who claim to love you are the ones who hurt you the most?

"That's hard to believe when you just shoved a fucking Plan B down my throat after you saw the test was negative." I deadpan.

A devilish chuckle leaves his mouth and his eyes bore into mine. "That smartass mouth of yours is what gets you into trouble, you know that? If for once in your life you could just shut the fuck up instead of making some sarcastic, bitchy comment, we'd all enjoy life a little bit more."

I throw my head back and laugh.

I'm so *fucking* tired of being his plaything. I won't allow myself to be for a moment longer. This is my opportunity to leave. This ends here. Now.

Throwing my hands out, I yell, "Okay, so I will make things a lot easier for the both of us. We're done, Leo. I'll come back for my stuff tomorrow." Turning on my heels, I head to the front door to put on my slippers. Footsteps sound from behind me, and I turn to see Leo barreling toward me, his arms up and reaching out. I open my mouth to speak, but his hands wrap around my neck and he slams my back into his front door.

His grip tightens around my neck and my vision begins to blur. My hands fly up to his wrists, digging my nails into his skin, but he won't let up. Tighter and tighter, he squeezes, dizziness overtaking me. My knees give out, and it isn't until then that Leo loosens his grasp around my neck.

My body falls to the floor with a hard thud and a piercing tone sounds throughout the room.

"Fuck!" I hear Leo yell, and slowly my vision comes back. His phone is to his ear, and a man is frantically rambling on the other line.

"Alright. I'm on my way." He ends the call and shoves the device back into his pocket.

Leo runs his fingers through his hair in frustration and I start to think of how I'm going to make it out of here. Surely he won't just leave me with the choice of staying or leaving. I really do belong to him now. Now and forever.

I close my eyes and slow my breathing, hoping he doesn't notice that I'm still conscious. He paces around the living room, mumbling to himself about what to do with me.

"Shit. You should've just let the bitch go, Leo," he says to himself.

His footsteps retreat and he's gone for only a few minutes, but it feels like hours. The sooner he leaves, the sooner I can plan my escape.

Hearing his footsteps get closer, I try not to let my body tighten. He leans over and I feel a poke in my neck.

Fuck this shit.

I try my hardest not to react and remain relaxed, but he just fucking drugged me. How the hell am I supposed to break free now?

He scoops me up from the ground and carries me into his bedroom, placing me on his bed. Then stalks out of the door, shutting it behind him.

That wouldn't have been the worst scenario, but a moment later, the click of the lock reverberates in my ears.

My stomach sinks at the realization that I'm stuck here. Is this kidnapping? Of course, the prick of all fucking pricks would leave me locked in his bedroom. Rolling my eyes, I pat my pockets in search of my phone. My hand grazes my back pocket.

Bingo.

Bringing the phone up to my face, the light shines in my eyes and my vision begins to fade.

Shit. I need to be quick about this. I need help and only one person comes to mind. The only one who can truly set me free.

Opening the text thread, I see our messages from the last night we spent together. I woke up in his bed, surrounded by his scent, and draped in his arms. It felt so right and every moment without him since then has been complete and total agony.

As much as I hate to admit it, I fucking need him.

My eyes begin to flutter closed, but I manage to reach him before sleep overcomes me.

ME

Drops Location

I'M HERE. HELP.

12

GRIMM

THE DOORBELL RINGS and I rush down the stairs to answer it. Eli was already heading toward the door, but I barrel past him, knocking him in the shoulder.

"Hey fucker! Watch where you're going, you ass," Eli yells, but I don't pay him any mind as I whip the door open and scan our porch.

Nothing but a black envelope sits on our doorstep. Fuck. This wasn't what I was hoping for.

My vision was more along the lines of Verena standing on my doorstep, eager to hop into my bed and release all of our sexual frustrations on each other. But, nope. Just a fucking letter explaining our next assignment.

If it's not Verena, at least it's an opportunity to take out my pent-up exasperations on someone who deserves it.

Usually, Eli takes care of the planning. Emmett and Jaden initiate our takedowns and I come in for the execution. Picking up the envelope, I shut the door and walk down the hall to Eli's room and bang my fist against the wood. "Yo! Send me the details for the assignment we have tonight."

Slipping the letter under the door, I head upstairs to get ready and ponder what lengths of barbarity I'm willing to go to tonight.

I'M DOWNSTAIRS in the kitchen, pouring myself a glass of whiskey, thinking about none other than V. I wonder if she's okay, if Leo has tried something again.

But mostly, and I know it's selfish and fucked up, I can't stop wondering if she's stopped to think about me.

The rest of the guys trickle into the kitchen and sit at the island, pulling me from my thoughts. Emmett is the first to speak. "Grimm, you're going to fucking love this."

My eyes shoot up and a grin spreads on my face. "Yeah, I better. The monster wants to come out and play. Who's the prick we're knocking off the hit list?" I ask, turning to Eli.

"Tonight's mission is a bit different from our normal feat. A woman. A powerful one at that. Her name is Mallorie Mavros," he responds. He flips it open and pulls out a small portrait along with a piece of plain white paper. Holding up the picture, Eli begins to explain our assignment for the night.

"Mallorie has ties with the black market. A lady who likes lethal weapons. She started dealing with smaller blades like daggers and trench knives. More recently, she's been dipping her toes in the deep sea waters of firearms. The Brotherhood was looking to purchase some of these exclusive weapons from her inventory. Long story short, she fucked us over. She asked for a fifty-thousand dollar advance for the weapons and went radio silent for almost four months. Ms. Mavros resurfaced again at a motel near Ramsey about two weeks ago. She hasn't tried to contact us once. We've got eyes on her, but it's on us to either get the money or take her out."

I let out an unexpected laugh. "Ramsey? Why would she choose a hiding spot twenty minutes away from us? Is she trying to be slick, moving right under our noses, or is she really back to fix things?"

Eli shrugs, "I haven't read her journal, dude. I don't fucking know. Simply telling you what I *do* know. I tried to do some digging and found that her parents bought a house in Ramsey, secluded from the rest of the suburbs. Those that spotted her at the motel, followed her to the house. Jaden and I cross-checked the address with the eyes we have on her and it's a match. Looks like she's there alone, so we'll leave in a couple of hours." He states, tapping the island and walking out of the kitchen.

I lock eyes with Jaden, his typically charming grin has disappeared from his face. "I don't kill women. Those are against my rules of morality," he says, shaking his head.

Chuckling, I sip on my whiskey, "You don't have any rules of morality, moron."

As he walks by, Jaden clunks the back of my head with his hand. "Yeah, I do. Women. Children. They don't die."

Nodding, Emmett joins in. "Then you better hope she's got the money to save her ass. Not like you'd be the one to off her, anyway. We all know Grimm wouldn't be generous to give one of us his kill. Don't sweat it." Jaden sucks his teeth and retreats to his room, slamming the door behind him.

Sighing, I down the rest of my drink and immediately pour another one, repeating the process. Emmett rests his hand on my shoulder and pats. "Whoa, just a few weeks ago we were in this very spot and you were telling me to chill out with my drinking. You good?" He asks, his brows furrowing.

I nod. "Yeah I'm alright. Family stuff. It's complicated."

Giving me another pat on the back, he walks out of the kitchen, leaving me alone.

I don't know what's worse. The silence around me or the voices that fill my head when I'm alone telling me to reach out to Verena and make sure she's okay. I don't care about the weapons or the killing. The Brotherhood and these dumb assignments. They used to give me such an adrenaline rush. But there's nothing like the rush I get from being in the same vicinity as V. I'd much rather be in her company instead of doing dirty work for The Elders.

A sinking feeling settles in my stomach. Maybe I shouldn't go. It would be good for me to stay back in case Verena came by and needed me, I mean, a place to stay.

Even though I know it's really not possible, I can't help but wish my plans for the night were different.

I feel it. I feel it with every pump of my heart.

Something isn't right.

A FEW HOURS LATER, we're parked outside of an enormous white brick house, onyx lining every trim. There's a light on upstairs, but the rest of the house is blanketed in complete darkness.

We get out of the car and the guys start walking to the house. I pop the trunk, removing my bag and throwing it over my shoulder. Gently, I close the trunk, then jog to catch up with the guys.

As we come up to the residence, I let my intentions be known. "Alright. In and out. I don't want to be here all night." I look around and their faces are twisted and confused.

"Since when don't you enjoy this stuff? What the fuck is going on with you?" Jaden asks.

"Nothing. I'm just tired. Let's go," I answer, pushing past them and stopping at the door. I stand in silence while patiently waiting for Eli to work his handy magic. Within ten seconds, the front lock is picked. The less time this takes, the better.

Reaching in my waistband, I pull out my gun and step into the foyer. I tiptoe into the house with Jaden behind me and together we scan the sitting room and bathrooms, while Eli and Emmett scope out the kitchen and dining room.

We meet again in the foyer in front of a massive staircase, and Emmett flashes a grin and a smile. "All good!" he whispers excitedly.

I nod and Emmett points up, letting everyone know where to go from here. Slowly, we file up the stairs and around the banister. At the end of the hall, a door is open and light pours out of the room. A laugh breaks out and Emmett's hand goes up, signaling us to freeze.

It wasn't a feminine laugh. That was a man. Irritated, I turn to Eli and whisper, "You said she was alone. Who is that?"

He side-eyes me, not up for my attitude. "I said it *looked* like she was alone, dipshit. It was an assumption. Or is that too big of a word for you to comprehend?"

Emmett turns, giving his gun to Jaden and flicks us both on the nose. "Both of you stop it. Right now. It doesn't matter who is here. There's enough of us to take care of it." Focusing on me, he speaks again. "In and out, right?"

"Yeah," I agree, lifting up my gun and heading towards the room.

Faintly, I hear someone behind me ask, "Grimm, what the hell are you doing?"

Unfortunately, I've got tunnel vision; the only thing I see is the dim light of the room. So I'm going in and ending this shit.

I walk into the room and Mallorie has some Johnny Bravo knockoff underneath her. Raising my gun, I squeeze the trigger, letting a bullet fly through the ceiling and alert them of my presence. They jolt and scramble to cover themselves.

"Who the fuck are you?!" Johnny shouts at me; his blonde coiffed hair puts a grimace on my face and it is too hard to contain my composure.

I laugh. "I could be your friend and give you some pointers. Or I could be your worst fucking nightmare and make the remainder of your life absolute hell. The choice is yours."

Mallorie cuts in. "This is *my* house and I have a right to know what the fuck you think you're doing in it!"

Slowly nodding my head, I answer. "You're right. Ms. Marvos is it? Mallorie?"

"Well…who's asking?" she responds cautiously. Her porcelain skin turns paler than before and I see her icy eyes dilate from where I'm standing.

I fire another round, the bullet just grazing her arm. She yelps in pain, blood trickling down her arm. It isn't until then that Johnny finally decides to be useful, and jumps in front of Mallorie.

"Answer me!" I yell, irritated that this is already taking longer than I wanted it to. My mind flickers back to Verena; images of her snuggled in my blanket flash through my mind and I want nothing more than to go home to her.

"You are in debt to The Red Skull Brotherhood. Whether it's money, weapons, or your lives, we're taking it. Hell, I'd be fine with snagging all three." I'm met with silence. Mallorie glances at the man, telling him something with her eyes.

He doesn't spare her a look, so she spits out a confession. "It wasn't me. I didn't take the money; it was him. It was Zachary! Please, don't hurt me. He works for my father, I was only doing what was asked of m-"

She's cut off mid sentence because of the bullet I put through her head. Mallorie lays motionless at the foot of the bed, crimson pouring out, turning her platinum hair into a bright red.

Zach starts screaming his head off, and I really do not have time for this.

Bang!

Bang!

Two more shots are fired, blaring throughout the room. Mr. Zachary screams out in pain, dropping to his knees.

Looking behind me, I see Emmett with his gun pointed at Zach's feet. Giving him an acknowledging nod, I return the gun to my waistband and walk over to our guy.

We got him.

I grab his neck and rear my fist back. Driving it forward, it connects with his nose and there's a satisfying crunch. Blood sprays out, covering my fist and his face, and it looks fucking beautiful. He falls to the floor cradling his face.

Grabbing his arms, I drag him up and over to a chair. I signal the guys to tie him up, but only Eli and Emmett step forward. Jaden shakes his head and leaves the room.

Pussy.

Letting my bag slip off my arm and drop at my feet, I flash my newest victim a big, toothy grin. Excitement pumps through my veins and my cock twitches at the prospect of getting to bust this motherfucker up. It's about damn time!

"Anyone else need to excuse themselves?" I ask the guys and they both flip me off. I return the gesture before they turn and leave the room.

"Hurry up, we'll be downstairs," Eli says.

Reaching into my bag, I pull out the photo I printed before heading here. Leo's ugly ass face greets me and I clench my jaw to refrain from squeezing and crumpling the photo in my fists.

"You see, Zachary, I don't care *why* The Brotherhood wants you dead. All I care about is being the executioner. That big guy that just fucked up your feet? That was Emmett. Looks like a sweetie-pie, but is a fucking psychopath. I've been learning a lot from him lately about tapping into my inner demons and letting my monster come out to play. It's fun, I'll show you."

Grabbing the strap of my backpack, I drag it across the floor to where he's tied up in the chair. I crouch down in front of him and shove my hand inside to grab a cloth and the container of pins I had brought with me.

I wrap the cloth around his mouth and shove it between his teeth for good measure. He screams behind his gag and I look up and smile at him. "What was that? You think I should play some music?" I ask. Slapping his cheek twice, I dig around in my bag for a speaker.

"That was such a great idea, Zach," I say, while pulling my phone from my pocket and opening up my music app. My playlist, *Grimm's Greatest Hits*, begins to play, and I set the device down as *Two Dope Boyz (In a Cadillac)* by Outkast fills the room.

Lifting the photo up to Zach's face, I can't fight the smile that splits my cheeks. Without tearing my eyes away from the sight in front of me, I reach down and snatch a pin from the container. The pins prick my fingers with the sharp points but I don't care. I'm so fucking excited right now.

Zachary attempts to scream once more, the gag doing its job to silence him. With the picture of Leo's face pressed against him, I take the first pin and push it through the paper at the top of his forehead. The sound of the paper being punctured before the skin breaks around the sharp point fills my ears. With a single pin at the top of his forehead holding the photo of Leo, I let go and it hangs beautifully.

"Much better." I smile. A small amount of crimson begins to leak from where the pin is, turning the white paper red. I hum along to the song while reaching for more pins. Continuing to push them through the paper and into his skin, I insert pins all along the perimeter of the paper.

Blood leaks from each tack hole through the black-and-white photo and satisfaction skirts down my spine. It looks perfect.

I just wish it was the real fucking thing.

With Zach's face covered by Leo's photograph, I grab some scissors and cut down the center of his shirt.

I rummage in my bag once more for the right tool. When my fingers graze the thin knife, I smile. The skinny, long knife is perfect for what I have planned.

I pull out the tool and turn it, letting the blade reflect the light. The clean surface shows my reflection and the big smile that fills my face.

Walking back over to my latest victim, I twirl the knife in my hand. "I've taken an interest in darts recently, you know? I've found that it's pretty satisfying watching that sharp point burrow into the target." He whimpers at my words, the tears that pour from his eyes wet the paper I have pinned to his face.

I press the tip of the knife between his collarbones and create my very own dartboard on Zachary's chest. Blood drips down his skin in a beautiful pattern.

I'm crouched down to ensure I create the perfect bullseye and my eyes lift up to his. "Perfect." I smile while standing back to my full height. I tilt my head and look over my handy work.

My hands twitch by my sides and my cock aches for blood. I grab my darts and give myself enough room to let them soar.

Just as I'm getting ready to throw the first dart, the song changes and the melody of my favorite song fills the room, drowning out Zach's cries.

"Zachary-y-y-y!" I singsong. "This is my favorite song! It's like the torture gods knew the fun was about to start." I can't dance for fucking shit, but I don't care. I shimmy and shake my ass while singing along to *Everywhere I Go* by Hollywood Undead.

Getting lost in the haze of the bloodlust. Forgetting about everything that threatens to fall apart. Distracting my mind from the girl that I want so fucking bad but can't seem to catch. No matter if I try to help her, save her, I won't be enough for her. After Leo, she needs a prince charming, and that is just not me.

I'm a monster. But I know she is too.

Bringing my attention back to the dance party, I throw my ass in a circle. "Hey Zachy, do you like my dance moves?" I toss over my shoulder. When he doesn't respond, I straighten back to my full height, and without hesitation, fling the dart right at his chest. The sharp front disappears into his skin.

That gets me a response. His muffled scream behind the gag and paper echoes around the room and my lips split into a grin. I know he can't really see me, but if he can whimper he can say a simple, "Yes, Grimm, you dance beautifully. Teach me your ways."

"What was that?" I cup my hand over my ear. "I didn't hear you. Was that a no?" I grab a dart from the ground and toss it hard at the carved target in his chest.

His screams turn into grunts as he loses more blood. Soon his grunts turn to silence, but I'm not done with him just yet.

My heart pumps harder as every dart impales itself into his skin.

"How about a little game of she loves me, she loves me not?" I ask. Knowing I'm not going to get a response, I throw the dart and watch as it plants into the skin.

"She loves me."

I throw another one.

"She loves me not."

And another one.

"She loves me."

And another one.

"She loves me not."

My lips spread, showcasing all of my teeth as I smile at my latest victim. Looking at the last dart sticking out of the center of the makeshift dart board, I pump my fist up.

"Bullseye. She fucking loves me."

I'll happily take my delusions and let them burrow inside my heart. Wiping my bloody hands down on my pants, I reach into my pocket to pull out my phone. I'm pulling up my messaging app to notify The Brotherhood's cleaning crew that their presence is needed, when my fingers pause on the screen.

My blood turns to ice and I feel my heart stop as I stare down at the message on the screen.

VERENA

Drops Location

VERENA

I'M HERE. HELP.

13

GRIMM

WITH MY HEART hammering against my chest, I bolt downstairs and rush to Eli.

"Can you do you techy shit on your phone or do you need a laptop?" I rush out. My voice sounds far away, as if I'm not the one speaking.

"Yeah, my phone works fine. What do you need?" Eli questions, already whipping his phone out, loading up his system.

I turn the device and show him Verena's text message. "That address; we need to go there now. Hack into their cameras. See if there's any movement around the house. We need to leave."

My vision turns red. I knew something wasn't right. *Fuck.* I hope I'm not too late. I can't be. The one time she flat-out asked for my help and I wasn't there because I was too busy fucking around with a human dartboard.

"FUCK!" I shout. Bolting out the front door, I hear footsteps behind me and shoot out a command. "Call Barron, have him send someone to clean this up."

"Grimm, you need to breathe. She's okay. We'll get you to her. I promise." Emmett tries to soothe my anger but it does absolutely noth-

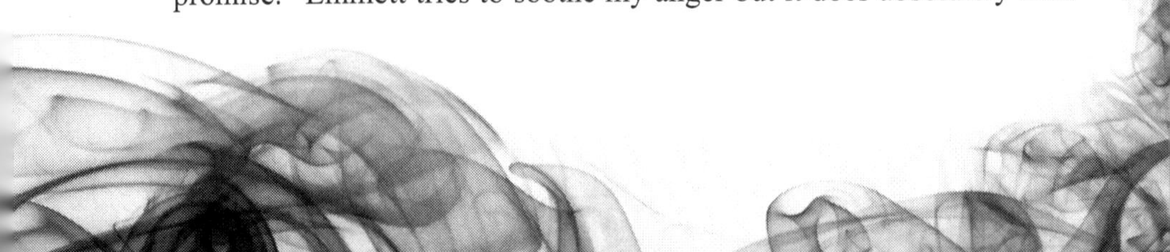

ing. Why would Verena call for help if it wasn't because of fucking Leo? I'm itching to paint my skin red with his blood.

"Let's go," is all I let out, before darting to the car.

I don't care about the blood splattered along my skin or staining my clothes. I don't care that someone could see me. I only care about one thing right now and that's getting to Verena.

Climbing into the car, the guys follow and I practically speed off before their doors are closed. The speedometer climbs at a fast rate. I whip in and out of traffic, never slowing down from the steady hundreds as I zip towards the address on my phone. I know how dangerous it is riding like this, that I could die in a split second, but with the way my heart slams in my chest and the fear that etches itself into my soul I'm certain that will kill me first, if anything.

That if Verena was hurt in an unfixable way, I would take this death over that one.

SHOWING UP TO THE APARTMENT, I find a fire escape and jump up, beginning my ascension to Leo's apartment. It's a three-story building and Leo is on the second floor. I had Eli confirm the details on the way here. With those cyber nerd skills, he secured Leo's door number, making my job that much easier. The cameras were clear. We had seen Leo leave a few minutes before Verena had texted me.

What did you do, you little shit?

Looking for the door number Eli gave me, I stop when I reach apartment eight. Of course his apartment number would be one of the most unlucky numbers. Standing in front of the door, I didn't stop to think about how I would get inside.

"V?" I call through the door, hoping she'll hear me and respond. When I'm met with silence my etched panic spikes again. Banging my shoulder against the door, I do it again and again until it becomes loose on its hinges. Pain radiates through my shoulder blades but I don't let up.

I lift my foot and kick my boot into it as hard as I can until the door breaks and I'm rushing my way inside. "Verena!" I shout, running through the apartment while trying to find her. Panic bubbles up in my throat, making me feel like I'm choking for air as I rush down the hall trying to find her.

Dots of blood trickle along the floor of the apartment and I barrel through every room trying to find her. The last door is locked and I don't let a single cohesive thought run through my brain before I'm pounding my body against the door to get it open.

"VERE-" My words die when my eyes catch on to the bruised and bloodied body laying in a bed. "Fuck. Fuck, fuck, FUCK!" I rush over to her, crouching down to her still body. As I bring my hand to her neck, I pray to a god I don't believe in, as my fingers press against where her pulse should flutter through.

"Please. Please don't take her from me," I whisper, bargaining with the man who many have and failed to get through too. I promise him, and myself, that if he lets her live, if I feel that pretty pulse against my fingers, I'll rid the world of evil in all forms.

I hold my breath and wait for what feels like hours until the faint bump of her pulse drums against my fingertips. "Shit," I curse. It comes out choked and cracked, a lump forming in my throat with emotions.

"I got you, baby," I whisper, my voice still cracking despite how hard I try to shove down the feelings flowing through me. It doesn't matter if she can't hear me, I have to be strong for her. I gently reach under her and lift her in my arms.

Her limp body moves easily for me as I carry her from the apartment and down the steps to where the car is. Jaden is the first one to jump out of the backseat and speak to me.

"What the hell is going on, Grimm? Is that Verena? Is she okay?" He steps away from the door to make room for us. I bend down into the car, being extremely careful with my movements.

"Just drive!" I order. Jaden sits in the driver's seat and peels out, bringing us back to the house.

IT'S BEEN a few days since I found Verena unconscious in Leo's apartment. I've spent the last seventy-two hours relentlessly catering to her. We called in the RSB doctor, Dr. Josiah.

He said Verena suffered a minor concussion and needed plenty of rest. Headaches were going to follow and so would some confusion, disorientation, and some slight irritation about the fact that she'll be stuck by my side until further notice. Dr. Josiah ran blood tests on Verena, checking for pregnancy and diseases. They all came up negative, but he did find something strange in her blood.

In addition to being knocked-out cold, she was drugged. Leo had poisoned her with Strychnine, a substance used to render patients unconscious. A little goes a long way and there was about two milligrams injected into her system. An amount lethal enough to end her life. I know he's in the medical field and I totally didn't expect more from his dumbass, but did he really think he'd never get caught?

I'm going to *love* delivering this reality check.

Dr. Josiah is positive that Verena will make a full recovery, but there's no guarantee she'll be able to recollect that trauma. He said the physical abuse was evident and we shouldn't rule out sexual abuse. "I can perform a SAFE exam, but that's up to Miss. Losado if she wants to go through with it. Ask her about it when she wakes up. If she chooses to do so, let me know within forty-eight hours." Dr. Josiah informed me.

My words get stuck in my throat at the possibility that Leo took advantage of V while she was unconscious and drugged. I want nothing more than to hurt him the same way he hurt her, or worse. The pure anger and rage that floods through my veins threaten to overtake my mind. He'll get what's coming to him. I'll make sure of it. Not a single inch of his body will be left untouched by the time I'm finished with him.

Justice will be hers. It'll be my life's mission until my dying day.

Aspen, Verena's roommate, blew up her phone when Verena went radio silent for the last few days. I informed her about what had happened as far as her concussion, but demanded she keep it under wraps. V doesn't want anyone in her business, especially when it comes to Leo and his habit of taking his frustrations out on her physically. No one knew except for me, I'm sure. She would want to keep it that way and I am nothing if not the one who fulfills her every wish.

Emmett has been a bit quiet, too. I'm not sure if he's been tied up in between Blair's legs or if Verena's situation traumatized him. But for all that we've done together, you'd think it'd be just another day at Blackwood for him.

Eli has been a huge help. He's stepped up in a way so out of his character, I'd kiss him if he wasn't such a detached soul. Every moment I haven't been able to be by V's side, he agreed to remain with her when I needed to be elsewhere and alert me when she finally woke up.

Every free moment I have is dedicated to crafting the perfect hell for when I takedown Leo. His days are numbered.

I'm coming for him.

14

GRIMM

STANDING OUTSIDE THE AUTOMATIC DOORS, I watch as nurses, doctors, and technicians weave between each other, floating from room to room. They are completely oblivious to the danger standing just outside their door. Luckily for them, I'm here for one dipshit, and one dipshit only.

My fists clench and unclench at my sides, my jaw grinding. I take a step forward and my eyes narrow, tunnel-vision taking over. The smell of nitrile gloves and antiseptic fill the hospital as I make my way through.

My boots are silent against the tiled floors. A rag doused in chloroform sits snugly in my back pocket. Heads turn in my direction, looking at me warily. My 6'6" frame usually draws the eyes of others anyway, paired with the promise of death that gleams in my eyes.

Except everyone here is too busy to give a fuck about my reasoning for being here. There's only one person who should be afraid of me right now, and as my eyes lock on the back of his head, I watch his spine stiffen. He slowly turns to look at me from over his shoulder. My steps don't falter as we lock eyes and I continue straight toward him.

His head snaps forward as he walks in the opposite direction. He can try to avoid me all he wants, but it's not happening. I'm here for vengeance. I'm here for V, my little monster.

Leo continues to push his little legs to bring him to the safety of his office, but I make long strides and catch up, the predator ready and hungry to pounce on its prey.

He slides into his office and attempts to shut the door, but I'm faster and shove my foot between the door and its frame. My right hand catches the door, aiding my foot, and I make eye contact with Leo. A sinister grin spreads across my face. *Oh, I cannot wait to fuck him up.*

I push him inside and slam the door, locking it, before I turn to face Leo. He puffs out his chest and puts on his best tough guy act when addressing me. "What do you want, man? Give it up, Grimmothy. You don't think I see the way you look at her? As good as you *think* you are at hiding your true feelings, you fucking suck at it. There's plenty of puss for you at Blackwood. Do you have to relentlessly go after Verena? Yeah, I hear things. People talk. But you know what? She doesn't want you. I can offer her everything she needs in life. She's happy. We're happy. Move on and get out of her life."

"Alright, first of all, fuck you. That's not my name. Secondly, you offer her nothing but misery and pain. You think no one knows about what you've done to her? I've seen the bruises, Leo. She called *me* for help because you made her your fucking punching bag. You're done. From this moment on, you'll wish I gave you the privilege of a quick death," I say, my tone low and menacing.

"Now are you going to walk out of this building without causing a scene or do I need to kill you right here, right now, hm?" My eyebrows raise, the skin on my forehead wrinkling. Leo sighs and picks up his briefcase. He walks out of his office and through the front doors of the building, towards my car. He reaches for the backdoor, but I stop him and open the passenger seat.

He thinks I'm a fucking idiot. That I don't expect him to retaliate after I practically kidnapped him. Yeah, right. Like I'd take my chances.

Once he's seated, I grab his briefcase and move it to the backseat. Now behind him, I rip the chloroform cloth out of my back pocket and wrap my arm around the head of the seat, covering his mouth and nose. Within a few seconds, he's knocked out cold. "How do *you* like being drugged, dipshit? Not so fun, is it?" I scoff and shut the passenger side door.

TWENTY MINUTES LATER, we arrive at Blackwood Cemetery and I grab all my necessities from the car, including Leo. Hoisted over my shoulder, I carry him to join a good old friend of mine. Braxton, the Pumpkin King.

Hooks hang from the ceiling and my dick twitches just at the thought of Leo dangling from them, the hooks piercing his skin with blood dripping down his body.

That image of Verena pops into my mind again. Covered in crimson, she looks so beautiful, unlike anything I've ever seen before.

Leo begins to stir, bringing me out of my daydream. I make quick work of tying his wrists behind his back with rope. Once his hands are secured, I hoist him up and align his shoulder blades with the hooks on the ceiling. With force, the hooks rip through his skin and embed themselves underneath his flesh. I wiggle his body to make sure he's not going anywhere, and he lets out a roar.

"Oh! You're awake, awesome! You can hang out with my friend Braxton until I get back," I say enthusiastically.

Leo's eyes flutter open and he groans groggily. His head falls from side to side until, finally, he's able to focus on the rotting corpse in front of him.

"WHAT THE FUCK?! LET ME GO NOW, GRIMM!" he screams at the top of his lungs. I laugh. Did he think using his sorry excuse of a stern voice was going to make me obey him?

My phone pings and I whip it out. A text from Eli came through.

ELI

Verena woke up.

My heart beats with a primitive urge to see my girl as I say, "I have to run. Don't go too far!" Chuckling, I rear my fist backward and slam it into his stomach, for good measure, of course.

As good as it feels to take out my frustrations out on Leo, my heart begins to beat fiercely in my chest. Verena is awake. She can tell us what happened.

We can end him once and for all. Together.

15

VERENA

I WAKE up in a dark room, confused. My body aches and my mind is clouded, groggy. I attempt to push myself out of bed, but the room starts spinning. Lying back down, I close my eyes and try to jog my memory.

What the fuck happened? Where the hell am I?

There's a squeak on the floorboard and I turn to see a hooded figure sitting in the corner of the room. Before I can say anything, it speaks. "Hey, don't freak out. No sudden movements. It's Eli. Grimm is on his way."

My head hurts too much to question him any further. Rolling over gently, I shut my eyes and bury my face into a pillow, breathing in that familiar, musky scent. My eyes shoot open at the realization. I'm in Grimm's bed. How the fuck did I get in Grimm's bed and why isn't he here?

As if he could hear my thoughts, his bedroom door bursts open and he stands in the frame. His chest rises and falls, his breathing rapid. "I got here as fast as I could. Is she alright?" he asks Eli.

Eli stands and walks over to the door, giving Grimm a slight nod and a pat on the back. "She's good. I'll be in my room if you need me. Try not to need me."

I sit up slowly in the bed, gripping the covers and holding them close to my chest. The room starts to spin and I close my eyes, waiting for the dizziness to settle down. When I open them again, Grimm is standing next to the bed, staring down at me.

"May I sit?" he asks quietly.

"It's your bed." I deadpan. "What am I doing here? What time is it? Why was Eli watching me sleep?" I question, determined to get answers now that he's here with me.

Grimm pulls out his phone and shows me a text message that I had sent to him. I sent him my location and said I needed help. Looking at the pin, I realize it's Leo's address and the maddening memory begins to trickle back to me.

The pregnancy test and an angry Leo flash through my mind.

"Verena," Grimm starts, his expression the most serious I've ever seen on his face. The big goofball looks nothing like his usual self right now. His eyes are tired and sunken, with purple bags underneath. His worry lines are so pronounced, I'd recommend my mom's plastic surgeon but have a feeling now isn't the best time. "I know you're going through a lot right now, emotionally, mentally, and physically. But I need you to tell me what happened at Leo's. I'll tell you why you're here, but you need to give me something too," he begs.

I nod and take a deep breath before I begin. "My memory is still a bit fuzzy, but I was at my house and stressed about my period being late. There were no pregnancy tests there, but I remembered I stashed one at Leo's, so I went to take it." Grimm's expression hardens, and I'm hesitant to give him the gruesome details. "He came home and saw the test and we just had a fight. I'm okay, really. I'm sorry I worried you."

He grabs my wrist and brings my hand to lie flat over his heart. It's pounding so hard I fear it'll explode. His eyes darken and he speaks, his voice raspy and low. "Verena Losado, I will give you one more chance to tell me the truth. Leo's door came down because of my fucking foot. I carried you out of his house and brought you back here. The Brotherhood doctor came to examine you and diagnosed you with a concussion. I know it's a lot to take in, but I need you to be fucking honest with yourself and with me for once in your life."

Standing and turning on his heel, he retreats to the bathroom. After spending what felt like hours inside, Grimm finally reemerges, water droplets covering his shoulders, and his impossibly chiseled chest, taunting me. The tiniest towel clings to his waist and rests low enough for me to have the perfect view of the godly Adonis belt he sports.

Sighing, he grabs clothes out of his dresser and tosses them onto the edge of the bed. We make eye contact and it feels as if time stops completely. My thighs clench instantly and all I can think about is how I want to be under him, on top of him, and everything else in between. But his words bring me back to reality.

"I'm trying to be understanding and patient. I'm trying to be a good fucking friend. But you don't make it easy, you know? You walk away, V. Every single time. You run to me like a stray cat looking for shelter and I give it to you with no questions asked. I've been here waiting for you to realize that I'm all you need. I'm your protector, I'm your provider, I'm your safe haven *and* your weapon. I don't want to be your goddamn friend anymore. I could make you happier than any other man or woman on this fucking planet. But you won't give me the chance. How am I supposed to give you all of me if you refuse to let me in?"

Oh, fuck.

All this time I've been so worried about myself, I didn't even think about how it could be affecting Grimm. The one person who actually cares enough about my well-being and my situation to not only say something to me, but act on it for my own safety. I'd never find someone else like him.

At the very least, he deserves to know the truth.

I let go and tell him everything. From the pregnancy test, to Leo forcing himself on me in the bathroom, charging after me in the living room, and injecting me with *something* before leaving me in his bed.

I swear I see smoke leaving Grimm's ears and his anger towards Leo only fuels the desire I've been trying to fight for so long. If life was that simple, I'd straddle him right now, concussion and all. But if a happily ever after is in the cards for us, it's going to have to wait. He deserves an apology and I can't believe I've been so selfish.

"I- I'm sorry. It wasn't my intention to hurt you, Grimm. I tried to leave, I used the fight with Leo as a way out and I was almost out of the door when he pulled me back in and forced me to stay in his hell for a little while longer." Tears form in my eyes and I don't have the energy to blink them away. I don't have the strength to keep myself together anymore.

"I'm fucking scared, Grimm. Every day for the last two years I've lived in fear of him, his actions, his words. Our relationship was beautiful when we first got together and I've spent so much time trying to get us back to that place, but no matter what I do, I end up with cuts and bruises and burnt fucking hands. If I don't go back to him willingly, he'll take me by force and I don't want to drag you into this mess anymore than I already have. You're right, you've been an amazing friend and confidant, and I can't apologize enough for taking advantage of you. I don't blame you for hating me. I'm so fucking sorry."

Grimm sighs and walks around the bed. I feel the mattress sink in next to me, and then those strong, ink-covered arms wrap around my waist. He pulls me in close, whispering in my ear, "I could never hate you, V. From the moment I laid eyes on you, you've belonged to me. I'm not Prince Charming, Verena. I'm not the angel that's going to balance out your demons. I'm a monster. But I do think if you gave me a fucking chance, I would do a damn good job of making you feel loved and secure. I live to see that smile and hear your laugh. I want to heal all of your scars and put you back together the way you so desperately need. You did nothing to deserve your pain and I will spend every day for the rest of my life proving that to you. Open your fucking eyes and let me in."

Nodding, I whisper, "Okay. I'll let you in."

He places a soft kiss on the crown of my head and pulls back. "Fucking finally. Now, I need you to listen to me. Stay here with Eli. Invite the girls over, whatever you want. I'm going to take care of Leo."

My heart nearly drops out of my fucking ass at his last sentence.

"Maybe we can just forget about him. I'm sure if he sees us together, he'll back off. We don't have to provoke him, Grimm."

He laughs, "Provoke him? Honey, that's not what I'm doing. I'm ending this once and for all. There's no changing my mind. I'm doing what has to be done. You will stay here until I get back, unless you want to help me finish him off." A mischievous smirk forms on his lips, and my heart skips a beat. I'm not sure if it's the smile or the threat to Leo that's turning me on, but I don't mind it one bit.

Are these the side effects of my concussion?

"Yes, I'll come with you. What are you going to do to him?" I ask nervously.

"You'll see. Let's go!" He interlaces our fingers and we head downstairs to the garage. Grimm picks up a black backpack and slings it over his shoulder.

My eyes bulge. "What's in there?"

Oh, fuck me. I didn't think Grimm was actually going to kill Leo. Yes, he's protective and a borderline looney, but he couldn't be a killer. Right?

He flashes me another smile, dripping with a lust for murder. "Toys. Let's go play."

GRIMM'S MOTORCYCLE had just enough space for the two of us. He placed the spare helmet over my head and lowered the visor, giving me a small smile. He secures his helmet and a small beep sounds in mine. His voice surrounds me and I feel a burning in my core at the thought of him being so close to me. "Can you hear me?"

I nod, and he gives me a thumbs up. "Hold on tight, little monster." I'm wearing the backpack and it is decently heavy. I'm wondering what the fuck he packed in here, but the whole little monster thing cancels the thought out completely. My arousal rises and I'm not sure if it's because of the adrenaline of ending everything with Leo or starting something new with Grimm. I want to give him a chance and I'm hoping by the time we get out of here, we can start moving in that direction.

"You know you don't have to do anything you don't want to do, right?" he asks as we park and make our way through the cemetery. Arriving at the weeping angel statue, we walk toward the back and Grimm pulls out some rock, shoving it into an empty slot in the statue. One of Blair's extravagantly detailed encounters with Emmett pops into my mind. I thought the underground tunnel was a bit of an exaggeration, but look at that! She was telling the fucking truth.

"Oh, wow! Blair wasn't lying!" I exclaim.

With a small chuckle, he asks, "What do you mean?" Did he really not know? Here I am, daydreaming about Grimm whipping out his own clone and he has no idea about Emmett's. I lean in and sum up the events to him in a whisper. Blair left no stone unturned when telling me and Aspen about her time…down here.

"No fucking way!" Grimm doubles over, laughing. "That kid is something else. He's truly my hero." He professes. Grabbing my hand, he guides me down the dimly lit tunnels until we arrive at an immense metal door with all kinds of locks. I look at Grimm with an anxious furrow in my brow. He gives me the brightest smile and I notice him shifting…*himself* in his pants. Once he moves his hand, I see his budding erection.

Grimm clears his throat and our eyes meet. "Like what you see?"

We simultaneously break out into a fit of giggles before he undoes each lock and the door creaks open.

16

GRIMM

THE DOOR SCRAPES against the cement floor as I push it open. The scratching sound fills the room and Leo's eyes flutter open. I instruct V to drop the bag, my eyes never leaving the piece of shit in front of me. His eyes seem unfocused as they search around the room until they finally land on me.

He gags and scrunches his nose as his eyes narrow, anger seeping out of him. "You dumbass, what the fuck is this?! And is that-" Another gag comes from his throat as his eyes bounce to the remains of Braxton's head with bugs flying around it, picking at what's leftover. "-A fucking head?! What the fuck?!" This time he actually pukes.

I watch as he expels his vomit, and it sprays around him as he remains hung from the hooks on the ceiling, the biggest smile filling my face. Verena walks further into the room and her arm brushes against mine as she stands by me. The contact makes my dick jerk in my pants.

The minute that she comes into view, Leo's whole demeanor changes and my hands twitch at my sides with the urge to decapitate his head immediately. "Verena, baby, what's going on? I love you. I am so sorry. You know I didn't m-" His words die as my fist connects with his jaw and his head snaps to the side.

"What the fuck!" he shouts, spitting blood to the floor next to him.

"She doesn't need your bullshit apologies. It's over, Leo. You're fucking done, dipshit," I say confidently.

"Grimm… is that a head?" Verena hesitantly questions, her finger pointing over to the very obvious head of Braxton. "Who is that?" She brings her hand to her nose and squeezes.

"Don't worry about it, baby. I'll tell you later. Let's finish this fucker." I state while cocking my head to the side and peering down at Leo.

"Verena, please don't let him do this. Please." Leo begs.

V lifts her eyes to meet his. Rage burns behind mine. All I want is to kill. I want to see red, bathe in it, and brêathe it in. "Why would I stop him? I've tried to stop you from doing so much to me for years and my words haven't had any impact on your actions. What makes you think he'll listen to me?" Tears begin flowing from her eyes, but she contains her composure. Every word that leaves her mouth is crystal clear.

"You destroyed me. Little by little, you ruined every good thing about me and my life. But I loved you, and to be honest, Leo, you're not the easiest fucking person to love. There's nothing you could say that's going to get you out of here alive and in one piece. You deserve to die. There is-"

Leo cuts her off with a cry. "Verena, plea-"

Verena's voice booms throughout the cement room as a tear trails down her cheek, "Speaking to me is a fucking privilege! One you no longer have. This is my hell, bitch. I make the goddamn rules! You don't get to speak anymore."

Oh, my lanta. I could combust right here, right now. Her eyes have darkened and her face has a red tint from her own rage. Her hair is a bit disheveled from the helmet and the wind. She looks fucking perfect.

Fuck, I want her so bad.

Focus, Grimm. You can think with your dick once this asshole is dead.

"Do you like games, Leo?" I ask, slipping a blade into my back pocket and pulling an axe from my bag, twirling it around like a baton. "Because me, personally, I love games and I'm assuming you do too.

Since you loved toying with Ms. Verena so much, I figured we could play a few of my favorites. Participate in one last family game night." I let the axe drop and the blade clacks against the ground.

Walking towards him, the sharp edge of the axe drags along the cement, eliciting a high-pitched scratching noise. "And one thing about me and games, Leo, is that I don't like to lose." I bring my face to his, so close I can smell the bile lingering on his breath. His eyes widen and the fear seeping into them makes my smile stretch even further.

I lean back from his face, a laugh bursting from my throat. Placing my hand on my belly, I laugh harder. "Wooo!" I bring the axe to my face and fakely swipe away a tear. "You should have seen your face, Leo. Truly priceless. No one told me you were so funny."

I drop the axe by his tied up body then head back toward my bag to grab the other tools I need. "What do you say, V. Want to have a game night?"

"Game night?" she asks, her pretty curious eyes going from Leo to me.

"Tic-Tac-Toe or Hangman, little monster?" I ask her. Looking over, I see her brows furrow; whether it's the nickname or the question I just asked, I don't know. What I do know is that after this, I will have most certainly created a monster.

My little monster.

Because there is no going back once this is done.

"Uhmm… Hangman?" she answers in a questioning tone. A smile starts to creep up my face. "Great choice." I praise her, unable to hide the excitement lacing my words. "I hope you two are ready to have some fun! I sure am. It's been a hot minute since I've been able to enjoy this shit."

Leo starts to shake his head at me while chanting "No's" and "Please's" but the only thing I hear right now is the words V said to me about how he hurt her. Broke her down until she was so fragile and weak, it took outside interference to save her.

I face Verena and smile while clapping then rub my hands together. "Here are the rules, baby. It's time to play."

17

VERENA

MY EYES ARE STUCK on his movements and the shock of electricity that makes its way to my core confuses me. What I would give to fuck him here, right in front of Leo.

I never had this kind of reaction to anything Leo did. Is this what true attraction and lust felt like? There's a strong magnetic pull between Grimm and myself. I absolutely need to know if this is purely physical or something more.

Can your horny ass wait until Leo is dealt with before you go hopping to the next one, you whore?

A small smile breaks from my lips and I push the laughter down, hoping the boys don't notice. I bite my lip to hide my obvious smile. Of course, it's something more. Grimm wouldn't care about getting rid of Leo for me, if he didn't want something more. At least, I hope that's true. But his protective nature gets me every time.

Are we about to torture and murder the piece of trash that has eliminated my self-worth and sucked my life dry for years? Yeah, I'm one-hundred percent sure that's where this is headed right now. And I've never felt happier, or hotter for that matter.

He turns and gives Leo a slap on the cheek. "Are you paying attention? You're going to want to know how to play." He looks back toward me again, "As I was saying, Leo here will have to guess a letter to the word I have chosen and for every one he gets wrong, we get to remove a part of his body." His smile is so large it looks like it could split his cheeks open.

Grimm twirls the axe in his hand as he steps up to Leo's bare chest. My heart starts to hammer in my ribcage as he drops the axe and whips a blade out from his back pocket. I watch him as he carves lines into Leo's skin. Blood beads along the cuts and drips down his torso before falling off and staining the cement floor.

Seven lines later, the board is set. Leo sputters above him, spit leaking from his mouth as he shouts, "You're fucking crazy!"

Grimm just laughs as he brings his face to Leo's. "You have no fucking idea." He smiles, the image wickedly beautiful.

"Alright! Guess a letter," Grimm singsongs. "B," Grimm immediately starts laughing a full on belly laugh as he walks over to Leo's hand. He presses the knife to his pinky and cuts through the flesh and breaks the bone with such ease, I'm impressed. "What a fucking idiot. Who doesn't start with a vowel?" He scoffs. "Guess again."

"I! I!" Leo chants. "Very good. See? Now you're getting the *hang* of it. See what I did there, V?" he asks, facing me. Finally, free to release my giggles, I do, and my hand flies over my mouth. Leo looks at me, his eyes widening with shock at my participation.

Grimm carves the *I's* into their designated spots and I can't help but wonder what he's chosen. Leo get's the next two guesses wrong and Grimm removes two more fingers. He looks over at me before outstretching his hand, the bloody knife held between us. "Do you want to try, little monster?"

"I-I, um, I don't know. Maybe I should just watch," I say with hesitation. Grimm nods, accepting my answer. "Well, alright hon-"

No, fuck that. I deserve a chance at this too. It's not like I'd ever be in the position to kill someone again and who better than Leo? In all honesty, what the actual fuck am I waiting for? Interrupting Grimm, I take the knife from him and stare into Leo's eyes. "On second thought, why not?" A menacing grin creeps across my lips and Leo stares back in not only disbelief, but fear.

"What's your next guess, *baby*?" I mock him. Leo takes a deep breath and shakes his head. The fear is practically expelling from his pores and it feels so good to not be on the receiving end of things for once.

"Uhh, J?" he asks, his voice cracking and his hot breath touching my skin. I'm not pleased with our proximity but he's restrained and hanging like a piece of meat so I know I'm completely safe. I look back at Grimm to see if Leo's guess was correct. He shakes his head and I turn, my own heart racing.

Fuck, okay V. You can do it. Remember all the absolutely vile shit he's said to you over the years. The countless amount of times he's put his hands on you and forced you to bend over for him. Show him how much it hurts. Show him pain that he couldn't even fathom in his worst nightmare.

I glance at Grimm and he nods with great encouragement. His smile is proud, like a teacher watching their student pass a really hard test with flying colors.

Grabbing Leo's mutilated hand, I press the knife into his skin and begin to dig the point of the blade into each layer. It severs fairly quickly, blood trickling down my sleeve and blooming through the fabric. The bone is a bit hard to snap but with persistent pressure I break it cleanly, the sound like music to my motherfucking ears. I want to hear it again. I snatch the last finger on his hand and slice through it with more force this time. It takes less time for it to detach and the snapping of bones rings in my ears like a beautiful melody, once again.

His screams fill the dirty dungeon and I let out a guttural laugh. "VERENA! What the fuck, I didn't even have a chance to guess!" Leo shouts, upset at my deviation from the rules.

Pouting my lips, I ask, "Did you really think you were going to make it out alive either way? You heard the man; he said you're done. Muerto."

"Hey Leo, pretty soon living is a privilege you won't have either!" Grimm lets out a laugh filled with malicious promises. Gripping onto his stomach, he leans forward and places his other hand on his knee.

Only he would find the humor in this madness, and it is the farthest thing from sickening.

I walk over to Grimm and hand him the knife. "Fill in the blanks." He nods, stalking straight towards our plaything. Once the word is complete, Grimm steps back showcasing his latest piece of art. Blood oozes and drips down Leo's chest, a crimson puddle forming underneath him. I can't help but laugh when I read the word Grimm chose to mark him with.

DIPSHIT

Grimm raises his eyebrows and asks, "Well, what do you think, little monster? You like it?" *Yes the fuck I do and it's most certainly not the only thing I like.* The urge to rush and tackle him right now is strong. I'm not sure how much longer I'll be able to hold back.

Sauntering towards me, Grimm lowers his face until he's aligned with my ear. "Take a look in the bag; use whatever you'd like. You can do it. You are resilient, Verena. End it on the best fucking note possible. I've got your back and I'm always here for you, but I want you to slay your demon on your own."

Walking over to the duffle bag, I look inside at the contents. Blades of every size and grit stare back at me, but one sticks out like a sore thumb. Its handle is jet black but intricate carvings filled with silver blanket every inch. The blade is long and clean, begging to be used. Begging to be covered in that copper scent.

I pick it up and turn towards Leo. My emotions flow to the forefront of my mind. My lips tremble as I take in where I am and what is seriously about to go down. I am taking Leo's life. I am the one he will succumb to.

"Fuck you!" I scream at the top of my lungs. Tears begin streaming down my face like a waterfall and all control I've had over my emotions diminishes into ashes. "I'm tired of being your punching bag! You ruined me, Leo. You broke me down, weathered and eroded my spirit, time and time again. You've done it for the last time!" I cry out, my chest heaving.

The adrenaline rushes throughout my body and it feels breathtaking. Heat funnels to my core and I beeline to Grimm. I wrap my arms around his neck and bring him in close. Our lips brush and I inhale. Taking in his scent, I exhale and say, "Thank you for fighting for me. Before we kill him, we need to do one more thing."

Grimm frantically nods and responds breathlessly, "As you wish, little monster. Name it and I'll do it."

Dropping the machete, I say, "Fuck me, Grimm. Take me. Own me. Show this prick who I really belong to." I look into his eyes and bite my lip.

His eyes train on my mouth as he wets his own lips. A sinful smile forms and those craters he calls dimples, make me weak in the knees. His hands rest on the small of my back and pull at the hem of my shirt. I nod and he begins to drag the fabric up and over my head. Faint bruises line my arms and his head snaps to Leo.

"Look at her." He commands. Leo picks up his head to the best of his ability, his eyelids falling heavily. "I said, look!" Grimm shouts, gaining his full attention. Leo's eyes snap open and he fixes his gaze on my olive skin littered with yellow patches of healing bruises. They're finally starting to heal. For good.

Grimm steps back, lifting his own shirt over his head and tossing it to the side. He kicks off his shoes and undoes his belt simultaneously. His pants fall to the floor and my jaw falls right with them, noticing the beast that's tenting his boxers. Curls fall over his eyes and frame his face, and all I can think about is pulling on them as he buries his cock inside me.

My heart rate picks up as he steps closer and begins to undress me. We're left in nothing but our underwear and his focus shifts back towards Leo.

"Oh, sweet, sweet dipshit. Love hurts, doesn't it? Believe me, I know. For years, I had to see you mosey around campus with *my* woman, not giving her an ounce of the treatment she truly deserves. And because I'm such a nice guy," he pauses, breaking into another malicious smile, "I'm going to give you some pointers. A 'How-To' guide, if you will. I'll have her screaming, but unlike when she's with you, it'll be for all the right reasons."

Leo groans, unable to form a coherent sentence. Seeing him in a helpless state, blood trickling down his chest and creating a pool underneath his feet, brings so much satisfaction to my being. I clench my thighs together, feeling my arousal build with every drop of blood that hits the floor.

Drip. Clench.

Drip. Clench.

Removing my bra and panties, I regain Grimm's attention. His jaw clenches and I reach out to grab his hand, pulling him closer to me.

"Fuck. Me." I order, and he wastes no time doing just that. Gripping my chin with both hands, he brings me in for a kiss. Our lips touch and in that moment, I realize what a fucking idiot I've been. Nothing has ever felt this right. Nothing will ever feel as wrong as it did with Leo, ever again.

Grimm slides his tongue into my mouth and mine meets his, wrapping itself around the muscle as if they were long-lost lovers reunited. He groans and his hand comes up to my breast, massaging it. As big as his hands are, my chest is bigger. He kneads my breast, pinching my pert nipple, eliciting a moan from my lips.

Pulling back, he angles his mouth so it's directly over my ear. "I've waited a lifetime for this. I've imagined this moment down to every last detail," he rasps as he brings his hand and wraps it around the column of my throat and squeezes. "But I need you on your knees, begging for me. Let's give him the best show of his life, baby."

His hand drops, and he steps forward, directly in front of Leo. I follow suit and Leo uses his last ounce of energy to convince me to set him free. "V-Ver…ena. P-pl-please. H-help."

Grimm removes the item from his waistband and clicks it open. Pulling out a joint and a match. He sparks it up and takes a hit, then passes it to me. The match is still lit, and he grabs Leo's mutilated hand, grazing the bloodied flesh with the flame. Not the best cauterization, but it'll do for the time being, I suppose. "You think V is as hot for me as this flame is for you?" he asks with a laugh. "Let's see, shall we?"

Putting out the match and tossing it, he turns to face me and orders, "On your back. Open those legs for me. Don't let that go out." I do exactly as he says and take a hit of the joint, then lay down. Grimm walks past me, no longer in my line of sight. I hear him rustle out of his boxers and toss them with the rest of our clothes. Within a couple of seconds, his voice fills the room again.

"You are mine. You have always been mine. Whether you knew it or not, that doesn't matter. What does matter is that now, you know and now, you're here. Mine to love, mine to cherish, mine to keep." He says, his deep rasp sending chills down my spine. My heavy breathing betrays me, giving Grimm the reassurance he so desperately needs to continue.

He grabs my wrist and guides the joint to his mouth, taking another hit. Letting go, his hand trails up my arm, his fingertips grazing my shoulder. Slowly, he runs his hand over my shoulder and down my breast, teasing my nipple as he goes. Gliding past my belly button and stopping just above my pussy. His fingertips land on my clit as he begins to rub slow, agonizing circles.

I've fallen into a rhythm of moaning and taking a hit, then bringing the joint to Grimm's lips. The high feels insurmountable, unlike any other high I've experienced before. Who knew getting off and getting high in front of your shitty ex-boyfriend who is on his last leg of life would be so…erotic?

Grimm picks up his speed, building the ache in my core. I lean back, placing my head on his chest and feel his cock press against my back. His gravelly whisper fills my ears, "Cum for me, V. Cum all over my fingers so I can lick them clean and please you again. You'll have them stretching out your pussy while my throbbing cock does the same to that pretty little asshole."

With that, he shoves two fingers into my cunt, slicking them with my juices and driving me to my climax. "Yes, please. I want everything. I want it all." My moans echo throughout the room and Leo's head snaps up, using whatever energy he has left to narrow his eyes at me in anger and disbelief.

I can't believe it either, fucker. I guess dreams really do come true.

A small chuckle slips past my lips and I relish the feeling of Grimm's fingers inside of me. But I want more. The blunt falls next to a drop of blood and the cherry goes out. A devious grin finds its way to his lips and goosebumps surface on my skin. "I'm so close," I whisper and the hungry growl that leaves Grimm sends a shiver down my spine. My eyes flutter and roll back as the orgasm rips through my body. "Oh fuck yes, baby. Give it to me. Show him that you've got all you need right here with me."

Regaining my composure, Grimm slips his fingers out of my pussy causing me to feel an emptiness so broad and heavy. Bringing his hand up to his lips, he sticks out his tongue, and weaves it through his fingers slurping up every single drop that was left behind. "So fucking sweet."

Pushing onto my knees, I face Grimm and press my hand to his chest, guiding him to lay down. Leo loved making me ride him solely because he knew I didn't fucking want to. I didn't want to put in the work for someone who didn't put the work in for me. He used the control he had over me to his advantage. Now I'll use it for mine.

Straddling Grimm, I lock eyes with Leo as I sink myself down onto Grimm's thick cock. It stretches me just like he promised it would. Imagining him going through the back door is both a blessing and a curse because I have no clue how he's going to fit back there.

Grimm's hands find my hips and guide my motions, building the perfect rhythm with me. I grind against him, our sweat slicking our bodies together. I lay my hands on his chest, caressing his godly figure.

He's fucking mine.

I've never felt so hungry for someone before. I moan and scream Grimm's name at the top of my lungs, Leo's head bobbing to attention every time I hit a new octave. My nails hook onto Grimm's arms, digging into his muscle as another orgasm builds and rocks through my body. "Yes! Yes! Fuck, you feel amazing." I admit breathlessly.

"It's all for you, baby. I'm all yours. Every inch of my cock is for you. Every inch of *me* is for you. It's always been for you, Verena." He responds, something stronger than lust slinking into his gaze. He wraps his hand around my back and flips us over, changing our position.

Keeping one hand under my head as a pillow, his other reaches down and gathers my wetness. He spreads it along that sensitive ring of muscle and I suck in a breath. "If you don't want to, tell me to stop. It'll all end on your word. Otherwise, this dick is getting buried in your asshole, little monster." His words cause me to relax, knowing it's all up to me.

"Yes. I want it. Keep going, don't stop." I answer. That devilish smile covers his face as he lines the head of his cock with my asshole. His fingers swirl in circles over my clit, stimulating me and pulling a plethora of moans from me. Slowly, he pushes past the barrier and fills me up. He enters me slowly, allowing me to adjust to his girth. In one swift motion he pulls out and thrusts himself back in. He pumps into me with such ferocity, that I feel like I may die if he stopped.

Slipping his fingers in between our bodies, he inserts two into my pussy causing my stomach to do flips. *This is how a real man fucks.*

"Yes, V. Squeeze this cock. Milk me for everything I have." His words pour out of him and bring me closer to my climax. Slamming into me a few more times, my orgasm begins spreading like flames throughout my entire body. There isn't a single inch that doesn't feel the pleasure flowing through me. Grimm kisses me with such passion, I combust the moment our lips touch. I feel his cock pulse, his releasing spilling inside of me, letting me know our kiss had the same affect on him.

"Everything I have ever dreamed of and more." He says before placing a quick kiss on my lips. Withdrawing, he stands and walks over to our clothes and brings them over to me. We dress and give our attention to Leo during the last few minutes of his life.

Walking over to him, I place my fingers on his neck, checking his pulse. It's faint, but it's there. "You just won't fucking die. Will you." I mumble my voice laced with frustration.

"How do you want to end this, baby?" Grimm asks, fishing for the joint case. He lights a second joint and inhales loudly.

Eyeing the machete, I pick it up and take a good look at Leo. I never thought I'd see the day where I was the one with the upperhand. Moments of hurt and struggle play in my head like a movie.

The bruises have faded but the scars will remain forever and tattoos can only cover so much.

I grab a fistfull of his bloodied hair and yank his head back. His eyes are drooping over and the last bit of his soul is lingering, still hoping I'll have a change of heart and set him free.

He can't hurt you anymore, V. You have the power. The power to end your pain. The power to take his life. Do it. He deserves it.

Do it. Do it. Do it.

DO IT!

"Asesinado por una mujer. Dulces sueños, cabrón." Taking the machete, I lift it above my head and drive it straight into his heart. His mouth falls open in shock and it sends a thrilling shiver down my spine. A lightbulb goes off in my head and I smile, hoping to make Grimm proud.

Putting pressure on the handle of the machete, I slice through Leo's body, nearly splitting him in two. His organs fall to the floor with a thud, the squelching sound bringing me satisfaction as his blood covers my face.

I drop the machete and turn to face Grimm, but all I see is the massive erection tenting his pants.

"Up for round two?"

18

GRIMM

MY COCK JERKS against my zipper as I look at the beautiful little monster in front of me. Blood is scattered along her face, arms, and clothes. I've dreamed of a moment like this one for so long. Her perfect body bathed in blood and Leo hanging lifeless, his flesh and bone scattered across the floor.

I think I died along with Leo and made it to the pearly white gates of heaven. My two favorite things, Verena and murder, have now become a cohesive pair. They fit one another as well as my cock fits into her pussy. A key that unlocked a new part of her, if you will.

"Oh my fucking gosh!" Verena whips around, her eyes bulging out of her head. "What the *fuck* did I just do?!" Her voice trembling. I rush to stand by her side and wrap my arms around her.

"You did what needed to be done. For your safety, Verena. No one will know about this." I promise her, cupping her face and raising it to meet mine. "I'll take care of the body and dispose of it in a way no one would know it was *us*, okay?" She continues to stare at me, shock running through her system. "Okay?" I ask again, a little louder this time. Verena nods slowly and a droplet escapes her tear duct.

When I begin to guide her out the door, Verena stops me. "We aren't just going to leave him here, right?" Her eyes filled with anxiousness and fear make her innocence shine through. Dipshit was her first love. The man she thought she was going to spend her life with, first out of want and then out of fear, is now dead at her hand because of his own piss poor choices. She did what needed to be done and I'd never ask her to do more, unless that's what her heart desired.

Shaking my head, I bring my hands up to her bloodied face and cup it, bringing her eyes to mine. "I'll take care of everything. You don't have to worry." I reassure her, her amber eyes search mine for a more direct answer, one she won't get until she pushes for it.

Her hands wrap around my waist and when she presses her lips to mine, I swear I'm ready to spill in my pants yet again. I kiss her back with hunger, swallowing every little whimper from her as I pull back, searching her face for a hint of regret or anger.

This is where we're supposed to be. She's filled the void in my soul without even realizing it. My little monster, if you only knew what you were capable of. There's nothing in this world that doesn't already belong to you, to us. Nothing I won't help you achieve.

My chest is heaving, matching the rhythm of her own. My hands twitch at my sides to bring her back to me. Like a man who's been starved and finally got a taste of food. "Grimm, he's dead." She pants, trying to regain her breath. A smirk slips onto my face and I chuckle.

"I know. It was fucking amazing. You're the hottest killer I've ever met. I am for sure your number one fan. Can I have your autograph?"

She grabs my shirt, yanking me back to her. Her lips immediately find mine again. "You're fucking crazy," she says against my lips, her own forming a soft smile.

"Does it scare you?" I ask, desperately hoping for it not to. By her reaction, I doubt she is but she was scared shitless just a moment ago. Her adrenaline is running and controlling her emotions may be tricky.

Verena inhales, thinking about her answer. On the exhale, she slowly shakes her head. "No." My cock swells behind my zipper at her response. My little fucking monster. She was made just for me, mind, body, and soul. She sees me for who I truly am and isn't running for the hills.

I may have finally met my match. Time to really ignite her flame.

VERENA

Back at the RSB house, after a shower and a blunt, Grimm and I cuddle underneath his blankets. Thoughts of Leo's lifeless body and puddles of his blood run through my mind. He's the second dead person I've seen. The only other one besides Ronnie. I should feel broken, destroyed, and terrified of the police finding out I was the one to take his life. But I feel…nothing.

Whether that's because Leo was a raging piece of shit or because I was already numb and broken before his death, I'm not sure. Ronnie's death left me a constant blubbering mess. I didn't eat or sleep for a week, only eating meals when my grandmother came to stay with us and noticed my self-destructive routine.

Because it would've taken too much time out of my parents' schedules to care if their other daughter was on the brink of death. As much as they were cold before Ronnie's death, the loss of their youngest made them hypothermic.

Just then, my mind shifts from my stone-cold parents to Leo's. His mother was practically obsessed with him. They spoke every single day. He'd send her flowers every week and I was considered fucking lucky and blessed if he remembered to get me a bouquet for our anniversary or my goddamn birthday. Unfortunately, his mother isn't any better to me than my own.

If she has the chance to insult my clothing, my cooking, and my culture, she will and *oh*, she does. The way I dress has never been up to her standards. Mrs. Leila Barlay pictured Leo settling down with someone more like Aspen or Blair. My olive skin and gloomy exterior should have stayed far away from her bright and cheerful baby boy. It was no match for their simple, clean girl personas. Effortlessly beautiful, with creamy skin and minus the Puerto Rican background.

Not that she actually cares to remember where my family comes from. There were plenty of instances where Leila would make remarks about Mexican restaurants being her favorite and Columbia having beautiful weather at a certain time of year. But the only logical explanation was that she didn't know I was Puerto Rican and my entire family, with the exception of my parents, is in Puerto Rico.

Leo and I had been together for almost three years. All throughout our relationship, we had weekly family dinners and I can confidently say that not one thing I've ever said about myself has stuck with her. She usually spent the night talking to Leo about Leo and his accomplishments. If she were to speak to me, I'd get lectured about what Leo needs and how I should consider changing certain things about myself to be the "appropriate woman for him."

Fuck her.

Everything revolved around Leo. She would give him two-week vacations every birthday and Christmas for "Mommy and Leo time," as she called it. I want to gag just thinking about it.

I switch my thoughts from her hollow heart to her finding out about Leo. A part of me wishes I could see her and fucking rub it in. But the other part of me remembers what I went through after Ronnie. I knew I shouldn't want anyone to feel that way, including enemies, but I couldn't help but be wishful to see the look on her face when she finds out that I took everything she loves in this lifetime.

The other part of my heart rages to spill the realities of the monster he truly was. To tell everyone how there were plenty of times he was seconds away from taking my life and instead graced me with another day by his side, living in evergrowing fear and anxiety. He was never remorseful, never apologetic or caring for the marks and scars he left behi-

"V, what are you thinking about? You look like you're having a stroke. Are you okay, babe?" Grimm's deep voice snaps me out of my thoughts. I blink a few times finding myself back under the covers wrapped in his arms, my hair still damp from our shower.

Sitting up, I untangle myself from his arms and he grips my wrist. My eyes snap to his and he shakes his head. He grabs my legs and drapes them on top of his and pulls the covers over us. "Go ahead, tell me what's on your mind." He lays an open palm on my lap, offering a hand to hold.

I slap my palm into his and take a deep breath. My nerves cause me to spit out my words and ramble a shit-ton of nonsense. "A lot happened today. I'm worried I went too far with killing Leo. But I'm proud of myself for finally standing up to him, although I would've never done it without your help, Grimm. I appreciate it so much but I'm also terrified that my life will be over soon and I'll have to spend the rest of my days in an orange jumper. I trust you wholeheartedly but I've never murdered someone before. I don't know how this process works and what happens with the body. But do I want to know? I'm not entirely sure. Even though it doesn't matter because I was the one to actually murder him! Do you see where I'm frustrated?"

He chuckles, "I see. Are you finished with your speech or is there more?"

My eyes shoot daggers at him. "No, there's no more." Squeezing my hand, he looks me in the eyes and brings my fingers to his lips. He kisses a knuckle then speaks a few words in a repeated manner.

"I can tell you my plan."

Kiss.

"For Leo's body, that is."

Kiss.

"If you want to know, I'll tell you."

Kiss.

"If you don't, I won't say a word."

Kiss.

His lips hover over the back of my hand as he whispers once more, "I can guarantee you, no one will find out you had any part in this, Verena."

Kiss.

He said my full name. He only says my full name when he's fucking serious. Now I'm questioning how often he really does shit like this to have it all figured out. He's too calm and collected. But as of right now, I have no other choice but to breathe and trust Grimm. He said he would help save me from Leo and he did just that. Grimm is promising me innocence and safety. Just like he's always done.

Suddenly, my worries seem to fade away and I begin to think how silly it was to question his devotion to me. He's been proving that to me for a very long time, I've just been too blind to see it.

I was in good hands, that I knew for sure. "I do want to know."

Grimm raises an eyebrow at me, "Are you sure, V? I don't want you to be upset. You experienced something very traumatic and you may need a moment to handle that first."

Shaking my head I protest, "No, Grimm. I want to be all in. I suffered at his hand for so long and I ended his life. It's only right I know where his body ends up."

Grimm is silent for a moment. He's unsure if this is the best decision for me but he's going to tell me anyway, I can see it in his expression. "Stop trying to save my innocence and tell me, please," I beg.

"I'm going to chop up his body and stick him through a meat grinder." He says bluntly. I break out into a laugh buckling over because holy fuck, was that unexpected. "Grimm, this is not the time for joking." I clear my throat, trying to regain my composure.

His expression doesn't falter, still the same straight face as when he told me he was going to grind up Leo into a big fucking pile of burger meat. There was no way he was serious.

My heart drops and my jaw falls slack, "Oh, you're fucking serious?"

Nodding his head, he laughs and says, "You'd be surprised at how many people buy ground meat off of the dark web."

The *little monster* in me, as Grimm likes to call it, comes to the forefront and takes over. Leaning over, I whisper into Grimm's ear suggesting a deviation in his plan. I know I've done good when his own chiseled jaw drops, rendering him speechless.

"Yes, please. Let's do that. Way better than what I said." His hand slips under the blanket to adjust his cock and he groans. "Fuck, I'm so hard right now."

Licking my lips, I rub my foot along his length. His stare meets mine as he slowly shakes his head. "No, little monster. No more tonight. I just want to hold you." His arm wraps around my waist and we slide back into our respective spots from earlier. My head on his chest, his strong hands on my body, and his fresh scent with a hint of pot was similar to what one would call, "heaven on earth."

Safe in Grimm's arms, I feel so ready for sleep to overtake me. But before I fall out, I hear his whispers. "I'm so proud of you, Verena. You got out. I'm happy you never stopped fighting for you. I'm happy *I* never stopped fighting for you. You're my missing piece."

19

GRIMM

VERENA'S BEEN SLEEPING SOUNDLY for hours. We came home and I washed off every inch of her body before giving her one of my old t-shirts and a pair of sweats. Her eyes instantly shut after our conversation ended and she's been sleeping like a fucking rock ever since. I don't want to move and disturb her peace, but I wanted to get a head start in mutilating Leo. I know she said she wants to be involved but personally, I think the action of murder was enough for her psyche for now.

My phone begins buzzing, taking my mind away from dipshit's soulless body. Dad's face and name light up my screen. Another invite to another dinner with people I don't want to fucking be near. I'll let it go to voicemail.

He leaves a message and my phone pings, notifying me, but then begins buzzing again. Verena stirs and I'll be damned if I let the slightest pin drop disturb her rest. Her breathing returns to a soft, steady pace as she rolls over and out of my arms. I use the chance to leave the bed, creep down the stairs, and answer the phone.

"Hey, dad. What's going on?" I ask, but we both know why he's calling.

"My boy! How are you? I feel like it's been forever since I've heard your voice." He cheerily greets me.

Usually, I decline his dinner invitations through text. The RSB has always given me an excuse to miss. But I don't want to hear the disappointment in his voice because I'm flaking, again. "I'm good, dad. Just been busy with school and The Brotherhood. Emmett's been keeping my schedule filled with extracurriculars too." I add with a tired chuckle.

"That's good. Listen, I wanted to talk to you about dinner this weekend."

There it is.

"I know it's been hard building a relationship with your siblings but I think you should come home. It'll be good for you, Grimm." He says, his words as unconvincing as the first time he gave me this speech. "I'd love to see you, too. You're still the baby after all and I'm tired of family dinners without my boy. So don't try to find an excuse to get out of this one. Come for your old man if not for anything…or anyone else."

Sighing, I drop my head. Being around my brothers and sister does not sound like a fun way to spend my Saturday night.

In fact, I was planning to spend this Saturday night buried to the fucking hilt inside the little monster snoozing peacefully in my bed.

"Alright. I'll be there. I'm bringing someone." I answer.

I'm met with silence for a moment before dad whispers his response. "Is it a special someone?" His tone returns back to normal before continuing. "Because that would be wonderfu-"

"Yes. She's special." I cut him off. "We'll come by just for dinner. Once the plates are clear, we're out the door."

"Alright, alright. We'll start with dinner. I can't wait to meet her. And I know Flame can't wait to see you, either." He states and my heart swells at the thought of my baby girl.

My Flame. I'm excited to see her too.

A warm sensation came over me and suddenly I was actually looking forward to visiting my family.

Gross.

But also, kind of nice?

The realization of what I'm bringing Verena into hits me and it's not nice or gross. It's collateral. It's diabolical. We just got together, there's no way she wants to meet my cracked out, fucked up family.

But I don't think I'd be able to go alone. Being with her felt right. Being with her *feels* right. I never want to be without her for as long as I walk this shitty earth. She gives me the strength to do things I wouldn't normally do.

You'd think that means stringing her ex boyfriend up by the meat on his back would be out of the norm, but it's right up my alley. What's really out of my norm is having my fucking dream girl in my bed and after she meets my family, she'll be running for the hills.

I sneak into my room and softly close the door when a voice startles me. "I'm awake, no need to be quiet." My spine stiffens and so does the little Grimm in my pants. Her voice awakens something in me so insatiable and uncontrollable. I quickly adjust myself before turning around. "Where'd you run off to? Took care of Leo without me?" She asks.

Scoffing, I walk past the bed and towards my dresser, changing into clothes that I don't care about to do just that. "Actually, my dad called to invite me to dinner with my family this weekend. I told him you're coming." Her face drops at the proposition of meeting my family so soon.

A smirk grows on my face and I continue. "Yeah, I'll give you the laydown before we go. Dinner with the Griswolds is a lot similar to, how do you say, telenovellas." I grab a hair tie and slip my hair into a ponytail.

"Oh! Grimmy's bilingual, who would've thunk." Her eyes shift to my hair, "How cute. I've never seen you rock a pony before." Verena giggles.

Giving her an eye-roll, I toss a middle finger and a wink her way, then respond. "Ponytails are strictly for cleaning up dead bodies. So, you coming or not, monster?"

There's a thick silence in the air and when I make eye contact with her, I see she's removed the sweats I gave her earlier. Slowly, she grabs the hem of my shirt and begins to raise it up and over her arms. Her breasts peak out of the bottom before spilling out, her body on full display for me. “Am I?” She whispers, her siren eyes reaching the depths of my soul and pulling me closer to her.

My feet are moving me to the bed and I’m nodding my head slowly. Who am I to deny my little monster of what she wants? I’m here to make her every wish come true. That doesn’t stop with Leo’s death. That’ll never stop. I am hers forever. There’s no length I wouldn’t go to make her happy. As long as the day ends and she has a smile on her face, I know I’ve done my job.

I make it to the bed in record time and her hands are on me, removing my shirt and sweats. Her palms roam my torso, feeling the curve of every muscle. She wraps one arm around my neck and her fingers thread through my curls. Pulling me close, our lips brush and sparks of electricity flow through my body.

Fuck, I hope she feels the same way about me. I don’t want to rush her but shit, all I want is her.

My arms envelop her body and I lean on her, our bodies flush with one another. Our lips touch again and this time, there’s no stopping. Her tongue tangles itself with mine and she tastes like candy canes on Christmas. My hands roam over her soft skin, worshipping every inch. I don’t want this moment to end, but I have a dead fucking body to clean up.

Pulling away, I sigh and shake my head. “That body will start decaying and I don’t want to be around it when it does.” Verena pulls back but doesn’t look nearly as disgusted as I thought she’d be.

“Strangely, I do.” She laughs. “Only because it’s Leo.” The smile drops from her face and she looks deep into my eyes while speaking again. “Does that make me a horrible person?” Her pupils shift back and forth, studying my face for any hint of a fabrication in my response.

“I think it makes you human, little monster.” Standing, I extend my hand and pull her off the bed. Chest to chest, I grip her chin between my thumb and forefinger, bringing her face inches from mine. I kiss her nose softly, then move to her lips. “I’ll make you forget all about it later on, I promise." My voice returns to its normal octave, "Until then, how about I distract you with all the wonderful details about my family? You have a lot to learn today, young grasshopper."

"Yes, Sir." She breezes past me, into the bathroom, a sly smile on her face and those slender fingers slightly grazing my bulge.

Fuck, there's nothing in this world I wouldn't do just to see that woman smile. To make her truly happy. You better fucking do it all, Grimm. No stone left unturned.

20

GRIMM

OUTSIDE AND ON our way to grind and pack up Dipshit, Verena wastes no time gaining knowledge about my family. "So what's up with your family? I know you have a lot of siblings but is it really that bad?"

Chuckling, I side-eye her and shake my head. "You waste no time, Losado." She smiles, her eyes twinkling. It's the most genuine smile I've yet to see on her face.

"My siblings are half siblings. We don't have the same mom. Their mom is my dad's first wife. They were separated but raised us all under one roof. They were high school sweethearts, got married, had a bunch of babies, the whole nine. From what I've been told, they were having some financial troubles which added stress to their already stressful lives with trying to care for a small tribe. Their mom had a family thing in Spain and needed to take a trip. While she was gone, my dad stepped out and had a one-night stand with my mom. Long story short, she got pregnant with me and decided to keep it." I let out a sigh.

"Why she didn't just abort me is what I never understood. She had an affair with a married man, chose to keep the baby even after finding out about his situation, has the baby, and then to top it all off, she fucking leaves." My mother walking out of our lives isn't something I talk about often. Because when I do, my emotions take over. Emmett is the only one who saw the changes within me after she left. The facade I had to put on everyday was taxing enough. "So I have a runaway mother, a step-mom who despised my existence all my life, and siblings who think I was a mistake–granted, they aren't wrong–that shouldn't have had any relation to their family. Growing up in that house was utter chaos and treachery. Going back isn't as easy as it sounds. Even if it's just for dinner."

We reach the tunnels and Verena hasn't said a word. I'm hoping I didn't scare her off with the truth of my family. It can get pretty heavy, but I made sure to only share the lightest bits. Outside of the room where Leo's body resides, she places a hand on my arm, stopping me from entering. "I'm sorry. You're always such a big goof. I figured that came from having a functional family. I hope you know you aren't a mistake. There's a reason you're here."

My gaze fixates on hers and my lips curve into a smirk, "Yeah. You." Her cheeks grow red from my comment and my cock throbs at her innocence. The slightest bit of flirting drives her up the walls. She acts like a young schoolgirl who's never felt true romance.

Well all of that is about to change, my little monster.

"You're an incredible man, Grimm. I can't thank you enough for all you've done."

Shaking my head, I reach for her hand still placed on my arm and bring her knuckles to my lips. I place a kiss on each one and whisper, "It's all for you."

21

VERENA

MY HEART BEATS ERRATICALLY at Grimm's words. The feeling he gives me is unmatched, unlike anything I've ever felt before. Towards anyone, including the man we're about to–dare I say–grind up.

The shock of Leo's death has lessened but my anxiety still runs rampant at the possibility of getting caught. My life would be fucking over. All of my plans to make sure the world remembered Ronnie, to make sure I made a name for myself instead of solely being known as my parents' child. Can't do that stuck in a 4x4 jail cell.

Grimm leads us down a dark hallway and I know right then, we're not going back to the room we were in last night. He senses my hesitation and stops. I don't notice until it's too late and bump into his chest. When did he even turn around?

"You can wait here if it's too much. I'll be quick." He whispers as his hand reaches for mine. Our fingers intertwine naturally and the warmth of his skin on mine sends chills down my spine. I shake my head in defiance and speak, "We're in this together. Forever and always."

The side of his mouth tips up into a grin and a dimple makes itself known. Oh boy, I am in trouble. There isn't a single thing wrong with this man. Grimm is a character. Funny, caring, unapologetically unfucking-hinged, and committed. He doesn't go back on his word and I'm certain he won't stop at literally anything to make sure I'm happy, healthy, and safe.

He will either make me the happiest woman in the world or ruin my fucking life.

Walking hand in hand, we reach a metal door at the end of the hall and he pulls out a key to unlock the door. We walk in and immediately I'm retching at the smell that floats throughout the room. "Grimm, what the fuck is that smell?!" I ask, my hand covering my nose and mouth, my eyes wide with shock.

"That is Mr. Dipshit in the flesh! I had someone come and hack his body into smaller bits to cut the job in half for us, well me." He shrugs. How is he talking so nonchalantly about hacked up body parts! My blood runs cold at the mention of someone else seeing and touching Leo's dead body.

Someone has proof that Leo is dead. Someone knows and if they spoke to Grimm, they know he was involved. How could he be so careless? He told me he'd protect me! In my rising anxiety, I snap. "Grimm! You told me no one would ever know. What the fuck?"

He raises his head to look at me and stares into my eyes blankly. He's looking at me like I'm the crazy one. I know I split a man in two with a machete but I didn't hire someone to chop up what was left of him like an onion.

"C'mon, V. This is your third year at Blackwell. You know about the society. I have people who answer to me and once I graduate, I'll pretty much be untouchable. Same thing goes for my lady." I blush at his last statement and he notices, another smirk making an appearance and bringing out his dimple right along with it. "Also, my dad is head chief of police. He knows all about it, knows I'm in it. We. Are. Golden. Trust me, please."

There's been plenty of rumors circulating about the Red Skull Brotherhood. They've been referred to as trained killers and assassins, and it's said they do the dirty work for higher ups at the university. Last week, there was a group of girls in the bathroom talking about the RSB and how to find out if the rumors were true. They wanted their pick at a man who would protect them from all the suspicious happenings on campus.

Students were going missing and they weren't taking any chances. Shouldn't I be ecstatic that I have Grimm in my corner? He has made it crystal clear he'd do quite literally anything I request of him, no matter how unreasonable. Either way, it's not easy to let my walls down when I'm looking at the scattered pieces of the man who shattered everything within me.

How long would it be until someone realizes Leo is missing?

If Grimm wants me to trust him completely, he'll answer my questions without hesitation. Right?

He gathers Leo's body parts and piles them by the meat grinder. He digs into a bag and pulls out two face coverings and slides one over each of our faces. Grabbing a plastic bag, he fluffs it out and hands it to me. "Keep this spread open under the mouth of the grinder. Shit can get a little messy."

I do as he says and waste no more time. "If you want me to stop questioning your motives I need you to answer some questions I have."

He nods, "Go ahead. Ask away. I'll tell you everything you want to know, little monster."

Holding up a finger telling me to hold my thoughts for a moment, Grimm picks up Leo's disfigured hand and throws it into the grinder. His flesh and bones crackle through the machine, the sound traumatizing me indefinitely. How the fuck does he sleep at night?

Once every bit makes it through the grinder, he drops his finger, signaling for me to continue with my interrogation.

"Who runs the RSB?"

"Emmett's dad."

My mouth drops. "The *dean* runs the secret society? I guess it makes sense, but what does he have you guys do?"

"Nothing out of the ordinary. He's a businessman and dabbles in some illegal shit. He has enemies like the rest of us. A guy like him doesn't have the time to take care of everything himself and that's where we come in. He needs money, we get it for him. Weapons? We do the pickup. Drugs? Us, again. It also helps separate his identity from cult leader to university dean." He ends with a chuckle.

"If you think it's a cult, why are you in it?" I ask.

"I'd like to say I had no other choice but that'd be a lie. I never knew what I was going to do with my life. I didn't have goals or ambitions. I liked to party. I liked to get high. I liked to fuck. The only other thing I was good at was intimidating people. I'm big as fuck. One look at me and both men and women are quivering in their boots, V. The society made my life simple. It gave me purpose and the opportunity to explore doing something I was actually good at. Books and tests weren't for me." He shrugs.

"How are you enrolled into the university then? Do you not go to classes? What do you major in? How has no one said anything to you about it before?" I spit out, not getting the answers fast enough.

He repeats the process of grinding another chunk of Leo's body before responding to me.

"The university doesn't question me for two reasons. Emmett's father and mine. I'm the son of the chief of police, there's a lot I can get away with scot-free and I do, but I promise I'm not a spoiled asshole. But if I do get caught up with the law one day, I'll have automatic immunity because of the connections I hold and the men I work for. When I graduate I'll have a liberal arts degree in communications. With that, I'd have the qualifications to be the university's human resource specialist."

Grimm has not hesitated after a single question. Is he just a really good liar?

Well there's another option, Negative Nancy. Maybe Grimm is telling the truth.

In my silence, he's moved on to grind up a few more chunks of Leo's body. The first plastic bag fills quickly and when it does, he ties it up and tosses it against the wall, then hands me another one.

As I fluff out the bag, I continue my inquisition. "So, what would you do as the school's human resource specialist?"

Grimm halts in his movements and looks at me. His body relaxes as he breaks out into a laugh, "Fuck if I know, V!" He's practically doubled over, his eyes crinkling above his face mask. Gaining his composure back, he continues, "I'd continue my work in the Brotherhood. The job will be filled with a stand-in, but if it's easier and less expensive to forge paperwork, that's another option. Usually, the men of the society are majoring in fields that will lead them to more specific paths. Things like finance, marketing, technology, and so on. I told you, I never had goals. I never knew what I wanted to do with my life. I just wanted to be a part of something that I was good at and enjoyed. Since our dads have known each other forever and Emmett and I are practically brothers, he worked something out for me. I can't do much but be thankful for the opportunity."

Soon the second bag fills up and we fall into the routine of sealing the bag. Tie, toss, new bag, fluff.

I'm processing everything Grimm shared with me, but he wasn't done there. "But I'm not always killing people. Like I said, my size is intimidating. Sometimes that's all it takes. Plus, most assignments are done in groups so I'm always with one of the guys. Emmett is usually my partner in crime but he's been pretty occupied with Blair lately so I've been cozying up with Eli." He smirks.

Nodding my head, I start to put all of the pieces together. They sit nicely and begin to make sense, the connections forming a web in my brain. A thought settles in my mind and the lead feeling in my stomach dissipates. I really am in the clear.

We finish filling up the last bag and secure it with a double knot. "I'll have someone take care of those. You don't have to think about this asshole ever again, V. He's gone. For good. You're free."

Free. I thought "free" was impossible. I thought the only way to be "free" was to be dead. If Grimm hadn't stepped in when he did, my death would have been the one covered up.

But no, that's not the case.

I'm free.

22

VERENA

GRIMM DROPS me off at my place and I slip inside my window. I opted out of using the front door for two reasons: everyone would hear my arrival and therefore wake up at the thought of a burglar or something, and I'd be recorded on the security cameras strategically placed at the front of the house, in the bushes. I don't want them to even know I was here tonight. In the morning, I'll wait for everyone to leave and then shower. I knew I made the right decision picking Wednesdays as my "study day." Everyone leaves for 8AM classes and I'll be left all by my lonesome.

THE SUN SHINING through my curtains awakens me the next morning. I yawn and pat my bed in search of my phone. It's nine in the morning, which means everyone has left for class. I race into the bathroom to wash off the grime from my skin and hair. Once I'm clean and dressed, I throw my sheets in the wash for good measure. After they're dried and back on my bed, I lay down already needing a nap. The adrenaline rush has bounced up and down, first with the actual murder and then again grinding up his body.

I'm coming down now and feeling exhausted. I curl into the still-warm sheets but my phone buzzes with incoming messages.

Grimm

Hey little monster, what're you doing?

A faint smile falls on my lips as I text him back.

ME

Laying down. Tired out from the last couple of days, WBU?

GRIMM

That's so funny. I'm laying down too. Except I'm naked and thinking of you.

ME

How do you find the energy?

GRIMM

You give me the energy.

Wish I was with you.

Do you need anything?

My heart swells at his messages. Each one that comes through feels as if it's wrapping a hand around the organ in my chest and squeezing at it tightly.

Him. I need him. That's all.

ME

I wouldn't mind some company. Throw some clothes on. You can take them back off before you hop into bed with me.

GRIMM

Hope you're prepared for the dragon.

I burst out laughing. This man is truly insane in the best way possible. Keeping him by my side doesn't sound like such a bad idea after all.

I send him an incentive. Shrugging off the blanket, I sit up and go to the camera app on my phone. I'm wearing a lacy black bralette and pushing my boobs together to give myself just enough cleavage for the picture. My nipples hardened from the loss of the blanket so I know they'll make an appearance in the photo.

I send the image to Grimm, nervous and impatient for his response. I've never done this before. Leo wasn't exactly encouraging when it came to me showing off my body and if he saw nudes on my phone, he would've gone berserk. Doesn't matter if they were meant for him. They were still sitting on my phone. What if I had a change of heart and decided to send them to every person in my contact list?

I can't believe I stayed with him for so long! His reasonings for acting the way he did were fucking bullshit! Good fucking riddance!

The phone vibrates, breaking my thoughts.

GRIMM

Fuck, V.

I'm hard.

I'm almost there. Door or window?

I can't wait to feel you.

My cheeks heat as I drag my teeth along my bottom lip. Flashbacks of the last time I felt every inch of Grimm inside me play through my mind and I shudder. A dull ache forms between my legs, anxious with anticipation to have him again. I send a reply without thinking too hard about its contents. Play it cool, V.

ME

Window. You're my dirty little secret. 💋

Easy. Light. Or too much? I hope it's not too much. I hope I don't offend him. Fuck, so much for playing it cool.

GRIMM

Here. Open up, please.

I stand and open the window for Grimm. His stature is so big, practically double the size of the window itself. He contorts his body skillfully as he slithers through the opening, away from the brisk atmosphere. Straightening his back, he stands before me dressed in all black looking down at me.

"Hey there, good looking." He says, his baritone voice filling my room and sending chills down my spine.

"Hi." I whisper so quiet, I consider repeating myself because I'm not sure if he heard me.

"So, V, baby, before we move on with our day, I just want to get one thing straight." His fingertips trace down my arm to my wrist, and swirl in my palm before reversing the pattern. My heart rate picks up at his touch, his proximity. I catch a waft of sandalwood and sage as his body towers over me. I take a few steps back and he follows until I'm lined up with the wall.

Unzipping his hoodie, Grimm shrugs it off and places it on my desk chair. His shirt clings to his muscles and his hair is wet as if he's fresh out of the shower. He raises his arm and places his palm on the wall directly next to my head. The other hand slips under my chin and brings my eyes to his. His voice reverberates through every inch of my body.

"I will not be your dirty little secret. Everyone will know you're mine." He states and I'm not sure if I'm terrified or exhilarated. Or both?

I wouldn't want people to notice my moving on so quickly. Little do they know I've been fighting for survival for years while being with Leo. Maybe the worst thing to do in my situation would be exactly what I'm choosing to do here with Grimm, but there is such a magnetic pull between the two of us. I need to give this a chance and see where it goes.

And I don't want to fucking wait.

GRIMM

She licks her lips, uncertain of how to answer. I know her concerns with people knowing about us too soon. And I have every intention to protect her for the rest of my life.

"But-" My finger moves from her chin to cover her lips.

"For now, I'll be a good boy. You don't have to worry about me, Verena. I'll be your secret until the time is right. Then every single person who crosses either of our paths will know that I belong to you and you belong to me."

She nods softly and a small smirk graces her face for just a second. "Are you okay with that?" I ask, afraid that I completely scared her off. If it wasn't the ten tons of baggage I brought along, maybe it was that right there. Claiming her after we just fucking murdered her abusive, piece of shit ex-boyfriend.

Fuck, I just want her to understand I'd do anything for her. I'd tell any lie, kill any man or woman, and burn down the world before I see her hurt or aching. Her smile makes my heart pound like a fucking kick-drum. No one has made me feel an ounce of what I feel towards V. She's my agony, my moonlight. I replay every moment I've had with her in my head like it's my favorite movie.

"Yes." She says more confidently. "I'm perfectly fine with that." I nod and focus my eyes on her chest. I softly hook my finger into her strap and rub it.

"This is pretty." I whisper, my eyes lingering at her chest gazing between her breasts. "You look beautiful." My tongue darts out to wet my lips and I can tell it's causing her pussy to pulse with need, begging for my attention.

My arms find the small of her back and bring her in close to me. Her arms wrap around my neck, our eyes locked on one another. "I know." She whispers, a smirk gracing her lips.

I lightly scoff, mocking shock and she giggles. "You should know. I'll spend every day reminding you, you know, in case there's a moment you slip up and forget."

Her eyes bat lustfully in response to my promise and her cheeks turn a coral hue. The blush compliments her olive skin so wonderfully, the sight makes my heart pound in my chest.

Looking into her eyes, I don't just see her *now*. I don't see a quick hook-up to feed my selfish desires. I see every morning and every night for the rest of my life. Every "I love you," saved just for her and I. I see stolen kisses in the kitchen because our kids find it gross that we show each other so much affection, they feel the need to yell at us to get a room. I see myself walking through the front door of our home and V running into my arms, stuck to me like glue, because a few hours separated was a few hours too long.

One moment turns into another, images flashing through my mind of what the future could be. Verena wearing my ring on her finger, Verena in a wedding dress, Verena's belly swollen with our baby, Verena holding our newborn, our happy little family.

Having my own family was something I've dreamed of for a long time, I just never thought it possible. With The Brotherhood being my career, my mind blocked out all chances of finding real love. I've always known that if I'd end up with anyone, it would be her. It took a lot of patience, but here we are. I finally get to worship her the way she deserves and right now is the perfect time to do so.

"Verena, I-" I say, my breathing heavy and erection growing by the second, thinking of her in all stages of life.

"Just do it, Grimm." She cuts me off. "You've got me. I'm yours." Reaching up, she loops her thumb through her strap and guides it off her shoulder. She repeats the motion with the other strap and pushes her bra to lay around her stomach. Grabbing my hand, she leads me to the bed and completely removes her bra before laying down, pulling me with her.

"Are you sure?" I whisper. "I know it's soon and if you aren't ready, I'm okay with that, I promise you."

She giggles and I furrow my brows in confusion. "I want you, Grimm. It's not too soon. I've been mourning a relationship for almost two years. I am finally at peace. I'm free and I can be with anyone I choose. I choose you."

I can't help but let a real smile breakthrough. My lips connect with hers, unable to blend fully because my smile is so big I can't keep my damn lips closed long enough for it to be considered an actual kiss. But fuck, her smile brings a warmth to my body that has been missing since fucking forever. Her caress starts my heart back up again, like a beat up car fresh out of the body shop with a new battery. Infinite life.

Her hands tangle in my hair as she pulls me in. Our lips collide and I feel a complete primal urge to overtake her. I massage her breasts and pinch her nipples, eliciting small gasps and moans from her, a sweet symphony I could listen to for hours on repeat. My hands move down her body, hooking my thumbs into her bottoms and removing them swiftly.

Verena pulls my shirt up and I take over, peeling the rest of the fabric from my skin as she undoes my belt. Right now is about love but it's also about feeling wanted. Finding the one that accepts your imperfections and faults. The one that will turn your faults and imperfections into highlights. The one that will help you acknowledge the love you deserve and not just what you *think* you deserve.

Both of us undressed, I kiss her forehead then trail down the bridge of her nose to her cupid's bow. I press my lips against hers and continue down her neck, across her clavicle and down the middle of her chest. On my descent, I appreciate her breasts more thoroughly this time. They spill out of my hands as I knead them and I take turns swirling my tongue around her brown peaked nipples. A louder moan slips from her lips and it's the most delicious sound I've ever heard. *I want more.*

I hear a door close in the distance but it doesn't fully register that someone is home. We all have roommates and the guys in my house always stay to themselves. The footsteps get closer to the door. It swings open and Aspen screams, bringing her hands up to cover her eyes.

"Verena! Grimm?! What the hell!" She gasps. V and I stay put, but she snatches the closest pillow and hurls it at the door. "Out!" She yells back at Aspen who runs for the hills, slamming the door as she exits.

"Anyways." She says, pushing my shoulders down towards her

perfectly wet pussy. Spreading her legs open, she bares herself to me, welcoming me into my new home.

Home sweet home, am I right?

Eye level with her core, I soak up the sight of her and lick my lips in anticipation. Lightly blowing on her slit, she breathes heavily and whines, anxious for my mouth to be on her. Gripping her thighs, I take in a deep breath, her arousal the sweetest smell, and dive in. My tongue lays flat on her clit and I swirl and suck in every which way to pull out those harmonic melodies from her. It's not long before she's unraveling on my tongue.

Her erratic breathing slows down, but I'm nowhere near finished with her yet. Sliding two fingers into her center, I pump them into her and suck her clit, pulling another orgasm from her. She places her hand on the back of my head and tugs lightly on my hair before pushing my face deeper into my blissful meal.

"Play with yourself, little monster. Show me exactly how you like to be touched. I want to give you everything you want." I say as I come up for air. Verena places her fingers on her clit and rubs softly, her whines grow louder as she's closer to her climax. With my free hand, I begin stroking my aching cock. Hard and ready to be buried inside of her.

Standing, I step back and admire her for a moment. She's the definition of ethereal. She's imperfect for me and that's all I'd ever ask of her. Appreciating her curves, I flip her over to get a better view. Her ass jiggles as she gets comfortable and I can't help but smack it to see it move like the waves once more. My handprint on her ass also looks mighty fucking fine, if I do say so myself. I imagine it tattooed, marking her permanently as mine.

How could I convince her to do that? I'll revisit at a later time.

Positioning herself onto her knees, her back arches and her holes are fully displayed to me. Bending down, I slide my tongue from her clit to her backside and don't leave an inch untouched. She continues to pleasure herself and I'm close to busting my nut just by listening to her. If that wasn't enough, she turns her head to the side and confesses,

"I need you inside of me, Grimm. Please, I can't go another second without you."

What my queen wants, she gets. Leaning forward, I line myself up with her core and whisper in her ear, "As you wish, my little monster."

Slowly, I watch her pussy stretch to fit my girth. Seeing my cock swallowed by her body feels like such a fucking privilege, I don't have any idea as to why Leo fucked this shit up for himself. Verena is a literal goddess on earth. Access to her mind, body, and soul shouldn't have been given away so carelessly. I silently vow to never take her for granted, in any facet of the word.

Once I've got every inch inside of her, I pick up my pace and rub her asshole with my thumb. It causes her to gasp and she tightens around my length, pulling me closer to my release. I hold onto her hips and watch as her ass moves in waves from the force of my thrusts. She continues to moan as she cums on my cock, twice, before I feel my balls draw up and a tingle in my spine.

"I want to give you everything, Verena. Every drop of cum. Every inch of my soul. I promise to always give you the love you want and deserve. You're irreplaceable. You're my alpha and my omega. My beginning and my end. I don't think I started breathing until you looked at me, and I mean really looked at me. You are all I need. You hear me?" My speed picks up and my grip turns aggressive, strong enough to leave bruises in her skin.

"You." *Thrust.*

"Are." *Thrust.*

"My." *Thrust.*

"Everything." *Thrust.*

My release spills into her, as we both scream out in pleasure. Pulling out, Verena snaps her legs closed and I worry I've done something wrong to hurt her. "Everything okay?" I ask, hesitantly.

"I like having you inside me. That goes for your cum, too. I want it dripping out of me, reminding me of every second we just spent intertwined." Hair sticks to her glistening skin and she's never looked so beautiful. My heart is holding so much happiness, it's painful.

Isn't it beautiful when the person you love loves you back whole-

heartedly? Isn't is fucking mesmerizing when they smile just for you, making you feel so accomplished and special for experiencing a part of them most never will?

I want to bask in the moment for a while longer, but alas reality sets in. Footsteps begin to pace in front of V's door before Aspen raps on the wood once again, impatient and insistent on speaking with Verena. "Are you freaks dressed yet? It's a fucking emergency, Verena!"

Verena rolls her eyes and rises from the bed, throwing on her clothes that were strewn across the floor. "Cover yourself, I'm opening the door."

I salute her and hop under the covers before she opens the door and Aspen stands there. I didn't get a good look at her when she interrupted us before, but it's clear she's in distress. Her mascara runs down her face and her hair is disheveled as she tries to explain that she's been trying to contact Blair for hours but to no avail.

"Blair's missing. What the fuck do we do?"

23

GRIMM

VERENA DASHES TO ASPEN, dragging her to the living room to drain every detail from her. My phone goes off, a loud ping within the silence and I hop out of bed to fish the device out of my pants.

DAD

> Dinner on Saturday at 7. Excited to see you. Can you bring a dessert? Your sister and I are putting together a last minute birthday celebration for Greer.

I roll my eyes at the idea of doing anything nice for Greer. Dude's the biggest prick I've met in this lifetime. He doesn't deserve an ounce of celebration towards his life. *I'll celebrate when he's six feet under.*

Greer was my childhood bully. Yeah, older siblings pick on you and beat you up, but he took shit to the next level.

Swiping out of the message thread, I click on my conversation with Emmett. Blair is missing and I haven't heard from him? A while back he drunk himself into oblivion over god-knows-what. I can't imagine what he'd do if something happened to her.

ME

Hey bro, just checking in. Everything all good?

V storms back into the room and asks, "Have you heard anything from Emmett?" I shake my head, not wanting to say it out loud.

"Yeah. I got Blair's voicemail. Aspen's been texting her for hours and hasn't gotten anything back." Verena sighs.

"She shouldn't be alone. Stay with her and I'll get in touch with Emmett. Let me know if you hear from Blair. I'll be back." I promise, kissing the crown of her head and slipping out of the window. Hurrying back to my house, I text Eli to let him know we've got a problem.

ME

Emmett MIA. Blair, too. Be on standby.

ELI

Fuck.

Got it.

AS IF EMMETT going missing wasn't enough for one day, Baron called to tell me whoever was supposed to pick up the bags of…Leo, flaked. My mind shifts to a playful idea Verena had when we spoke about what to do with Leo's remains and I wonder if she'd be willing to go through with it.

"Where the hell could they be?" I think out loud, pacing Eli's room. Verena stayed at her place with Aspen. She's in so much distress about Blair's uncertain status, and I know Verena is feeling it too. It's one thing when you know something sinister is going on, it's another when you're directly affected or affected by association.

The guys and I are at the house, waiting to hear from Emmett.

A call comes through and I reach for my phone so quickly, it slips out of my hand and Eli catches it. He looks at the name and then tosses it back, "Verena. Potentially useless."

I imagine daggers shooting out at him from my eyes, directly into his. I know he means she most likely has no new information but there's a million other ways to say that. Picking up the phone, Verena skips the formalities and gives me her update.

"Still no word from Blair. There's really nothing for us to do except wait to hear from one of them? What about some fancy location trackers?" Verena questions.

Walking downstairs and into the kitchen, I pour myself a glass of whiskey and down it. "Trackers have to be implanted. We don't have trackers, at least, none that I know of." My hand skims over the skin of my neck and behind my ears, double-checking that I'm not sporting an unknown chip beneath the surface of my skin.

"While I have you, there's something I need to tell you. The pickup for Leo was delayed and so I was wondering if we could use Plan B." I say, my voice low. Silence greets me at the other end of the line.

"What was Plan B?" She asks.

I chuckle. "You know, make it into something delicious and deliver it to someone insufferable."

She chokes on a laugh and my smile grows. "We're going to make one hundred pounds of lasagna and deliver it to our enemies?"

Her giggles grow louder and my heart aches to hear it in person. She laughs a lot now and it's the most beautiful sound ever made. A slight lump forms in my throat when the realization hits. I've always known I love her. But now I get the chance to fall in love with her. That's the greatest thing in life I may ever experience.

No drug, kill, or bit of blood can compare to what she does to me.

Her laughter slows and she continues, "Alright. Which tunnel leads to a kitchen because there's no way in hell I'm cooking Leo in my house."

"Oh, of course not, darling. We have a wonderful kitchen down there. State of the art. You will love it." Chuckling, I down my second glass of whiskey, when my phone rings. Emmett's name flashes on the screen and I pick up without a second thought, ending my call with Verena. "Long time, no talk. Nice to finally hear from you."

Emmett goes on a tirade about his dad being behind the disappearances. He orders me to bring James to the shed behind their house and sends me his location. I hang up, inform the guys, and shoot V a quick text.

ME

He's okay. Meeting him now. I'll update you later.

Her reply comes back quickly. My heart melts and my dick hardens at her words.

VERENA

Stay safe.

VERENA

LEILA

Hello, Verena. Haven't heard from Leo in a few days. I'm sure he's busy but can you just let him know that Mommy is missing him and just wanted to talk? Thanks.

My eyes roll so far back, they almost get stuck. I leave her on read and toss the phone to the side. My mind is occupied by the lack of Blair's presence. She walked the straight and narrow. She always had her nose in a book, what trouble could she have possibly gotten into? Aspen has been a mess and I've spent most of this time comforting her. She hasn't been able to spend a single second alone. Eli has been ordering us take-out for dinner because we don't have the energy to think or cook.

I have to admit, it's been nice to be part of a circle of people who care for one another. Aspen, Grimm, and even Eli, they're like this newfound family I don't ever want to let go of.

When Leila's texts go unanswered by me, there's no concern for my well being. I understand Leo is her son, but this family has known me throughout my entire college experience and there's not an ounce of concern for me. In fact, her texts went from "innocent mother looking for her son," to "vile bitch showing her true colors" and I'm so thankful that soon, I'll never have to see or hear from her again.

When you pop a kid out of your cunt, I don't think you expect to become one. I'm sure Leila didn't anticipate it but she's a fully fledged "C U Next Tuesday."

LEILA

Is everything okay with Leo? He's not answering and I'm getting worried.

Did you tell him to ignore my calls, you little wrench? Why isn't he answering his phone?

If you don't tell me where my son is, I'm going to the police. I just went to his apartment and he clearly hasn't been home for days.

I always knew you were evil, your clothing–if you can even call it that–was convincing enough, but I'm sure you did something to my son.

Fucking brewha.

My heart pounds ferociously at her words as my blood pressure spikes along with my anxiety. I snap a screenshot and send it to Grimm. His response is almost immediate.

GRIMM

What a bitch. If you want to take her out too, let me know. But I'm sure once she's tasted your lasagna, she'll turn a corner.

We're in the clear. I promise. Don't stress about it, little monster.

I miss you.

He's been on a vengeance streak with Emmett for the last couple of days. Grimm gave me all the details about Blair's disappearance. He keeps true to his word and updates me regularly, sometimes with too much detail. I delete our messages periodically because I'm so goddamn paranoid he's going to get my ass thrown into jail with the stories he tells me.

I need to speak with Eli and have him wipe it all from the inter-web for good. Before that, I have some meal prep to do.

Huffing out a breath, I look at Leila's messages again. The utter disbelief that courses through my veins sets ablaze my anger. I do what I do best and laugh about the situation at hand, because if I don't, I'll spiral.

Looking at Leila's texts, my mind dissociates to that night underground with Leo and Grimm. The machete driving straight through his chest and tearing him to pieces. A laugh of relief bubbles up my throat at the reminder that Leo is no longer in control of my life.

But if I want to successfully deliver my Leo-sagna to her, I need her to think I'm innocent in his disappearance.

ME

We aren't together. I haven't heard much from him lately, either.

Can I stop by this weekend? I would love to have a chance to say a formal goodbye.

Also, it's bruja.

I fucking hate playing nice. I'd much rather keep to myself because it drains me a lot less than plastering a fake smile on my face to empathize with twatwaffles.

Her response comes in faster than it usually took Leo to get it up.

LEILA

Whatever.

Saturday at 6.

A devious smirk splays on my lips as I feel a sense of accomplishment in weaseling my way into her house one last time to serve up delicious, meaty revenge.

24

GRIMM

THE LAST FEW days have been fucking wild. As much as I've hated spending time away from V, the thrill of killing douchebags that deserve it has been fulfilling in her absence.

The craziness has settled down. Emmett and Blair are back, or what's left of them anyway. They've stayed to themselves mostly, soaking up every minute with one another and I've done the same with Verena whenever she's not consoling Aspen.

But tonight is *finally* the night. Tonight we will cook. Tonight we take vengeance.

Verena also meets your family tonight. Woohoo! Don't forget a dessert!

Shit. I crawl out of bed and dress in jeans and a black tee. Slipping on my boots, I reach for my phone and text my little monster.

ME

Be ready in an hour?

VERENA

I'll be waiting, loverboy.

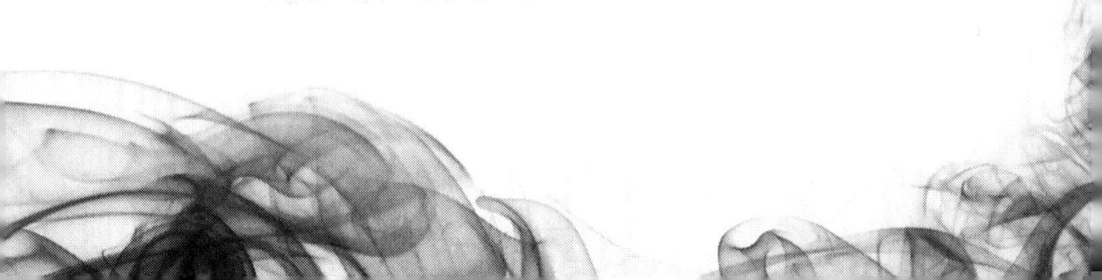

My dick practically jumps out of my jeans at my newly acquired nickname. She keeps that up, we won't get any real work done.

I finish getting my shit together, pick up V, and head to the tunnels.

"WOW, you were right. This is a very fancy setup. Does The Brotherhood use it often for similar...purposes?" Verena asks with a chuckle.

I shrug my shoulders in response. "Not sure. Usually, I sell the meat. But there's a first time for everything, right? I'm glad I get to pop my human lasagna cherry with you."

Her smile grows and she shakes her head. I collect gloves, aprons, goggles, and hairnets for us in preparation for our roles as Head Chef and Sous Chef. "You look dashing in a hairnet." She compliments me before breaking into a fit of giggles.

"Not as good as you, little monster." I respond, her cheeks flushing instantly.

We move around the kitchen flawlessly. Two halves working as one whole. Verena calls out ingredients and seasonings, I fetch them for her, and she adds it all into a big dish.

Three hours later, we have two large trays ready to be devoured by cunts and douchebags who aided in making our lives hell at one point or another.

We clean up and head back to my place to get ready for dinner at my dad's. I thought I'd loathe this day when it came, but Verena and her willingness to participate in my mischief sends signals to my little man and changes my attitude toward the night.

My angel of darkness has brought so much light into my life without realizing it. Clouds of questions don't hang around anymore because I found all of the answers in those amber eyes.

Maybe I saved her, but she resurrected me.

BACK AT THE HOUSE, we shower and change before our presence is expected at my dad's place. V swiped some of my clothes while I was still in the shower. When I walked into my room, she was already swallowed by one of my large t-shirts with the covers pulled up to her chin. Her faint snores filled the room and my heart almost jumps out of my chest to lay in bed with her.

The last few weeks have been insane for both of us. The disappearance of our friends, the whole Leo fiasco, and now we have to face two more enemies, Leila and Greer.

When Verena sent me the screenshot of the nasty things Leila was saying to her, I wanted to hatch up my own plan and dispose of her in the middle of the night. No one deserves to be spoken to like that, but especially not my little monster. The shit she had to put up with from Leo all these years was more than enough and I'll be damned if I let anyone think they can treat her like that for even a mere second,

Verena should be treated like the goddess that she is, and I will stay true to my word to show her that.

I hang up my towel and sit at my desk to roll up a joint. Once it's rolled, I walk over to my nightstand and fish out the gift I bought for her recently. Opening the box, I power on the wand and it roars to life. The smirk on my face grows and I'm gleeful for Verena to wake up so I can treat her the way she deserves to be treated.

She stirs from the vibration and I turn it off, setting it down carefully so I don't wake her yet. I peel the blanket from her body and slowly slip off the pair of basketball shorts she stole from my dresser.

Starting at her feet, I peck her skin, appreciating every inch. The smoothness of her body against my lips feels like heaven and my cock hardens immediately at the collision.

I kiss my way up to her chest, peeling up my shirt from her chest as I go. She moans softly and her eyes flicker open. "Hey, do we have to go? Did I oversleep?" She questions.

"We have all the time in the world, little monster." I reassure her. "But I've got a lot of pent up anger and nerves, figured you do too. I wanted to do something for you to take the edge off."

She smiles, still half asleep, and asks another question. "You woke me up to smoke? What a gentleman." Her hand falls on my back and she rubs in circles, her talon shaped nails graze over my skin, making me shudder.

I reach over her and grab the wand from the nightstand. "Yes, but also," I place the wand between us, against her center, and power it on. "I had other ideas."

Her breath hitches and her words get caught in her throat. "Just relax and let me take care of you, okay?"

Verena nods and her eyes open fully, locking with mine, and following my every move. I bring the toy past her pussy and glide it along her hips, up her stomach and to her nipple. Circling the vibrator around the hardened bud, I reach down to my leaking cock between us and gather the precum on my thumb before rubbing it along her other nipple.

The most lustful chuckle slips past her lips and I almost bust on the spot. She has no idea the power she holds over my heart, and my cock.

I wrap my lips around her nipple, sucking on it and pulling blissful moans from her. Every breath, every mewl, every sound that falls from her mouth contributes to the pulsing in my lower half, my cock becoming impossibly stiff.

Bringing the vibrator back down to her entrance, I slide it in, soaking it with her wetness and pull it out slowly. Verena's mouth falls open and creates the prettiest "O" any man or woman on this earth has ever seen. I raise the wand to my lips and suck on it, savoring her taste. I repeat the process and raise the wand to her lips and order her, "Taste yourself, little monster. You're fucking delicious."

She sticks out her tongue and obeys without a second thought. "That's my good girl." I whisper in her ear before removing the wand, increasing the vibration, and inserting it inside her core once more.

I stand and find my preroll along with a lighter. Grabbing my desk chair, I swivel it across the floor and position it right at the foot of my bed. Lighting the preroll, I inhale and walk over to Verena. Bending down, I tap her lips and she opens up as I lean in and blow the smoke into her mouth. She holds it in for a moment, before exhaling.

Taking a seat, I lean back with my legs spread wide, my still exposed and hard cock bobbing between them. I take another deep inhale, letting the soothing smoke fill my lungs. I peer down my nose at her while exhaling. The smoke creates a haze between us and my lips tip up in a grimace. "Let's see how many times we can get that pretty pussy to cum for me before I finish this joint," I rasp.

"Grimm, I'm already so close. I want to feel you inside of me." She begs. Oh, how fucking sweet she sounds when she's begging. But it's going to take a lot more than that to get me to obey her at this moment. She looks too good, sprawled out just for me. I want to soak up every second so I can replay it in my mind whenever she's not here with me.

I shake my head and take another hit. "Soon, but not yet, little monster. What you need to focus on right now is coming around that wand while I smoke this." I hold up the joint and bring it back to my lips, hitting it a few more times. Clouds of smoke permeate the air and my dick pulses, begging to be touched.

I wrap my hand around my shaft as V's cries get louder and more frequent. "O-oh fuck. I'm coming, Grimm." She tips her head back. From here I can see as her first orgasm washes through her. Her limbs stiffen and her back arches. My eyes rake over every inch of her, cataloging every twitch and movement until landing on her pussy as it clamps around the wand as she comes undone.

"That's one. Such a good little slut. Keep going for me, baby." I bring the joint back to my lips and watch the amber glow at the end as I inhale.

A tear falls down her cheek and her limbs shake and another orgasm ricochets through her body. Her whines grow louder as I reach over and turn up the wand to its highest setting. "You got another one for me, pretty lady? I know you do. Give it to me. Give it all to me."

Verena nods furiously and her eyes squeeze shut as her pleasure takes over and courses through every vein beneath her skin. Her toes curl and her back arches once more, displaying her perfectly stuffed pussy to me. I pump my length a few times and that tingling sensation shoots down my spine as my release nears.

"Who do you belong to, Verena?" I ask, thrusting into my hand. "Tell me, baby. Who owns you?"

Breathlessly, she responds. "You, Grimm. You own me. I'm all yours. Now and forever. Forever and always."

Nodding, I push her to continue. "Keep saying my name. I want you to call out to me over and over again until we're both spent."

"Grimm." She whines, "Grimm, fuck I'm coming."

Finishing the blunt, I put it out on my tongue, the touch of the ash sizzling my muscle before the fiery glow fades to black. I walk over to the ashtray and drop the roach in there then stalk over to Verena. Lining up my cock with her mouth, I bark one more order her way.

"Open up, baby. Swallow every drop and take every inch." She obliges like the perfect little whore she is. Not a speck of my load leaves her lips and I gently wrap my palm around her dainty neck to feel her swallow me down.

"Good girl. You follow directions beautifully." I praise her and her smile brightens.

"Only for you, Grimm. It's all for you"

Not only is my little man at full attention after not even getting the chance to soften, my heart thrums against its confines at her words.

Only for me. Her love is only for me and I'm more than certain there's nothing in this world that could make me happier or feel more fulfilled than Verena Losado.

25

VERENA

THAT WAS FUCKING AMAZING. Never in my life have I experienced an orgasm so riveting and toe-curling. *And he didn't need to lift a finger to touch me.*

It's official, Grimm Griswold has me wrapped around his finger. He could tell me to get on all fours and bark in the campus square and I'd happily oblige as long as I get a taste of him again.

We dress and prepare to head out. I made sure to wear the perfect outfit that Leila would absolutely despise. A black leather halter corset pushes my girls together giving me the perfect amount of cleavage. I opted for a shirt with no sleeves just so she can see the lingering bruises her precious little boy left on my skin before he disappeared into thin air…or into my pasta dish.

Leo preferred my straight hair to my natural curls and after my shower today, I decided to embrace everything about myself that he hated. My skin, where he preferred his indigo kisses to my olive tone. My hair, falling in ringlets down my back. My outfit, showing off all the glorious curves I was given.

My jeans are skin tight and do wonders for my legs. Heeled combat boots and loads of silver jewelry complete my look. Little machetes hang from my ears and I giggle at the irony of it all. I've had these earrings for years and never gave them a second glance. Overnight, they've become my favorite pair and have more meaning than any other piece in my closet.

The cherry on top of it all is my smokey black eye makeup. I spent an hour watching "siren eyes" tutorials, perfecting the look. The last time this bitch sees me I need to present myself in a way where I feel the most powerful.

Grimm emerges from the bathroom dressed in black jeans and a black fitted long-sleeve, the accessory of a preroll tucked behind his ear. His muscles can be seen clear as day through his shirt and my mind wanders to all the things I'd do to him if he was shirtless. It's obvious he has the same idea as his eyes roam over every inch of my body and I can't help but bask in his attention. My heart thumps in my chest and I feel my cheeks heat as they redden.

"Black is your color, little monster. You look ravishing." He compliments, stepping closer to me. His nose burrows into the crook of my neck as he inhales my scent and whispers, "I could devour you whole, right here, right now."

Smiling, I respond, "I have no objections to that."

Pulling back, he straightens and shakes his head, "If we start, we won't stop. And this cunt needs a taste of her own bitchy medicine." He lowers his hand to cup my ass and then taps it lightly. "Let's go fuck some shit up."

Grimm tucks his hair behind his ear and I grab the preroll before noticing a glint coming in the direction of his ear.

He has a fucking earring. A silver chain dangles from his left ear and my mouth goes slack.

"Yes, I have an earring. No, I don't wear it all the time. It's only for special occasions and being with you, bringing you to meet my family, is special. It's not something I've done before and I wouldn't do with anyone else." He pauses as his smile widens, "Yes, I'll keep it on while I fuck your brains out later."

I'm utterly speechless. "Yes," is all I can make out before we're both doubled over laughing at my lame ass reaction to something as simple as an earring.

Grimm wraps his arm around my waist and we grab the trays of lasagna from the kitchen before entering the garage.

His blacked out McLaren is sleek and sexy. The leather interior smells just like him. He hands me a lighter and revs the engine. Before peeling out of the garage, he flashes me a smile. “Spark that, baby. It’s showtime.”

26

VERENA

WE TOSS the joint back and forth throughout the car ride, Grimm's playlist blasting through the speakers as we go. Some songs that come up are the epitome of who Grimm Griswold is, like *Killing in the Name Of* by Rage Against the Machine and *We Do This Shit* by MODSUN featuring DeJLoaf. Other songs catch me by surprise, a few by Sabrina Carpenter, Raye, and Qveen Herby made his playlist, and he belts out every word.

I look at him in disbelief, but it's the kind that's followed by lust. His charismatic and goofy personality has always been one of his best attributes. Any time he's in the room, it's filled with laughter, smiles, and a good fucking time. It's the number one thing that caused me to gravitate towards him, his protective nature is a close second. I had never seen him pick on anyone or start a fight. He was the kid who stood up to bullies and took them down from their pedestals, reminding them that they were no better than anyone else, especially if they had to go through all the trouble of putting another person down to prove it.

For the first time in my life, I don't feel like I have to pretend to be something I'm not. When I lived at home, I had so much pressure to have high ranking academics because my parents preferred nothing less. They only saw us kids as an extension of them and their success.

For Ronnie, I pretended to be the strong, invincible older sister. I had to wear a poker face every time I walked into her room and saw her hooked up to a bunch of machines. I wanted her to think I didn't see her in her fragile state, she was always the same old Ronnie she had been. I'll never know of the demons that seeped into her mind when she was left alone and I could only hope she would have confided in me if they were. But alas, those days are gone and I'm not that studious daughter or overly positive sister anymore.

I'm not the grief stricken girl that Leo met and took under his wing. I'm not the "bruja" Leila claims me to be, but I'm over the moon that I get to be both his worst nightmare and her reality check.

With Grimm, I can just be Verena. I'm not someone's daughter, someone's girlfriend, someone's sister. I'm just me and this feeling is better than any high I've experienced in this lifetime.

WE PULL up to Leila's house and I wipe my palms against my jeans. "Go get 'em, baby. I'll be right here if you need me." He reaches over and squeezes my thigh, and places a peck on my head.

Nodding, I get out of the car, open the backdoor, and grab the lasagna from the backseat. A smile threatens to break out across my face but I tamper it down as I walk up to the door and ring the bell.

No more than three seconds pass before it swings open and Leila greets me with her snooty, upturned nose and a smile so fake, it doesn't reach her eyes.

Reminds me of my own mother, how sweet.

"Hi, Leila. Nice to see yo-"

"Yeah, get inside quick before someone sees you." She spits, grabbing my arm and yanking me into the house.

Stumbling into the foyer, I come face-to-face with a wall full of Leo. There's more pictures of him than there are of Leila and her… fourth husband?

Looking out of the bay window, I see Grimm's McLaren parked out front and my heart rate calms. He's with me. I'm not alone anymore.

I'll never be alone again.

Leila trots off to the kitchen and ushers me to follow. "So, what do you have there? You've always shown up empty-handed. Why bring food now?" She questions.

"I brought pasteles one Christmas, Leo said you tossed them after we left. Then there was that time I brought empanadas that you refused to eat because oil and tortillas weren't part of your diet. I can keep going." I offer but it's clear she gets the point.

Sighing, she displays a smile of defeat and nods toward the dish in my hand. "What is it, Velma?"

My patience is thinning. This woman is going to end up in my next batch of empanadas if she doesn't cut this shit out soon.

"It's Verena, actually. I made lasagna for you. It was…Leo's special recipe." It physically pains me to speak positively about Leo, but I need her to believe that I wasn't the one to take his life so I can leave this hell house and her in the past, once and for all. "He even let me in on his secret ingredient."

She stares at me with empathetic eyes, "Lasagna was always his favorite."

I offer no response and quietness blankets the room, the sound of a pin drop would be equivalent to a nuclear bomb.

"Alright." Leila breaks the silence. "When did you last see Leo? It's been about two weeks since I've heard from him and he missed our weekly lunch the other day with no phone call or text. What's going on with you two?"

Game time. Bring out those puppy dog eyes and pouty lip.

My eyes begin to water on cue and I tell her everything about Leo's abuse. She uncovers the lasagna and grabs a corner for herself. She heats it up and sits down at the small booth in the corner. I tell her when it started, how it escalated, and what happened the last time I saw him, alive and well that is.

She scoops up a spoonful and chomps it down. Bile rises in my throat at the thought of putting that lasagna anywhere near my mouth, but I just give her an innocent smile and continue. I showed her the burn on my hand that's in the midst of healing. I repeated every vile comment I could recount. I told her he drugged me and locked me in his apartment. Then I told her that when he got back, he broke up with me and tossed me on the street like a bag full of trash.

Leila pauses after I finish and picks a chunk of meat from her teeth. She musters up all of the audacity in her fucking being to ask me something so outrageous, I fear I may just cook her into the empanadas tonight and tell Grimm we need to take a raincheck on this birthday dinner.

"What did you do to cause him to act out?" She questions, genuinely concerned for how I've been treating her son rather than the physical evidence I've just shown her that was left on me because he chose to throw temper tantrums instead of conversing with me like an adult. I didn't need to explain myself any further.

"Wow. That's my cue to leave." I say, rising to my feet and walking out of the kitchen.

"Velma, wait!"

"My name is fucking Verena!" I yell, bumping into a side table and knocking down a vase. "Address me with the correct name or don't fucking address me at all. I don't know where the fuck your bitch-ass son is and I don't fucking care anymore. He's given me nothing but trouble and for the first time in years, I can be myself without him bitching in my ear about what *he* prefers every two seconds." Tears stream down my face, but they aren't tears of pain. They're tears of joy. I'm getting out of here and never looking back.

"If you don't help me find him, I'll go to the police. I'll tell them it was you. You know we have friends in high places. It wouldn't take a lot to get you convicted. You don't have the same connections and safety that we do, you little bitch, and you know it!"

My heart just about falls out of my ass until I remember one small detail. My lips tip up into a sinister grin, "I have a friend too, Leila. Chief of Police, Greg Griswold. Are you familiar with him?"

Her eyes widen as I step closer to her until our noses are just inches apart. My voice lowers to an intimidating octave I've never spoken in before. "You tell them I had anything to do with Leo's disappearance, and I will do everything in my power to make sure that I drain you of every asset, every dollar, and every fucking jewel you own." Pointing to the vase, I continue my threat, "Clean that shit up and pray to every bruja you know, besides me that is, that your precious boy finally makes it home one day. If not on his own two legs, preferably in a silk-lined casket."

Turning on my heel, I storm out the front door and back into Grimm's McLaren. My chest rises and falls as I dab the tears from my face, careful not to smear my makeup.

"Everything okay?" Grimm asks, his eyes searching my body to confirm I'm not injured.

"Yeah, I'm good." I turn to him and break out in a smile. A laugh follows shortly after. "She fucking ate the Leosagna. Let's go before she runs out here to pester me about the secret ingredient."

With that, Grimm speeds off down the road.

Time to meet the Griswolds.

27

GRIMM

MY CHILDHOOD HOME should bring fun and nostalgic memories. Instead I think of every bad moment I've experienced within those walls.

When I was five, my older brothers were teaching me how to swim. I had gotten out of the water to use the bathroom and left my floaties by the pool. When I came back, my floaties were gone. I don't know how, but I slipped and fell into the pool and couldn't find my way to the surface. My brother Griffin yanked me out and gave me CPR. If it wasn't for him, my life would have ended right then and there.

Would've saved me a whole lot of fucking trouble, too.

But then you wouldn't have met Verena, dingbat. And she would've been stuck with Leo. You know how that would've turned out.

I turn the car off and pull out another preroll to delay the inevitable. V senses my hesitation and brings it to light. "Does your leg always bounce when you're nervous?"

She's the first to notice. The first to care. I've never spoken about my anxiety and the feelings that override my golden retriever personality most days. My spark was lit when Verena came into my life for good. The anxiety has been almost non-existent. At first, I didn't think it was possible for another person to do a better job of ridding the anxiety better than good old Mary-Jane, but she continues to prove me wrong.

I don't want to spill out my whole life's trauma so I settle on a simple answer for now. "My siblings and I, we don't really get along the best. I'm sure you'll see it firsthand tonight, so if that happens, I'm sorry. Greer is the worst one so just stay away from him. Gracie isn't all that bad and she's the only girl, so I'm sure your presence will excite her."

She places her hand over mine and squeezes. "What I'm sure of is you. You're a great person. Whatever sibling feud you have doesn't define who you are. I'm pretty certain siblings are supposed to hate each other." She says with a small laugh.

"What about you and Ronnie?" I ask. "Did you guys ever go at each other?"

Her smile softens and she's quiet for a moment. "She did steal a few pairs of shoes from me without asking," she chuckles, "but other than that, no. We didn't have time to fight about regular sibling things. I was too busy making sure every moment we spent together was centered around things that brought her joy. I wanted her to think of our time together as an escape from all the scary stuff. So I did whatever I could to make that possible."

Her smile grows as she turns the conversation back towards me. "Anyways, this dinner is going to be great. Your asshole brother will eat the Leosagna and we'll get a good laugh out of it. Then we'll be on our merry way, hopefully back to your place, and we'll get stoned off our asses." She nudges me and winks, "Before the night ends, you can fuck me while you still have that pretty little earring on."

How can I not get a fucking boner when she says shit like that?

I spark the roll and we smoke to calm my nerves before heading inside.

"MY BOY!" Dad shouts, rounding the kitchen. He beelines to Verena and I, sweeping me into a bearhug. "Is this your someone special?" He whispers before pulling back.

With a tight-lipped smile, I nod. "Dad, this is Verena. Verena, this is my dad, Greg."

Her smile brightens the entire house and my nerves relax. "It's so lovely to meet you, Greg. Your home is beautiful."

"Thank you! We're excited to have you for dinner tonight. Grimm, your siblings are in the den. Go introduce her while Graciela and I finish setting the table. We'll let you know when we're ready for you all!"

Nodding, I grab V's hand and lead her to the den. "There's a lot of us, seven to be exact. We've all got names that start with Gr, so if it takes you a while to commit all the names and faces to memory, just know we won't judge you. Well, I won't." I say with a shrug.

We round the corner and walk down the hall. Laughter and chatter echoes throughout the hallway. My stomach churns and I pray to whoever is controlling our simulation that the night goes smoothly and Verena doesn't backtrack on her feelings toward me, or us.

Stopping at the door frame, all eyes turn in our direction and there's not a friendly face in sight. Each one of my brothers are scattered around the room. Griffin, the oldest, sits on a leather couch, a glass of whiskey already in hand.

The twins, Graylin and Grayson, wrestle each other across the rug like football pricks at a highschool house party. Graham is nowhere to be seen, which irritates me because he's the only one besides Gracie that I can tolerate being in the same room with.

My eyes sweep across the room and spot him in a lone chair, with his ankle propped on his knee. Greer stares at us, more specifically, Verena. *My* little monster.

I'll make a nice fat burger and grill this motherfucker if he so much as breathes in her direction.

"Gracie's in the kitchen with Dad so you'll meet her in a bit. These are my brothers." I point to each one and give her their names. "Graham is somewhere nearby, hopefully."

No one has noticed our presence besides Greer. His voice booms throughout the den, quieting everyone and turning their focus towards us. "Hey, lookie here! Little Grimmy brought home some fresh meat. It's a lot more exciting to see you when you come home with presents."

The twins cackle and it amazes me that there's a six year difference between myself and them. You'd think I'm twenty years older with the way they behave and bicker with one another. As much as they butt heads, they're inseparable. They live together, play on the same hockey team, professionally, and even shared the same girl for a hot minute.

Griffin stands and strides over to us. He scoops up Verena's hand and introduces himself. "Griffin, nice to meet you. Your name?"

Verena smiles and replies, "Verena."

Griffin's lips tip into a smile. *I've literally never seen him smile before.*

"Verena. Beautiful. A respectful name." He compliments.

What the fuck is going on? He isn't nice to anyone but his own reflection. He admitted to me that he saved my life out of obligation, not want or love.

"Thank you, Griffin." Verena says with a friendly smile that subtly lets him know he's not getting any further than this no matter how hard he tries.

Griffin kisses her knuckles softly and backs away, grabbing his drink and leaving the room. Presumably for a refill.

"Hey! Grimmeister!" A palm comes down on my shoulder and I turn to face Graham.

I nod in his direction and give him a curt hello before introducing him and Verena. Gracie calls from down the hall that the table is ready so everyone stands and walks down to the dining room together.

A large table sits in the middle of the room with just enough chairs for everyone to sit down. My dad and Griffin sit at the heads of the table. I sit on the corner next to Griffin and Verena sits to my left.

Gracie's eyes widen when she sees Verena enter the room and beelines to introduce herself. "Hi, I'm Graciela. Gracie or Grace is fine. Slim Grimm over here literally never brings anyone over and the rest of the guys are too full of themselves to have a full-time partner. It'll be fun to have another girl around."

V looks at me with a gentle smile and falls into easy conversation with Gracie, and invites her to sit next to her. The twins and Greer sit on the opposite side of the table.

One chair remains empty, Luna's. *Their mother. My step-mother and one of the first mortal enemies I created.*

Appetizers are displayed along the dining table and my stomach growls. I've hardly eaten in days due to my assistance in Emmett's "Prince Charming" escapades. The sight of ground meat has also made me a bit queasy as of late, but Dad uncovers two trays filled with nachos and empanadas and I'm done for.

Verena's eyes light up at the food, excited to dig in. Gracie helps uncover a few more platters and Verena's eyes continue to widen and her mouth falls slack, drool practically dripping from the corner of her mouth.

"Escalivada, artichoke chips, and espinacas a la catalana!" Gracie beams," So Verena, Escalivada is-"

"I know what it is." She says with a smile. "I'm so sorry to cut you off."

It's Gracie's turn to widen her eyes. "You do? None of our guests know Catalan dishes. Is your family from Catalan also?" She questions.

Verena shakes her head,"My family is Puerto Rican, but there's a restaurant near campus that makes the most mouth-watering Escalivada."

Gracie's smiles grow wide. "¿Tu eres Boricua?" She asks Verena and she responds with a head nod.

Gracie lets out a squeal as she sits back in her seat,"Okay assholes, dig in!" Then she leans over to V and lowers her voice. "We're going to make really good friends." She wraps her arm around Verena and gives her a light squeeze before sitting upright and eating her food.

SO FAR, so good. No one's flipped over a table, myself included, so I'd say it's going pretty well. V hasn't run out the door in a fit of tears, either.

A win is a fucking win.

What doesn't make me feel so hot, is my fuckwad older brother making shifty eyes towards Verena all throughout dinner. Even as he's involved in other conversations, his eyes stay glued to Verena–more like her chest–as he eats. Greer has always gone out of his way to get under my skin. This is exactly what I didn't want.

Another fucking bozo thinking they could get close to Verena and rile me up. Newsflash assholes! I'm a cold-blooded killer and I'll do anything to make sure my woman remains protected, guarded.

We ground up her ex and made him into lasagna for crying out loud. I look at Greer, attempting to send him mind messages that scream, "You won't wake up with those eyes tomorrow if you look her way again. You won't wake up *at all*."

My jaw tightens in anger and my breathing gets heavier. But all the tension is released from my body when the feeling of her delicate fingers landing on my thigh has me instantly going half mast in my pants.

My eyes drag over to hers and a smirk creeps on her face. She bats her eyelashes in my direction and my cock jumps at the sight of her.

She trails her fingers further up my thigh until the tips lightly brush along the side of my dick. The feather light touch makes me ache for more. More of her attention. More of her touch. More of *her*. Her nails drag against my jeans and send shivers down my shaft.

She applies more pressure as her fingers continue their path along the side of my cock, before they journey along the crown. I jerk in response, my dick trying to burst free from its confines and settle between her lusciously thick thighs.

Attempting, and failing, to distract myself from the vixen, and from any prying eyes, I reach out and grab my drink. My hand has a slight shake to it as I bring the glass to my lips. She swirls her finger in a circle along the crown of my dick before flattening her hand and fully cupping me.

Her hold on me through my jeans has me choking on the whiskey and sputtering. She takes that distraction as her excuse to start rubbing me. Her hand rubs along my thick erection through my jeans. "You good?" Griffin asks, his eyes narrowing at me.

"Yeah, I'm good." The words come out raspy, both from the whiskey I just choked on and the death grip Verena has my cock in. She jerks her hand faster, rubbing me through the layers of clothes. I look over at her as she takes a spoonful of rice in her mouth.

I look around the table and fuckwad finally peeled his eyes off of her. When I get back around the table and look at V, her eyes lock on mine as she slowly pulls the spoon out, making a show of licking her lips seductively before giving me a smile, all while continuing her torment on my dick. The sight has my balls drawing up and cum spurting from my cock as it twitches.

"Fuck," I grunt in my blissful high, my eyes closing as hot cum fills my pants.

A throat clears and my eyes snap back open realizing that I cussed out loud. "I gotta go. Room-bath. Fuck. I mean bathroom," I stand up quickly, my chair tumbling to the ground as Verena pulls her arm back. I try my best to hide the wetness with my half erect cock as I stumble from my seat and over to the restroom.

"I'm going to make sure he's okay," I hear Verena tell them as her chair squeaks against the tiled floor. Her steps sound behind me until she reaches my side. I'm already pushing the bathroom door open before grabbing her arm and yanking her inside.

I shut and lock the door behind me before spinning around. V's devilish smile illuminates the room as she leans back against the sink, her arms behind her on the counter making her breasts jut out.

"Such a dirty fucking girl you are." I press my body against hers, my cock already growing hard again just from her touch. "You made such a mess," I say, unbuttoning my pants and pulling down the zipper. "Why don't you be a good little slut and clean it up."

I yank down my pants and boxers, my heavy cock springing free. White cum covers my shaft and drips from the crown. She drops to her knees without hesitation and leans forward, sticking her tongue out and dragging it from the base of my dick all the way to the dripping tip.

"That's it. Good little sluts always clean up their messes, don't they?" Her tongue drags down my shaft, collecting the cum that's stained me. Her lips wrap around the crown before sucking hard. She hollows her cheeks and peers up at me, those amber eyes locking on mine. The sight has cum leaking from me as she drinks it down, moaning around me.

"Fuck, I want to feel you wrapped around this dick." I bring my hand to the base of her head, gripping the hair and tugging her back to standing. She releases me with a pop and my mouth is immediately on hers. "I love the taste of me on your lips." I mumble into her mouth.

My lips trace a path to her jaw, then down to her neck. I bite on the soft skin as nails scrap against my scalp before gripping the curls that dance along my shoulders. The soft touch turns rough as fingers yank my head back by my hair. Opening my eyes, I see Verena with that same devilish smile on her face.

"I need you, Grimm. I can't wait any longer."

28

VERENA

"FUCK, SAY THAT AGAIN," he whimpers while pressing his lips to mine. He *whimpers.* Desire floods my core at him going soft for me. That the beast of a man that is Grimm turns into a pile of mush in my hands.

"Please," He kisses my lips softly as his hands find my waist and lift me onto the counter. "I've been such a good boy, haven't I?" His lips continue to pepper soft kisses against mine as his hands leave my waist and settle between my thighs. "Such a good boy for not fucking you on the table in front of my whole family," He grips the thin material of my tights that rests against my pussy and pulls.

"Such," *Rip.*

"A good," *Rip.*

"Boy," He yanks the rest of the way until a large hole is formed in my tights displaying my pussy. His hand grips the side of my thong before pulling it to the side and baring my soaked slit to him. "Say it again," he whispers while dragging his finger through my folds and pushing it inside.

He pumps his finger in me, his lips tracing along the pulse in my throat. I toss my head back as the words flow from my lips again, "I

need you, Grimm." My breathy words float around us, his finger pulls out and the head of his dick nudges against my entrance.

My head snaps forward and I lock eyes with him, our panting breaths mixing between us. "You've been such a good boy. Keep it up. Be a good boy and give me what I need." His hand clamps against my mouth as his other wraps around my waist, pulling me to the edge of the counter as his hips slam forward.

The scream I let out is muffled from his hand as my walls immediately clamp down around him. The stretch of his cock spearing into me is everything I've been craving since he placed a vibrator to my clit and forced me to cum over and over again. While he just watched me as he smoked a blunt.

He throws his head back, shutting his eyes. "Fuck." When he drops his head back down and tips his chin towards his chest, his eyes staring into mine as a strand of his long curls falls in front of his eyes, I almost combust right then and there.

Pulling out until just the tip of his cock sits inside me, he slams his hips back forward, bottoming out. He repeats the long, hard thrusts, his hand clamping down tighter around my mouth as he pounds into me. My labored breaths behind his hand are the only sound besides his soft grunts as he pumps his hips.

"I'm gonna remove my hand, and you're going to stay quiet. Isn't that right?" Pulling his hand back, he slams his hips forward somehow harder than he had been, the action making my whole body jerk backward and a surprised gasp to slip from my lips.

His tattooed hand immediately wraps around my throat, cutting off my oxygen. "Bad, bad girl, Verena. I told you to stay quiet," He squeezes harder. "Good sluts listen." He drags his cock from me before ruthlessly slamming back in, "Are you going to be my good little slut and listen?"

I nod my head quickly in his tight grip just as white spots start to dance against my vision. In my lightheaded haze, I let the words float around in my mind. When Leo would call me the degrading names it was like whip lashes against my skin, carving the words unto my flesh.

But with Grimm, it's… *Empowering*. It kisses my skin and seeps to my core. It makes me feel raw and alive.

It makes me feel sexy. Desirable. Free.

"Words, little monster." His hand leaves my throat and yanks at my halter top, exposing my nipples. "Yes," I gasp. His mouth attaches to my nipple, circling his tongue around the hardened bud. He bites down until pain morphs into pleasure and the shock of the contrasting feelings courses through me, straight to my clit.

"Yes what? Say it." His teeth graze my nipple again before he places a kiss over the assaulted bud. His hands go to my hips, gripping the sides of my waist as he yanks me forward to meet his thrusts. His fingers dig into the flesh of my sides as he pulls me forward so roughly my whole lower half slides off the counter.

A shriek leaves my lips as I put my weight on my arms behind me. Grimm holds me by my hips in the air like I weigh absolutely nothing, the corded veins of his arms pop and his muscles bulge as he continues to pull me in to meet every thrust. He shoves forward, his large frame holding me up and towering over me as he holds himself unmoving as deep as he can go.

He stays there, taunting me.

"Grimm, please," I beg, my hips wiggling while still suspended in the air, trying to encourage him to move.

In a languid thrust, he pulls out and slams back forward, "Fucking say it," he grunts.

"Yes! Yes, I'll be your good slut and listen!"

His lips slam to mine as he bucks his hips back forward, bottoming out every time. The pain from the stretch of him mixes with the pleasure and my limbs start to heat as my orgasm builds. Each thrust brings me closer and closer to heaven.

"I wanna feel you strangle my cock with your tight little pussy, V. Give it to me. Be a good slut and show me how much you like my thick cock when it's pounding you."

His words paired with the rhythm of his hips has my release barreling towards me. I throw my head back, my eyes rolling as heat washes over every bone in my body. I bite down on my tongue until a metallic tang fills my mouth to keep from crying out as he continues drilling into me.

"Fuck, fuck, fuck," his rhythm stutters as he curses, his balls slapping against my ass with every thrust. He sounds breathless, and as I come down from my high and look at him, my pussy flutters again at the sight.

His dark eyes bore into mine, pupils dilated with lust, red stains his cheeks, his angular jaw clenched. "I want you to fill me up with your cum, Grimm," I pant. Like my words are the flame to a firework, he ignites.

"Yes, baby," Grimm bottoms out and holds himself there. "Fuck, V. You're going to be the death of me."

His hips buck forward in his hold. My eyes widen as he continues to cum, the warm substance seeping into me and dripping to the counter.

When the last drop is spilled, he tucks himself back into his pants before taking my underwear and pulling it back over my pussy, trapping his cum against the material and my skin.

"I can't wait to taste you later, little monster." He whispers into my ear. My heart does backflips and cartwheels thinking about later with Grimm, his talented tongue, and that sexy little earring.

Pulling my dress back over my hips, I fix myself up the best I can before we leave the bathroom. It's hard to pretend that nothing happened when there's a hole between my legs from where he ripped my tights and cum coats my underwear as it sticks to my skin.

Grimm pushes the door open and I begin to follow him out, but run into his back as he halts in his tracks. I try to peer around him to see what made him stop abruptly. When I do though, my blood turns cold in my veins at the sight of Greer leaning against the wall right next to the bathroom door.

The smug look on his face and the bulge in his pants tells me everything I need to know. His eyes skim Grimm before landing on me. They start at my toes before dragging up my legs, pausing for a moment where the rip in my tights begin. It feels as if he knows there's a hole there despite the fact my skirt is covering me. He drags his gaze up, pausing to stare at my breasts, then lips, before finally stopping at my eyes.

The way his eyes assessed me as if I had nothing on makes disgust turn in my stomach. Unease knocks on my subconscious as I stare back at him. "What the fuck, Greer?" Grimm shields me from his brother who's stare hasn't left mine. His dark eyes glimmer as his smirk grows wider.

"Little brother, you didn't tell me what a screamer she was. Do I get a turn with our lovely guest?"

I feel Grimm stiffen against me as I harden my stare, my eyes narrowing and my fists balling at my sides. I may have let one man make me feel as if I was weak but the reality is that I'm anything but. I am not a victim. I'm a survivor.

I survived him.

I won't let another man think he can intimidate or degrade me. Think that he can speak to me in any way outside of respect. While Leo may have been breaking me down, I took those broken pieces to form a new me. A version that's cracked with jagged edges, yet those pieces are stronger, sharper, and aren't afraid to cut a bitch.

I step around Grimm, to let his brother know just how well I can scream when Grimm's hand flies out and grabs Greer by the neck. His fist tightens, the knuckles turning white as Greer's smile shapes into something more sinister.

"What the fuck did you just say?" Grimm yanks his face closer to Greer's, their noses practically touching.

"I asked if I get a turn," he chokes from Grimm's grip, his smile never faltering.

"Say that shit again, *big brother.*" Greer's face turns tomato red, his eyes bulging as Grimm's grip somehow grows tighter. He releases him, but before anything else happens, he rears his fist back and slams it into Greer's face.

Greer's nose cracks and blood starts trickling from the newly crooked bone. Grimm's hand wraps around my wrist before he's yanking me away from his brother and his eerie smile that still has not faltered.

"Enjoy the lasagna, asshole!" I spit out, angry at his treatment, but content that my revenge–and Grimm's too–is already in motion.

Grabbing my wrist, Grimm pulls me down the hall and up the stairs. "There's someone else we have to see before we go."

29

GRIMM

WE REACH the top of the landing and I whistle. Within seconds, the jingle of her collar sounds and I hear the tippity-tap of her nails on the wooden floor.

My Flame.

Flame beelines for me, jumping into the air, and taking me down to the ground. I land on my back and she begins furiously licking my face. Her tail wags like a door stopper in excitement. "Hi, baby. It's good to see you, too." I say to her, scratching behind her ears and along her sides.

"Is she yours?" Verena asks, her eyes sparkling at the sight of my Dobermann. I nod and stand as Flame makes her way over to smell Verena.

"Be careful, she's a killer just like her daddy." I say with a wink. Flame doesn't tolerate anyone else besides my dad. More than that, she doesn't tolerate anyone within close proximity of *me*, so I'm shocked to see when she sits at Verena's feet and raises a paw to her leg to gain her attention.

"Hi, sweet girl! I'm Verena." V pets her head and immediately, Flame is mush in her hands.

Did I just lose my dog to Verena? Of course, the two greatest females in my life would band against me.

Seeing them bond so quickly causes an ache to settle in my chest. I'm ecstatic that they're getting along, but Flame can't come with us. She has to stay.

Verena notices the shift in my mood and wastes no time questioning it. "Why so glum? Flame is super excited to see you."

A sad smile forms on my face, "Yeah. I'm stoked to see her. I wish I could bring her back with me, but I can't. Jaden is allergic."

A few beats of silence pass before Verena speaks again, "I can keep her at my place." Her eyes meet mine and the amber irises sparkle with love and adoration.

"What? No, I couldn't ask you to do that. She's good here. Tons of food, a nice big yard, and all the toys she could want." Although it pains me to say it, Flame needs to stay here. I couldn't possibly put the responsibility on Verena when she has classes and a life of her own.

"I don't remember you asking me. I just remember offering. If she's trained to only go outside, and isn't violent or aggressive, I can take her with me. I want to." She rebuttals. "Come on, let's pack up her stuff and head out."

With that, she stands and walks, Flame trotting down the hall by her side. I watch them as I feel a blush creep up my cheeks and that familiar ache seeps into my heart.

My girls are coming home with me.

My girls. Home. With me.

I could get used to this.

30

GRIMM

FLAME HAS BEEN at Verena's for a few weeks and has loved every second of it. Verena went on a spree to get Flame all new bedding, leashes, collars, and toys. She has her own corner of the room equipped with a luxurious dog bed, a bowl of water, a basket of toys, and the softest rug that displays a neon pink flame

She's spoiled fucking rotten.

And I thought I couldn't fall in love with Verena any more.

Everyday with her has been a dream. We spend so much time together, you'd think she'd be sick of me by now. But she keeps me around. Keeps *us* around. I'd do anything to savor this feeling, bottle it up, and wear it around my neck so it lays close to my heart.

You can't bottle your butterflies, but you can bottle her blood.

My dick tents my pants at the thought of having a vial of Verena's blood around my neck. Now, I just need to figure out how the hell I'll convince her to do that.

I adjust myself in my pants as I wait for Verena outside of her last class for the semester. We get three uninterrupted weeks together. She has no idea, but I've got something up my sleeve for this upcoming break.

A moment later, the door bursts open and out pours what feels like half of Blackwood's student body. My eyes scan over the crowd, thankful for the advantage of my height. I spot Verena quickly, my little grumpy amongst all the sunshine in her all black ensemble.

There's a large portion of students that come from old money and Blackwood legacy who wear nothing but neutrals and argyle. Verena was the complete opposite. Hues of black and red headed in my direction and it wasn't until she spotted me, that the little grump morphed into the brightest sunshine this world has ever seen.

Her eyes light up, her smile widens, and she gently catches her bottom lip between her teeth.

"Hey there, lovely." I say to her as she makes her way closer to me, laces our fingers together, and rises onto her tiptoes to kiss me.

"Hi, handsome. We're free! Well, I guess you're always free so now *I'm* free." She responds with a chuckle.

I wrap my arm around her shoulder and we walk to her house making small talk and cracking jokes. One thing that surprised me about Verena is how fucking goofy she is. I thought I was a jokester, she's a goddamn clown. Sometimes the most outlandish shit comes out of her mouth, and it's even better when she's stoned. It's perfect.

She's perfect and she's perfect for me.

My heart flutters once again at my reality and I don't think there will ever be a moment in time where I'm not absolutely smitten by her. Cupid didn't just shoot the arrow, he dug that thing deep into my chest, piercing my heart and staking Verena's claim.

I have no problem with that at all. I belong to her just as she belongs to me.

BACK AT THE HOUSE, I get Flame ready for a walk and Verena rolls up a joint. We walk around campus and watch as students dispersed, leaving in cars or on foot to the campus bus stop. Verena doesn't usually go home for holidays. She said her relationship with her parents isn't the best and the rest of her family is in Puerto Rico. But since she never had the job she told me she was working due to Leo's dictatorship, she didn't have any money saved up to go and see her family. Staying at Blackwood was her only option.

My reasoning was plain and simple. I couldn't stand to be around Greer for more than an hour at most and even that was pushing it. To my knowledge, he still lives at home and I never wanted to subject myself to that for three days let alone three weeks. It was easier to stay away and I was never really alone.

Emmett and Eli aren't running back home to their fucked up families either. It's all super complicated for us.

Verena and I finish the joint before walking back to her place. Verena showers extends the invitation to me. I follow her into the bathroom and help her undress, placing kisses along her body from top to bottom. Her skin pebbles under my touch and she melts into my arms.

I lick a trail up her skin from her shoulder to her earlobe and bite gently. She gasps and throws her head back onto my chest. I tangle my fingers in her hair and tighten my grip a smidge. The sweetest moan slips from her mouth and I bring my lips down to hers. Kissing her feels like my every wish and want in this world has been granted. I want to worship her body every single day until I die. But even the afterlife won't keep us apart. I'll make sure of it.

"How do you feel about me wearing your blood around my neck?" I whisper in her ear. If she couldn't feel the pounding of my heart against her back, I'd be genuinely surprised. Her body stiffens against mine and I'm nervous I said the wrong thing, or brought it up too soon.

Verena turns around to face me and presses her hands against my chest. Her eyes lock with mine and my heart can't handle how fucking beautiful she is. The water runs down her back, soaking her dark hair. Her usual siren eyes compliment her cutthroat attitude but right now her bare face resembles that of an angel and those big brown orbs shine with innocence. The most breathtaking smile forms across her lips and she nods her head, "I'd like that very much."

The raging organ in my chest settles to a steady beat once again, relieved that she said yes.

After *thoroughly* cleaning Verena with my tongue and then with soap and water, we hop out of the shower and into bed. Verena's wearing my shirt, I'm in boxers, and we're snuggled under her blankets with Flame lying comfortably at our feet.

Verena starts up a horror movie but turns to face me, "How long have you had Flame?" she asks, reaching over to grab Flame by the belly and moves her closer to us.

I smile thinking about that fateful day. "I found her right after graduation. One night, I was driving home from work and it was really foggy. I saw something moving on the side of the road and thought it was a wild animal that needed help. After slowing down, our eyes locked and I opened my passenger door. She hopped in without a peep and curled her body into a ball, staring at me the entire drive home. She's been with me ever since."

Flame's tail pops up and begins to wag as if she knows I'm recounting our first moments. "A few months later, I took her on a walk and ran into her previous owner. The family had a young daughter and they were celebrating her birthday with a party in full-swing in their backyard. A bear had come through the yard and this brave little girl got lost chasing it out and away from the party. I'm telling you, she's a warrior through and through, like you." I wink and squeeze Verena's fingers with one hand, while rubbing Flame with my other.

"They didn't ask to bring her back home?" She questions, her eyes widening at the prospect of anyone leaving Flame behind.

"Not really, no. Flame wasn't her name, but it's my name for her. They called her Junebug." I respond and when Verena hears the name, she bursts into laughter.

"I can totally see it, but I think lame suits her perfectly." She raises her voice an octave and bends down closer to Flame, "Can I call you Junebug?" Flame responds by licking her nose and Verena giggles.

"DId you grow up with any pets?" I ask, eager to know more about her. Dying to know *everything* about her.

She nods but her smile fades. "None growing up, but in my senior year of high school my great-grandmother passed away. She had a beautiful white pitbull named Mística. Her husband wouldn't let the dog in the house and she didn't have a dog bed, so she slept on a birdbath in their backyard. When she died, her husband didn't want the dog or the house or anything she had left behind."

I blow out a breath at the bullet that dog dodged by someone like Verena having her on her radar. "So you took her in?" I ask, tucking her hair behind her ear.

"Yeah. I begged my parents and promised they wouldn't have to lift a finger for her. In Puerto Rico, it's common for owners to let their dogs out beyond the gate. They become strays and face so much hunger and cruelty. I didn't want that for her and I knew my great-grandmother wouldn't have wanted that for her either. It's inhumane."

Sighing, she continues, "I couldn't bring her with me to Blackwood because they only allowed service animals at the time, and my parents held me to my promise of them not doing a single thing for her. I brought her to a nearby shelter. I told her I'd visit her as much as I could, but then I started dating Leo and he made that impossible." A tear forms in her eye and slides down her cheek. I catch it with my thumb and stroke her face. "I haven't seen her in so long and I don't even know if she's still there. I just hope wherever she is, she's happy and healthy."

My heart sinks and I realize at that moment, my plans for this semester break are changing. "Maybe we can find her? Bring her home? I'm sure Flame would love to have a friend. I'm so thankful you offered to house her here. One less reason to go to my dad's."

"Does your dad know about your feud with Greer?" She changes the topic, tears still lining her eyes.

I shrug, "Yes and no. He knows about the small things. Greer used to pull pranks on me almost everyday. One day it'd be pantsing me at school, the next it'd be leaving a plate of peanut butter right outside my door first thing in the morning. I can't tell how many times I've had to wash peanut butter off of my feet at seven in the morning." I chuckle and pull her into me so her head rests on my chest.

"But as we got older, the pranks became a bit more ruthless. Greer cut the breaks on my first car and it almost ended with me driving off of a cliff nearby my dad's place. The night of my high school graduation, I got a text from my mom, but in reality it was Greer posing as her. I hadn't seen or heard from my mom in years and I had tried to reach her for months prior to my graduation to give her an invite. It was all I wanted from her. To show up. To prove to me that I wasn't easy to forget about. I was her first born, afterall. So when I got a text from her saying she changed her number and was ecstatic to see me walk across the stage, I was beyond fucking happy. Long story short, she didn't come because Greer was fucking with me." My tone sharpens at the end of my recountment.

Verena tilts her head to look at me, "You never told your dad?" I shake my head no but don't say a word. "Why?"

Blowing out a breath, I toss my head back, "I don't know. Seemed like more trouble than I cared to be involved in. I thought keeping my head down and staying out of his way was enough, but clearly it wasn't and still isn't. But all I have there is a room with a cold bed. Flame was my last tie. I love my dad, but his house isn't somewhere I'm welcome and that's okay. I can love him out in the open." I end with a laugh.

She gets up and retrieves a preroll of her desk, bringing it back into the bed and sparking it. We watch the movie and smoke in silence until she speaks again, her voice barely above a whisper.

"I think this is the first time in my life I've felt absolute peace since I was born." She chuckles and when she looks over at me, I can't help but join in on the laugh.

"Me too, little monster, me too."

31

VERENA

FOR ONCE IN MY LIFE, I have no complaints. No notes, chef's kiss, all the good things. Grimm and I spent the last week in bed, only leaving the house for walks with Flame. He cooks us breakfast every morning, orders lunch from my favorite Spanish restaurant in town, and then chefs it the fuck up for dinner. I don't have to lift a finger or strain a single muscle. He *wants* to cook for me. He *wants* to be there for me.

And I want to bounce on his dick later because of it. It's the simple things.

We've been at each other nonstop, like it's fucking mating season and we're a couple of rabbits. We fell into such a nice routine over this last week. It's given me a glimpse at what life would really be like with Grimm, without roommates and secret societies and art projects to worry about. There's no weird brothers or psycho ex-boyfriends. Just Flame, Grimm and me.

He's been acting funny for the last two days, though. I heard him murmuring on the phone earlier this morning but I don't know who was on the other end. His usual goofiness has dialed back and I'm unsure if he's having second thoughts about us getting together or if I'm just overthinking it.

Grimm left this morning to grab more clothes and things from his place and I've done nothing but think of him since he's been gone.

He ignited something in me creatively, and in our down time, I began drawing again. It has felt so nice to have my spark back. I can't recall the last time I was this happy with my life. Maybe when I first came to Blackwood, maybe even as far back as before Ronnie was diagnosed.

It's been a fucking while.

My phone lights up and I snatch it from the nightstand, and align my face with the screen. It unlocks to my thread with Grimm where a new text awaits my response.

AN HOUR LATER, Grimm pulls up in front of my house and rings the doorbell. My bags are packed, Flame's things are ready to go, and all that's left is to pack up the car and go.

I shout, "It's open!" and Grimm flies inside, slamming the door.

"And why, exactly, is it open, Verena?" He speaks, his tone harder than usual.

My brows furrow and I turn around to meet him in the hallway but he's already crowding my doorframe. "What's wrong?" I ask.

"What's wrong? Your roommate was literally kidnapped and then attacked in this very fucking house. Locked windows and locked doors unless I'm with you, please. I don't want anything happening to you."

I nod and my heart blooms. His protective nature forms a ball of butterflies in my stomach that travel lower and lower until it reaches the apex of my thighs. Grimm grabs all our bags and Flame follows him out of the house and to the car.

When I step outside, I'm surprised to see a blacked out Escalade instead of his usual ride, the McLaren. "New ride?"

His smile spreads and the sight of his dimples, or should I say craters, set that ball of butterflies on fire. "We may need the extra space," he says with a wink.

Yes, please. A thousand times yes. How have I resisted him for so long?

He loads our bags into the trunk, sets up Flame in the backseat, and I get comfortable in the passenger seat. When he's settled in the driver's seat, he turns the music up and tells me to relax. "Nap, draw, snack, smoke, do whatever you want. We've got a little bit of a drive ahead of us. We'll stop at rest stops whenever you need a bathroom, but other than that we're driving straight through so I'll do my best to keep you entertained." he says with a chuckle.

I spend the next few hours controlling the aux, sparking up, and drawing. After my initial burst of energy was depleted, we recharged with burgers, fries, and milkshakes, then continued on our journey to the mystery location.

Hours go by before I see that we're crossing state lines and there's signs welcoming us to California.

What in the hell could Grimm have planned in California?

GRIMM

Verena has no idea where we're going and more importantly, who we're bringing home. I'm surprising her with a trip to her hometown, Fremont, and we're getting her dog back.

I'm reuniting Verena with Mística and I can't wait to see her face. She never specified the shelter she was being held at, so I called every single one in the Fremont area, hoping to get lucky. Once I found what I thought was the correct place, I verified all of Verena's information and even asked them to send a picture. Verena's home screen is a collage consisting of Ronnie, Mística, and an older woman whom I assume is her grandmother. The dog looks identical to the one in her phone, and once everything was verified, I told them Mística would have a comfy new home back in Devil's Lake, with Verena and I.

We're currently at a rest stop. The girls had to piss and I needed something to eat. I'm chomping on a meatball sub as my mind fills with anxious thoughts of Verena not liking the gesture of bringing Mística home.

What if she doesn't want another dog in her house, dumbass?

What if she preferred you to talk to her about it first?

What if she appreciates the gesture but decides to leave her at the shelter?

What if it's the greatest thing someone could do for her and she'll love me forever because of it?

What if?

The girls enter the car as I'm finishing up my sub and V holds up a bag of snacks. "Flame befriended this adorable little girl and it turns out, her parents own a snack shop in there and gave me all of this for half off! All because she wagged her tail and handed out a few licks." She does a little dance before digging out a preroll and sparking it up. She inhales and hands it to me, then digs in the bag. Pulling out a bag of doggie snacks, her verbal enthusiasm continues, "Look! She even weaseled her own free treats out of them! That's what I'm talking about, girl. Gimme paw!"

Verena holds her hand out towards the backseat and Flame follows the command. Verena lifts her up to her lips and kisses her before murmuring a string of good girl's to Flame.

The ticker in my chest is ready to explode, the detonator pin feels like it's hanging on by a thread. Seeing my two girls together, knowing we're on our way to get a third and they don't even know it, gives me the most heartwarming feeling.

Maybe I'm a little bit anxious to know that I'll have three ladies hanging up against me from now on.

I DRIVE throughout the night and into the morning. V moved to the backseat and snuggled up with Flame a few hours ago. She wakes up any time I spark up a joint and we pass it back and forth for a few minutes before she drifts back into sleep again.

Sometime around noon we enter Fremont. Verena eyes me suspiciously and wastes no time interrogating me. "Why are we going to Fremont?"

"Heard it had some nice sights. What do you think?" I answer, without making eye contact. I hate not being transparent with her, but she'll find out the truth soon enough.

She shakes her head, "You know I live here, right?" I open my mouth in an exaggerated gasp and look at her in disbelief.

"I'm with a Fremont local?" I answer sarcastically and continue. "You can show me all the best spots. Just have to stop by a couple places first."

We pull up to a white brick building that has a metal plate on the left side of the front wall in the shape of a paw print. To the right, in shiny metallic lettering reads, Pitbull Paradise. Verena's eyes widen and she looks at me in complete shock. "You did not."

I smile and turn off the engine, then grab her hand and give it a squeeze. I bring my other hand up to her chin and softly stroke her skin. "There's not a thing in this world I wouldn't do to see you smile. Anything you wish for is yours. Anything at all, Verena."

Her eyes water and a small tear slides out of her tear duct and slips down the bridge of her nose. Placing a soft kiss on her lips, I wipe the tear with my thumb and pull back to look at her fully. "Let's go get our girl." Her smile brightens and I swear I've been blinded by the brightest light ever to be shone.

Flame hops out of the car and walks alongside us into Pitbull Paradise. The front desk lady smiles brightly when she notices my little monster. "Verena! How nice to see you! It's been a long time. How's school?"

Verena swallows and nods slightly, "Hey, Liz. Good. I've been good. How has everything been here? How's Mística?"

The lady beams and waves her hands motioning for us to follow her. "She's alright. Been a bit sad lately. She had made a couple friends here and spent most of her free time with them. One was rehomed and the other passed. She hasn't wanted to connect with the other animals much since then."

The woman leads us down a hallway and turns left to a new corridor. Past the doors and down a few cages, she stops and takes out a large ring of keys. Finding the correct one, she unlocks the gate and calls out to Mística. "Hey, pretty girl, some special folks are here to see ya!" The scratch of Mística's nails tick against the floor as she pads her way out of the small room. Verena drops to her knees, her eyes watering when she sees that first spot of snow white fur.

"Mística! Hi, baby." Verena chokes out. Mística's eyes light up when her eyes meet V's and her tail wags furiously. She dashes into Verena's arms, tackling her and pinning her to the ground. Mística licks V's face, making up for the years of kisses that they've lost. Verena breaks out into a laugh as she remains splayed on her back, her arms around her four-legged best friend. I'll never get over that feeling that consumes me when her happiness shines brighter than every glittering star in the sky.

Verena sits up as Mística backs off of her. I step to the side and Flame walks out from her spot behind me. She treads carefully near Místic as Verena introduces the two. "Místi, this is Flame. She's a very good girl, just like you, and I think you'll love her." She pats her leg and calls Flame over to her. The dogs sniff each other for a few seconds and before we know it, their tails are wagging and Flame rolls over in front of Mística. Her tongue hangs out the side of her mouth and Mística swats her in a playful manner.

I look at Verena and her giddiness tugs at my heartstrings. She whistles, getting Mística's attention and her head swivels in my direction. "Come here, mamíta. There's someone else you need to meet. He's the whole reason we came here." Her nails click against the floor as she inches toward me, a familiar light glinting in her eyes. It's one that is reminiscent of the one Flame had when I first picked her up from the side of the road. She sniffs my shoes and then moves higher and sniffs my jeans. Her tail wags slightly before she brushes her side against me and looks up at me, her tail still wagging, tongue hanging out of her mouth now.

Verena chuckles, "She wants you to pet her."

I bend down and pet her winter white coat. It's the complete opposite of Flame's short-haired pelage. "Hey there, beauty. Let's go home, yeah?" She wags her tail in response and Verena stands.

She faces Liz and thanks her for her time. Five minutes later, we're packed into the car and getting back on the road.

32

VERENA

HOW DO I thank him properly? Never in a million years would Leo have offered to bring Mística home. *I mean, I do have a few things in mind that I know he'd like.*

A lightbulb goes off, and just like that, I know the perfect way to show him my genuine appreciation for his heart. "I figured maybe we could take them to your place for a little while. There's another place I'd like to take you but it's not exactly the best place for dogs, let alone the two most stereotyped dogs." Grimm says with a shrug. "Is that cool?"

My spine stiffens in my chair. This trip has been fucking phenomenal. It's felt like an endless dream and I'm not ready for reality to seep back in just yet. I can't go back home. I can't see my parents. Grimm notices my hesitation. He's looking my way with one eyebrow arched because he knows there are thoughts reeling through my mind and I won't share a single one unless he asks. I swallow and smile, "I don't think my parents would want two dogs running a muck in their pristine palace."

He nods, "Understandable. Good thing they aren't home."

My head snaps to face him as I question, "How do you know that?"

Grimm throws his head back with a chuckle and his dimple makes an appearance, "Elijah Denissova. The kid is good at what he does. Weaseled his way into your parents' emails and found that they're both away on separate business trips. Your mom left last night for New York and your dad left this morning for Illinois."

My heart rate amps up just thinking about all the digging and planning he did for this trip. *Sneaky little sucker.*

With my mind at ease that my parents won't be home anytime soon, I agree to leave the dogs at the house while Grimm takes me on whatever exciting excursions he has planned.

WE PULL up to the large white mansion, the neutral colored rocks and white siding sit perfectly in place, not a dent or scratch in sight. The lawn is greener than the bud we've got stored in the middle console and my favorite part, the driveway is empty.

I sigh, feeling relieved I won't be running into them during our trip.

Unbuckling my seatbelt, I exit the car, and open the backdoor to collect the dogs. We all head inside and I bring the girls out to the backyard. I set up their things in my bedroom and meet Grimm at the bottom of the stairs. He's staring out the back window that faces the yard. The dogs are running circles around each other, tails wagging, tongues hanging out of their mouths. They certainly enjoy each other's company and I know his heart is just as happy as mine.

I wrap my arms around his waist and press my face into his chest. "Thank you so much for this. Thank you so much for bringing back a piece of me I thought was gone forever."

His arms envelop me and squeeze. "The world is yours, baby. I'm just doing my due diligence by giving it to you." Kissing the crown of my head, he backs away and lets the dogs inside. We bring them up to my room and put out food and water for them before closing the door and heading back downstairs.

We're walking towards the front door when I hear the beep of a car being locked outside. My head whips to Grimm, just steps behind me. I grab his shirt and pull him into a hall closet, placing a finger over my mouth to signal him to be quiet.

I hear my father's voice, but can't make out his muffled words. My eyes widen. We haven't been within arms distance of each other in almost two years. Now I've got this six-foot-tall monster hiding in one of his coat closets and two small fucking horses in my bedroom. Grimm looks at me, a smug grin on his face. *What the fuck are you up to now?*

Placing his hands on my waist, he brings us face-to-face. He kisses my nose and pecks my lips, moving to my ear and whispering, "I'll be quiet. Will you be?"

Just as I'm about to ask him to clarify, his hand slips into the front of my leggings and he cups my center. I gasp and he puts his finger over his lips, that smug grin still holding on tight. "What's wrong? I thought you said we needed to be quiet?" He whispers, his thumb circling my clit.

My head falls back at his touch. His calloused hands have a way of making me feel like the most precious artifact in the world. He slips a finger into me, and then another, and one more. I groan and Grimm's free hand flies over my mouth as I begin rocking back and forth against his hand.

Whimpers fall from my lips as he pumps his fingers in and out. Just as I'm about to reach my climax, Grimm leans down next to my ear again. "You want me to stop so we can focus on being quiet? Seems like you're having a hard time there, pretty lady. I, on the other hand, can behave like a good boy whenever you need me to." His voice ignites the bomb that's building in my core and I detonate, my release spilling over his fingers. After removing his hand, he shoves his fingers in his mouth and savors every drop.

In a lust-filled haze, I drop to my knees and undo his belt and pants. Gripping the material, I pull it down, his underwear coming down with it, and let his cock spring free. Already hard and thick for me, there's a bead of precum at the tip and I swipe it with my tongue.

Grimm shudders and moans at my touch. "Shhh," I whisper before taking him fully into my mouth.

His hand rests on my head. He doesn't yank or pull. No, he pets me. Fucking pets me. Grimm caresses my head and even twirls my strands around his finger. Immediately, I feel that pulse again between my thighs and I throw all caution to the wind.

"Be a good boy, Grimm. Give your pretty lady what she needs." I bob my head on his cock, the tip hitting the back of my throat with every stroke. Once the head touches the back of my throat again, I close my mouth and swallow. Grimm's body reacts, sending him slightly forward. He catches himself on the coat rack in front of him, remaining inside my mouth the whole time.

"Fuck, V. That feels so good. You're a fucking goddess. I love when you take control of me. You're fucking perfect." My eyes look up to meet his. I keep sucking as we stare into each other's irises. He sees me for everything I am and doesn't expect me to be someone I'm not. Grimm has shown me the most pure and rawest forms of love. He's seen me at my lowest and chose to fight for me every single time. There's no getting past that.

I licked him, so he's mine.

He moans as I bring one hand to his ass and the other to his balls. I gently massage them both and he unravels before me, his release filling my mouth. I swallow all of his cum down before pulling his pants back up, tucking his *not-so* little guy back into his underwear, and redo his zipper and belt.

Footsteps sound just outside the door, before we hear the front door swing open and slam shut. A few moments later, a car engine starts and we hear my father peel out and away.

"That was close. Grab our little bitches and let's get the fuck out of here." I say, unable to contain my smile.

We slowly retreat from the closet and I peek out of the window to confirm that my father has left. Grimm runs upstairs to collect the girls and when he meets me outside, I ask, "I thought you said he left this morning for a business trip?"

Grimm shrugs, "That's what I was told. Take it up with Eli, not me." Once we're buckled in, we hit the road and I remember why the dogs were in the room in the first place.

"Wait! What about our little impromptu rendezvous?" I ask, with a giggle.

"It was just that. Impromptu because I like giving you everything you need and more. Nothing we can't do back home." He replies, his free hand stroking my thigh while his other guides the steering wheel. "What happened back there?"

I look out the window, wishing to avoid the discussion altogether. I knew it was coming, I was just hoping we'd never have to actually talk about it. "I'm not sure what you mean."

Grimm reaches up and pinches my nipple through my shirt. "Hey! Hands on the wheel!" I chuckle.

"You can talk to me, you know. I just want to understand you. Did you avoid him because he didn't know you were coming? Or because you don't *want* to see him?" He asks, patiently waiting for my answer.

My confessions spill from my lips, "I don't have a good relationship with them. While I was spending all of my free time with Ronnie, they were at fundraisers and meetings, caught up in temporary, unimportant matters. Ronnie's life was the only temporary thing that had any level of importance. They weren't there. She missed them. She wanted them around and they left it up to me, a fucking teenager, to make sure she was at peace before her life ended. They had no regard for what I was going through. All that's important is the money, the house, the cars. Materialistic bullshit."

"Sometimes I wonder if they went into overdrive because they had to pay for her medical treatment. But I'm almost positive they had more than enough sitting in a savings account, nestled away in a foreign bank. They had the luxury to take time off of work, to spend her last days with her, to reassure her that she was loved and valued. If my mom had time to get a fucking rhinoplasty a few days before Ronnie died, she had plenty of availability to spend time with her daughters. The one that was grieving *and* the one that was dying." Tears are streaming down my face before I can pull myself together. "That solidified it for me. They didn't care about us. They thought of us as extensions of them, heirs to their legacy. Those expectations died when I fought for a chance to study art and writing. Ronnie wasn't even going to make it to middle school." I blow out a breath and Grimm pulls the car over to the side of the road.

He unbuckles his seatbelt and reaches over the console to hold me. I wrap my arms around his neck and bury my face into him. "I don't know if they're even together anymore. They're married on paper but those business trips could be weekend getaways with mistresses and gigolos for all I know. But I truly don't care. I just needed them to pay for my tuition at Blackwood. Once I graduate, I'll be free from their shackles of pressure. I don't know what I'll do, where I'll work, or how I'll survive, but I'll do it. I always have."

"Stop right there," Grimm interrupts. "You're not alone anymore, V. You haven't been alone since the first day we met, and you certainly haven't been alone since coming to Blackwood. Feelings are a fickle thing. They trick us into believing that our emotions are fact. News-flash, that's a fucking lie. You have Aspen and Blair. They care for you so much. Even if they've got their own shit going on, you know if you call them, they will always be there for you. Also," he brings his hands down along his body to present himself as an obvious choice, "I've been here since day one. It may have taken you a while to notice, but this didn't start at the beginning of the school year or when I saw you hanging off of Leo's arm for the first time. The moment I saw your light brown hair, your pink high-top converse, paired with those low-rise jeans held up by that awesome black-and-white checkered belt," I can't help but laugh. At the same time, I'm fucking shocked he remembers the details that well. "I became yours. Even when you turned around and I saw that funny looking cartoon monkey on your shirt blowing up a glittery ball of bubblegum."

Now I'm cackling and regretting my previous outfit choices. Those styles were all the rage way back when, but I wouldn't be caught dead in anything remotely close to that now.

So many parts of me have changed and gotten lost along the way, some for the better, but there are parts that I wish remained. My innocence, my trust, my confidence. I just hope that in time, I'm able to build up all the best parts of myself once again.

Grimm brings his hand to my face and strokes his thumb across my cheek. "All jokes aside, it has always been you. It *will* always be you, V. My little monster. I love you." Grimm freezes and his Adam's apple bobs as he swallows, his face turning a bright shade of pink. My eyes widen as my mouth falls open in disbelief.

He WHAT?

33

GRIMM

YOU GOTTA BE SHITTING ME. No fucking way I just dropped the L word on her. *This is what happens when you speak faster than you think, dude.*

V stares at me, eyes wide, mouth agape, and I just feel the heat of my body turning my face the color of a fucking tomato. Out of all the things I could have said, it had to be that. *I love you.*

I told Verena I love her.

She clears her throat and speaks, but her voice cracks, "Sorry. That caught me off guard."

It caught her off guard, and she's not going to tell me she feels the same. It was too fucking soon.

I drop my hand and face straight ahead. I clear my throat and punch the campus address into my GPS. Starting up the car, I pull back onto the road and keep driving. A feather light touch grazes my thigh, sending shivers up my spine, causing my heart to do backflips, and goosebumps trail down my leg.

"Hey," she whispers, and I toss her a quick look. "I'm sorry I-"

I shake my head, "Don't worry about it, pretty lady. You don't have to say anything you don't feel. It's alright." I throw her a quick smile and dig into the middle console for yet another preroll. Once it's lit, we pass it back and forth until we hit the filter. I toss the tip into my ashtray filling up one of the cupholders up front, then pluck another preroll and repeat.

A few hours of excruciating silence pass by before Verena speaks again. "I wasn't apologizing for not feeling that way about you, Grimm. I was apologizing for my reaction. I was stunned. It was unexpected. But that doesn't mean that I don't share the same feelings you do."

The same feelings. I'm borderline obsessed. There's nothing in this world I wouldn't do to see her smiling, succeeding, and achieving everything she wants out of this life. I'd kill a thousand Leos if it meant she was safe and unharmed from the universe's cruelness. All I want is to tear down her walls, brick by brick, until I unearth all her darkness and set it free. I just want to see her grow into her true, authentic self. The woman she is, is just the beginning. The woman she'll become, will be a fucking menace to society. She's a goddess and I want nothing more than to worship her until my very last breath.

I don't say anything because I don't know what the hell I'm supposed to say. I keep my eyes on the road and my focus on us getting home. I have no time to feel. The woman I love doesn't share the same sentiment, and that's perfectly fine. Very on brand for me, if I'm being honest.

"Grimm, I love you too." The words falling from her lips make my heart race. It beats so aggressively, I question for a moment if she's sending me into cardiac arrest.

"I'm not saying it because I feel like I have to. I'm done doing things that I'm not obligated to do. Thanks to you. So, I love you. Because I want to. Because I can. Because even if I wanted to fight it, it'd be impossible. I love you, Grimm. I'll say it as many times as you need to hear it until you believe it."

Nope. No cardiac arrest, just the hardest hard-on harding it on in my jeans right now. We need to find a hotel, and soon.

Grabbing my phone, I hand it to Verena and instruct her to find the nearest hotel that's animal friendly. There's an inn not too far away from us, so I tell her to go ahead and book a room for the night.

Ten minutes later, we arrive at the hotel and park by the entrance. Verena steps out to stretch and I get a cart for our luggage. "Load the bags and I'll check us in?" I rest a hand on her lower back and kiss the crown of her head. She smiles up at me and nods, my heart somersaults and my stomach does backflips. *The way her eyes glint with love turn my organs into an olympic gymnastics team. She's absolutely perfect. Don't fuck this up, Grimm. Don't. Fuck. This. Up.*

Remembering my mission at hand, I dash to the check-in desk and ask the receptionist to upgrade us to the biggest room with the best view. An extra six-hundred dollars later, we've got ourselves a penthouse suite, baby.

I grab our key cards and meet Verena and the dogs at the front entrance. I direct the luggage and Flame, while Verena walks with Mística by her side. We reach our room, and when I open the door, the dogs creep in, smelling and inspecting the place before our entry.

Our little bodyguards, how sweet.

"Grimm, why'd you go so big? We're only here for one night, right?" Verena asks, removing Mística's leash before removing Flame's as well. I push the luggage cart into the room and shut the door.

"Go big or go home. Since we aren't going home, yet, we go big." I answer, matter-of-factly.

The suite has a full kitchen and living room, floor-to-ceiling windows, and a view to die for. I set-up the dogs' necessities, then snatch Verena by the waist and run to find our bedroom. She laughs at the unexpected ride, but we're just getting started.

We didn't get a hotel room because I needed a nap or a break from driving. I had her reserve the room so I could fuck her brains out. There was no way in heaven, hell, or any otherworldly land, that she was going to proclaim and profess her love for me and I wasn't going to show my appreciation for her in return. I wasn't kidding when I told her she's a goddess. Now I'll make good on my word and worship her the way she deserves.

Down a small hallway, there's a double door that leads to a pristine, white master suite. *I can't wait to fuck this shit up with her.*

Throwing her down on the bed as she giggles. I walk over to our bags, grab a few prerolls and a lighter, then trek over to the mini bar in the corner of the room. I whip us up a couple drinks, a Maker's Mark and ginger ale for myself, and a Malibu Bay Breeze for my lady.

"Grimm! There's a balcony! Look at this fucking view." Verena exclaims as she pads to the sliding door and steps onto the lookout point. I follow her onto the balcony and set our drinks on the small table in the middle of the balcony. I bring the preroll to my lips and ignite the flame against the tip. The paper crackles and that satisfying first hit, sends a shiver down my spine and straight to my cock.

"I know. You're fucking perfect." I rasp, and she turns around with the sexiest smirk along her lips.

She struts over to me, her hips swaying back and forth, and slinks her arms around my neck. "Thank you so much." She speaks softly.

"For what?" I ask.

"For the weekend getaway. For reuniting me with Mística. For saving me from Leo. For everything, Grimm." She confesses. "I can't tell you how much it means to me that she's here, with me, with us. Liz said she would keep a spot for her at the shelter for as long as she could, but she couldn't guarantee someone wouldn't want to adopt her. When I dropped her off, she also spoke about possible euthanasia. So, seeing her in the flesh, getting along with Flame, it's a dream that I can't even fathom came true. I can go on for hours talking about my gratitude, but it'd be better to show you instead."

Verena grabs my wrist and brings the preroll to her lips. She takes a drag and as she exhales, she interlaces our fingers and walks us over to the table. Verena places her hand on my chest and pushes me into the wide cushioned chair next to the table. Straddling me, she reaches for my drink, takes a small sip, then taps my mouth, directing me to open up for her. I do as instructed and she spits the alcohol into my mouth.

Holy mother of pearl. I think I just came in my pants.

"Are you going to be a good boy for me, Grimm?" She asks, her voice drips with the sexiest rasp. I could hear her speak about nonsense for hours on end. Her sultry voice consumes me, the second most addictive drug.

My erection tents my pants and she rolls her hips. I swallow and close my eyes, trying to restrain the urge to rip every inch of fabric from her body and fuck her senseless over this balcony.

I'll show everyone who she fucking belongs to.

"The very best boy. Just for you." I respond, my free hand wraps around her back, cupping her ass. She smiles and we each take a hit of the joint before she takes it from me and sets it down in a small black ashtray.

V stands and removes her top, her breasts spilling out of the fabric. She turns and bends over as she pulls her leggings off, giving me the most breathtaking image of her backside. My mouth waters as she faces me once again and softly drops to her knees in front of me.

Undoing my belt and zipper, she pulls my pants down and my cock springs free. Licking her lips, she wraps her hand around my dick and begins pumping it. Her free hand lays flat on my chest, her nails scratching my pecs gently. Grabbing the hairs on my chest, she moves her other hand from my dick to my balls and massages them as she takes me into her mouth.

"Fuck, baby." I moan. The warmth of her mouth has me ready to bust in just a few seconds and it takes everything in me to hold back my release.

Verena twirls her tongue around my shaft, showing every vein and inch appreciation. My hand finds her head and I thread my fingers through her silky soft strands. Twisting my hand, I make a fist and tighten my hold on her head gaining more control over her movements. She picks up speed and I'm right there with her, thrusting my hips to meet her, my dick touching the back of her throat.

She gags, her eyes watering. Tears begin to stream down her face, taking her mascara and eyeliner with it. *She couldn't be any more perfect. She is everything good and pure about this world. She's the lethal drug that could end my life, while she's also the antidote to all of my pains and suffering.*

The sound of her choking, her spit collecting at the base of my shaft, and the heat of her mouth work as the most perfect trifecta, urging my release to spill free.

"Yes, V. Right there." I groan as my balls tighten and my eyes close, no matter how much force I use to keep them open so I can keep watching my pretty lady do her thing, and not a moment later, my cum is filling her mouth. She stills, swallowing down all I have to offer her. The suction makes my dick jerk in response, eager to keep her right where she is.

V leans back, swipes at her bottom lip with her thumb, then stands. Her body is on full display. Her plump ass jiggles as she walks away from me and leans over the balcony, her elbows propped onto the edge. She arches her back, and throws a look at me over her shoulder. "Are you just gonna sit there or are you going to come and finish the job?" She asks, the sexiness venom lacing her tone.

I stand from my seat, pluck the joint from the ashtray, and relight it before walking over to her. My hands run over her smooth skin and my dick hardens immediately. My fingers travel to her core and I feel as her wetness drips down the sides of her thighs. I collect her arousal and bring it up to my lips, anxious to savor whatever little bits of herself she'll give me. I kiss her shoulder and trail my lips up to her ear. "Tell me what you want from me. I'll give it all to you." I whisper.

"You. I need you, Grimm." She straightens her back, her arm reaching up and behind her, snaking around my neck. Her fingers lock in a fist as she pulls gently on my hair.

In one swift motion, I thrust inside her. Her hand releases me and joins her other one in gripping onto the edge of the balcony for dear life. I pull on the joint, then pinch it between my fingers and bring it around to Verena's mouth. My thrusts never slow, never relent, never stop.

She's all fucking mine and I'm going to pound into her so hard, she'll have a hard time forgetting. The ache will be so prominent, she'll think of me and my little guy with every step she takes.

Verena's moans fill the balcony, her low-pitches alto sounds like the sweetest symphony. I'd love to listen to it on replay.

Pulling out of her, I walk over to my pants, fish out my phone, and open the voice memo app. I start recording and toss the device onto the table. Walking back over to V, I align the head of my cock with her entrance and bottom out. My balls smack against her ass with every thrust and her moans grow louder as my force grows harder.

"Yes, Grimm. Take me. I'm yours. I love being yours. Own me in every way. Please." Verena begs and it's enough to send me over the edge.

"Louder. I know who you belong to. It's about damn time everyone else knows it too, little monster." I growl and she erupts on my cock. Her pussy clenches my shaft and my orgasm rips through me, spots floating across my vision. Our mixture drips down the inside of her thigh and I pull out, swipe the sweet elixir with my fingers, and paint my initials onto her skin.

A "G" for each asscheek.

I turn her around and take her in. The flush of her pink cheeks against her olive skin tone make a remarkable pair. Her chest rises and falls as her breathing calms and her chocolate brown eyes melt any of the remaining ice around my heart.

She is mine and I am hers. There's no doubt about it. There's no going back. I'm looking my forever in the face and somehow, forever isn't fucking long enough with her.

I grip her chin and pull her closer, her lips meeting mine. She pulls back and speaks the most unexpected words, but they're everything I want to hear. "Verena Griswold. Has a nice ring to it, don't you think?"

There's no containing the smile that's bubbled within me. "Sounds fucking perfect."

34

VERENA

Three Weeks Later

AFTER OUR WEEKEND RENDEZVOUS, the four of us traveled the rest of the way back to Blackwood. I expanded Flame's corner to make space for Mística and her things. Those girls love each other. One doesn't do anything without the other. You name it, and they are paw-in-paw; they bounce back and forth between their beds, always cuddled up within each other. Dinner, walks, trips to the dog park, Flame will not leave without Mística and vice versa. *They remind me of myself and Ronnie when we were younger, unable to be without each other.* My heart pangs with both grief and satisfaction, hopeful that in another world, in another life, we have more time together.

In addition to the dogs loving each other, I've surprisingly found so much extra time in my days to focus on my creative mediums. School is back in session and even with projects and assignments, I've had more creativity flowing through my veins than I have in months, possibly years.

I've been working on a special piece since we returned from our trip. Two skeletons sit with their legs dangling at the edge of a cliff as they share a joint. The hues are dark and moody, and blend so melodically, that my heart blooms with pride. The red and black color palette represents us perfectly.

It's the most profound piece I've created. I honestly fear I may never create anything I love as much as this. It's called "Eternal Lovers" in honor of my growing feelings for Grimm. I've never been more sure of anything in my life, except for him. The feelings he's awoken in me are unhinged, unmatched, and unfortunate for every other bitch who had their eyes on him.

He's fucking mine. That'll never change. Not in this life, not in the next, not even in death.

Our love is eternal.

35

GRIMM

VERENA GRISWOLD.

Verena Losado Griswold.

Grimm Losado. Doesn't sound bad, I wouldn't mind taking her name.

I'm sitting in my writing class, doodling once again because I don't give a shit about this lecture. I don't want to learn about writing styles and techniques. I want to go back home. To Verena and our pampered princesses. To a place where I truly feel like I belong. Where I'm not some crazed outsider.

She loves the devil in me. She values my darkness. No drug could ever compare to the high she gives me. Not even the good old MaryJane.

Everyone just thinks I'm here to fuck around and murder motherfuckers. While it has been fun, that's not all I'm here to do. I've never had a reason to do anything else. My drive to train, to conquer, to see blood spill, it all came with the reason to protect myself. I was tired of being pushed around by my siblings, mainly Greer. I wanted to be ready. I wanted to be bigger and stronger than him physically because against him, brains didn't matter.

Although my strength helped me with my position here in the

Brotherhood, I thought my time here at Blackwood would help me find what I was meant to do. Because let's be so fucking for real, who the hell would be put on Earth with the sole purpose of murder?

Sounds fucking crazy if you ask me.

But nothing has sparked my interest. Tools and toys have filled up my room over the years. I've switched my major almost ten times in the span of these four years. That's how fucking lost I felt when it came to my future. The only thing that stuck was the power kick that courses through me when I slice a motherfucker's neck open.

The rush flows through me instantly and my mind brings the most perfect memory to the forefront.

Verena is coated in blood, standing before Leo, cutting his fingers off and carving letters into his fucking skin. My erection aches as his screams fill the room and the scent of his blood flows through the air. A sense of calmness washes over me and all I can think about is how fucking delectable Verena looks while she's in control.

Oh, how I'd wish she'd take control of me.

The power emanates off of her being, from the top of her head to the tips of her fingertips and toes. My little monster is fucking dynamic and dominating. I always knew she had it in her. All she had to do was believe it herself.

Look at her fucking go.

Professor Dimwit wraps up his lecture, his voice cutting through my memories and bringing my attention back to the somber reality I'm living every second I'm not in Verena's presence. He says his usual parting words and I'm racing out the door and back to my house in a flash.

ARRIVING AT MY PLACE, I check our mailbox and find a package and some small envelopes. There's one addressed to Eli with lipstick marks all over it.

Wonder who the special lady is. The initials "MD" are written in the top left corner with no return address. I shrug my shoulders and walk inside, sliding the envelope underneath his door. I toss the rest of the mail onto the table and look at who the package belongs to.

Me? Maybe it's that vial necklace I ordered for myself after we got back from our little road trip. My dick jerks at the thought of wearing Verena's blood around my neck, the vial resting over my heart.

I rip open the package but there's no necklace, no vial, nothing. Just...pictures?

Picking up the photos, I thoroughly examine them and when I recognize the luscious black hair and dark eyeliner, I know exactly who these photos are of.

My little monster.

My Verena.

My everything.

Photos of her walking the dogs, going to class, even one of us overlooking the balcony after sex on our road trip. On every picture, her face has been scratched out with red ink. Is someone threatening her by sending me these images? Who could be behind this?

Whoever they are. They better count their fucking days.

36

GRIMM

I HAVEN'T BEEN able to leave Verena's side. She's not aware there's a third trying to weasel their way into our relationship and won't take the hint that three is a fucking crowd and they aren't wanted here. But I have been her shield and shadow whether she's aware of it or not. I've skipped my classes and meetings this week in fear of someone getting to her the moment I took my eyes off her. I saw how that worked out with Emmett and I'll be damned if any one of us have to go through that fear and turmoil again.

My phone vibrates in my pocket and I retrieve it to see my little monster's contact lighting up my screen.

VERENA

I miss you. Wish I was in your arms and not in class. 😳

ME

Miss you more. Can't wait to kiss you.

VERENA

Yes, please! Kiss me to deathhh

ME

I'd love nothing more than that. Maybe choke you a little, rail you good, and then hold you gently in my arms before I kiss you to death.

VERENA

That idea sounds like a 10/10. I'm in class until 4:30. Pick me up and we can walk over to my place. No one will be home this afternoon so we have the whole place to ourselves. After we have Mom and Dad time, we can have a family snuggle date. 😉

My dick jerk in my jeans at her mention of family. The four of us create the only true family I've ever known. The only family to spark consistent joy in my life. The family I want to keep forever, same from pain and the evils of the world. The organ in my chest is sprung at the idea of a family snuggle date, but her referring to us as Mom and Dad did something else to me entirely.

I want nothing more than to worship her every inch, thank every god for her presence, her heart, and her soul.

With the anxiety in my chest growing, knowing I'd be with her soon, I confirm our date and take a deep breath, attempting to shove any negative thoughts out of my mind. I'd ask Eli for his help and we would figure it out together. I'll do everything possible to keep Verena out of harm's way. I'll get all the answers I'm looking for even if I regret ever knowing.

37

VERENA

BUTTERFLIES SWIRL in my stomach at the prospect of having family time with Grimm.

I never expected to use Grimm and family time in the same sentence, yet here I am.

It feels fucking *wonderful.*

My art professor wraps up the lesson for the day and hands out pieces of paper that list the guidelines for our final assignment of the year.

With my spark and flow back, I'm thrilled to be able to create again. Sketches have taken up the majority of my notebook and when I'm not drawing, I'm pouring out words. Whether I'm writing in my notes app, on pen and paper, or behind my laptop, my brain fires ideas off one after another and I race to catch the ideas on paper.

I'm almost done with the first draft of a short story I've been writing. I'm thinking of having him read it tonight after I give him a little present I have waiting for him at the house.

He's sneaky, but I'm sneakier.

I ordered myself a couple of those vial necklaces. Grimm doesn't ask for much and I want nothing more than to give him the one small thing he did request. He saved me in ways I never thought imaginable and I am forever grateful for my eternal lover. The other night, I swiped a knife from the kitchen and slid it across my palm.

The ruby liquid filled the vial quickly and after I reached the desired amount, I cleaned and wrapped the cut, then sealed the vial. My stomach flooded with butterflies both good and bad.

I really hope he was serious about this whole blood-on-a-necklace thing because I don't think I'd ever recover if he wasn't.

Along with the vial and the story, I want to show him the piece I created with us and our relationship as the inspiration. Tonight will be filled with surprises.

BACK AT THE HOUSE, we walk the dogs, feed them their dinner, and let them roam free. The suspicious eyes they give us every time we walk into the room without them makes me double over.

They know what Mom and Dad are up to.

As soon as the door closes behind us, Grimm wraps his arms around my waist, picks me up, and tosses me onto the bed. I fall on my back and break out in another fit of giggles.

Crawling across my bed, I pluck a preroll from my nightstand and spark it. Grimm undresses and only once he's fully naked, does he come over to take a hit.

"I'll hold this. You get naked." He orders. His voice sends shivers down my spine, causes every goosebump to raise along my body, and did I mention the absolute waterfall that he created between my thighs?

I sit on my heels and lift my shirt. Unclasping my bra, I let my heavy breasts fall out of the fabric. My nipples protrude, anxious to feel his hands caress my skin.

"Mm, you look so fucking perfect. I've been thinking about diving in between those thighs all goddamn day. No meal beats you. I'd have you for breakfast, lunch, and dinner if I could." He rumbles, as I flip onto my back and shimmy out of my jeans and thong.

"Well that wouldn't be sustainable, now would it?" I chuckle.

Grimm scoffs, "I'm positive it's the most sustainable food option I've got. Everything else is chemicals balled up in bright packaging. I'd take you over that, any day, any time."

I feel my cheeks redden at his words. He climbs into bed with me and we embrace under the sheets, passing the joint back and forth. We smoke it until it's nothing but the filter and toss it into the ashtray on my nightstand.

The smell of smoke on his breath, mixed with his usual sandalwood scent sends a rush throughout my body. That usual heat forms at the apex of my thighs and as Grimm runs his hands along my skin, I can't help but melt right into him. Being in his grasp is nothing short of lustful.

He tucks my hair behind my ear and cups my face, "You are everything I've ever wanted. I promise I'll spend the rest of my life making sure you never forget that."

And the basement is officially flooded.

I smile softly and place my hand on his cheek, "I love you. Let me show you just how much."

Slipping underneath the blanket, I align myself with Grimm's impossibly thick cock. It causes the blanket to tent and my mouth to water. I slide my tongue from the base of his shaft to his leaking crown. I want to trace every vein and commit its path to memory.

Grimm moans his approval, motivating me to continue on. I take him into my mouth, slowly coating all nine inches in my saliva. I bob my head along his shaft, pulling the sweetest whimpers from his lips.

I'll never get over how he responds to me. I drip for him, but he melts for me.

Releasing him from my mouth with a pop, I crawl back up his body and straddle him. When we come face-to-face, he's got one hand on the back of my neck pulling me into him, and another on my lower back holding me steady. We kiss passionately and there's no rush for the actual act of sex. Grimm is the first man I've been with that has showed me sex isn't only for his pleasure.

Yes, I've gotten myself off more than anyone else ever could. But that statement has officially been debunked, thanks to him. Every touch is filled with love, and the desire to not only make himself feel good, but me too.

I pull back from the kiss and reach a hand behind me to spread myself open. His cock slides right in and once I'm fully seated, we moan once more in unison. I rock back and forth against him, feeling every inch of him impale me. His hands grip onto my waist, most likely bruising the skin, but in the best way possible.

He guides my body against his and we move in unison. It's a dance we've done before but leaves me in shock every time. His attention to my pleasure is breathtaking and only brings me to my release that much quicker.

His hand comes up my clit and his thumb makes smooth circles, steadily building my already growing orgasm. My heart rate picks up as I continue to rock against him. I grip his chest hairs and pull slightly, making him wince, but a groan follows and I know he's floating in the same blissful paradise.

"Yes, baby. Show me who owns this cock. It's got your name written all over it. Claim it, claim me. I want to be yours. I want to be owned by you." His words, though unexpected, send a rush of adrenaline through me and my orgasm crescendos, crashing against me like a tsunami. It comes without warning, and I feel my release spill out of me. My eyes flutter to a close as I pulse around his cock.

Grimm growls as he props me up, spreads my cheeks, and starts pounding into me from underneath. He pumps with such ferocity I feel my soul ascend to another dimension. His length penetrates me and just when he's about to cum, I feel another rush of chills and my vision goes black.

We finish together, his release filling me up. Spent and sweaty, I remain seated on him and rest my head on his chest. His hand comes up to pet the crown of my head and I sink deeper into him, holding this perfect moment for as long as I can.

"You hungry? I can order us some food." Grimm offers, his chest rising and falling at a steady pace as his heart rate slows.

I nod my head, eager to refuel and he punches in our usual order from my favorite Spanish restaurant. Standing, we walk into the bathroom to rinse off before the food arrives.

BACK IN MY ROOM, we're dressed and setting up the bed for our family snuggle date.

"While we wait for the food, I have something for you." I say, feeling the blush creep along my cheeks. *Dammit, I know he's mine but he still makes me so fucking nervous. That smile, those muscles, his third leg, those dimples, the rasp of his voice...once again, his dimples!*

His eyebrow perks up, "I'm intrigued, do tell."

Padding over to my desk, I open the first drawer and take out the small black box that holds the vial of blood on a chain. I bought a second necklace in case Grimm wanted to return the favor, but there's no pressure. It'll remain in the drawer until he's ready.

Fuck, I hope it's not too much.

I present the box to him and his eyes twinkle as he beams at the idea of me giving him anything. Placing the box in his hands, he opens it up and pulls the necklace from its enclosure. When the vial dangles just around his eye level, his pupils almost pop out of his skull.

"You really did it? Is this a vial of your blood, little monster?" He asks and I nod my head slowly. I thought it was impossible for his smile to grow any larger, but Grimm has consistently proved me wrong in so many of the best ways, I shouldn't even be surprised.

Without hesitation, Grimm slips the chain over his head and the vial sits perfectly over his heart. His eyes meet mine and they're filled with lust but also, earnest and genuine happiness. "No one has ever done anything like this for me. I love it." His confession tugs at my heartstrings. Knowing his childhood was rough and he felt alone majority of the time, makes my heart ache. It only drives my point to make him feel just as loved as he does for me.

"There's one more thing," I say with more confidence. The loss of my nerves makes room for the excitement coursing through me. I walk to the painting sitting in the corner of my room. I hold it so the art is facing me, hidden from Grimm's line of sight. When I reach him, he's sitting on the bed with a huge grin plastered on his face, his fingers twirling the vial.

"Careful now. My ego may blow up if you start showering me with gifts." He chuckles. "My birthday isn't for another few weeks."

His birthday. Shit, I didn't even know his birthday was coming up. For all I know about him, his birthday never came up in conversation.

"This has nothing to do with your birthday and everything to do with how much I love you. I want to show you that. Though, you're probably right. Your head is already so big, I'm afraid if I keep it up with the gifts, you'll topple over from the weight of your ego." We bust out laughing and when the laughter calms down, I clear my throat. "Okay, ready for the reveal?"

He nods and I spin the canvas around. His eyes fly to the image and butterflies begin doing summersaults in my stomach. *Please, love it. Please, fucking love it.*

"Verena, this is beautiful. Is this supposed to be us?" He asks.

"Mhm," I return and point to the name of the painting on the lower left corner underneath my signature.

"Eternal Lovers," he reads out loud and sits back on the bed as he swallows hard. His eyes meet mine, and by golly fucking gee, a tear slips out of the corner of his eye. "It's perfect. I love it. Thank you."

Taking the painting from my grip, he places it against the wall and stalks over to me, gripping underneath my thighs and picking me up. My legs wrap around back and he holds me close as he peppers kisses along my neck, whispering sweet nothings into my ear.

OUR FOOD ARRIVES and the family night begins. We stuff our faces and watch movies until our eyes forcibly shut. Nothing feels as peaceful as this.

I found everything I'd ever need in Grimm, my killer Prince Charming, my dark happily ever after.

38

GRIMM

SHE DID IT. She actually fucking did it. I have the privilege of wearing her blood around my neck. The vial lays overtop my rapidly beating heart.

The heart that only beats for her.

Our night together was just as amazing as every other night that came before it, but there was something special about those moments. The painting, the necklace, movie night in V's bed with one dog between my legs and the other between hers. It all felt so fucking right.

My phone buzzes uncontrollably and I pull it out to see what the fuck is up.

Text messages from my dad, Verena, and Eli come through all at once. I open V's thread first.

VERENA

Hey, Flame was sick this morning, not sure what happened. She was acting a little weird before I left for class. Whenever you can, swing by my place and check on her, please. Key is taped underneath the mailbox.

ME

Sure thing, pretty lady. Weird how?

VERENA

She was really lethargic. She's usually super pumped in the morning. Plus, I had to get up twice throughout the night to fill up her water bowl. I checked for a spill, but there was nothing.

ME

Okay, I'll keep you updated. I love you.

VERENA

Thank you. I love you more. 💋

With that being said, I gather my things and head over to Verena's. I'll be going to my writing class straight from her place, so I make sure I have my doodle-pad and pencil because in all actuality those are the only two supplies I need.

When I open the front door, there's a black padded envelope on the doorstep. I swipe it and check who it's for.

Me. Again.

I shut the door and walk down the cobblestone walkway while ripping the envelope open.

Another picture of Verena slips out. She's walking to class alone and from where the picture was taken, they were in close range.

If anyone touches a hair on her end, this entire fucking world will burn.

A small white paper slides out of the envelope and falls to the floor. I snatch it and unfold the paper. Messy handwriting stares back at me. Handwriting that I recognize but can't pinpoint from who or where exactly. My heart almost stops beating at the words scrawled across the paper.

Meet at this address, 7PM tonight. Come alone if you want her to survive. Pull a no-show or try to have your goons attack us, and it's game over.

815 Sycamore Ave - enter through the backdoor

I look around at my surroundings, hoping to spot the dickwad in the shadows lurking. With no luck, I punch the code into my phone and find my thread with Eli. His text message about a Brotherhood meeting goes unread as I send him a picture of the note and photo, then tell him to find me any and all information on this place. His response is prompt.

ELI

The house belongs to someone named Griffin Griswold.

My heart stops. Griffin? My fucking brother, Griffin? He's the one behind this? What the fuck could he want with Verena? A few more texts buzz in.

ELI

I can hack into the security cameras, see what's been happening there. I'll forward some footage.

Before you go, take an earpiece and a tracker. If you do need backup, holler into the earpiece and I'll take care of it from there.

Blowing out a breath of frustration, I run a hand through my curls and down my face. As soon as things start looking up, some dipshit decides to come around and fuck it up.

Whatever. I'll do anything required of me to keep Verena safe. I've done it once, I'll do it again.

Remembering I also received a message from my dad, I open his thread to a text inviting Verena and I to another family dinner, this time to celebrate my own birthday.

Fuck me. I hate birthdays.

I cave in, unable to deal with his pestering right now. If something happens to my little monster, there will be no birthday dinner. I'll be preoccupied finding the cuntbags who hurt her and ripping them apart. Limb by motherfucking limb.

Was it foolish of me to think our problems died with Leo? Because I'd be delighted to resurrect him and kill him again.

Scratch that.

I'd be delighted to fuck Verena in front of him again, and then watch her kill him for a second time.

My cock aches just thinking about seeing her in her best form. My little monster.

Whoever this asshole is has dedicated the time to crossing state lines to follow us and take pictures of us without our knowledge.

All I'm trying to do is fuck my girl, cuddle my girl, and smoke her out. Why does the universe need to make that such a taxing task? This year has already added on enough extra turmoil onto our life.

Running back into the house, I dial Eli's number before grabbing my other backpack that holds my guns and knives.

He picks up after a few rings, "What's up?"

"Yo, I have no time to wait. Is there an earbud at the house I can grab? I'm going to this address. Don't want to wait any longer." I say as I race upstairs and beeline for his room.

"Uh, yeah. There should be one ready to go. It's in the blue case on the top left of my desk. Pop it in and power it up. I'll listen in and have guys on standby if you need backup." He answers.

"Awesome, thanks man." I hang up and bolt to the garage, hopping into my McLaren and speeding down the highway to 815 Sycamore Avenue.

MY CAR HIDES in the shadows as I watch the still mansion before me. Three blacked out cars sit in the driveway and I speak to Eli through my earpiece. "Eli, can you hear me?"

His voice sounds through the earpiece, "Yeah. Tell me everything you see. I'll be here."

Digging through my bag, I strategically hide three knives and two guns on my person. I've got one knife hidden in each boot, plus an additional one tucked into my belt. One gun rests in a holster on my side and the other is hidden away in the interior pocket of my leather jacket.

I step out of the car and walk around the building until the back-door is within my line of sight.

"There's no one here." I say to Eli.

"None that you know of. Be aware. Don't let your guard down for shit." He responds.

He's right. I need to be vigilant. This is a life or death matter and pertains to the person who means the most to me in this world. Without her, I am nothing. Without her, there is no me. I was a shell of myself before but now that I've felt that sensation of true love and harmony, I don't want to go back to the emptiness that held me captive before.

Knocking on the back door, I wait for an answer. When none comes, I turn the doorknob and it opens with ease. I step inside to the dimly lit entryway and close the door behind me.

"Door was unlocked. So far, I'm the only presence." I update.

I take two steps away from the door before the lights switch on and an unfamiliar man is seated before me at a large office desk.

"Hello, Mr. Griswold, is it?" The man asks, his voice deep and husky.

"Who's asking?"

"I am." Another voice sounds from the corner and a figure stands in the shadows. It walks toward the middle of the room coming into light.

Fucking Greer Griswold.

"You're the prick that's been following us around?" I ask in disbelief.

He laughs, "I thought you'd enjoy my company, little brother. I'm offended."

"Three's a fucking crowd. What the hell do you want, Greer?" I spit.

"Funny you should ask. I want vengeance. Not only did you fuck up my life, but you hurt my friend, Grimm. Where's Leo? I know Verena was his girl. But you seemed to snatch her up so effortlessly after he fell off the face of the fucking earth. Was that your plan all along? Manipulate her into thinking you loved her when really you just wanted to get to Leo." He takes a few steps closer to me and we stand toe-to-toe. "I mean, I get it. She's a fine piece of a-"

He doesn't get to finish his sentence. Before I can render my thoughts, my fist rears back and connects with Greer's ugly ass face. "Don't say another fucking word about her."

Greer licks the blood pouring from his upper lip and smiles a wicked grin. "Or what? You're going to kill me the same way you killed Leo?"

I stand tall, hovering above Greer. He's not a big guy but his confidence is what makes people fear him. I've feared him for far too long. He's nothing but another person, made of flesh, blood, and bone, same as me. Instead of running away from my fears, they need to be conquered. I'm done tolerating his bullshit.

"I just might." I say, my tone even though I can feel my blood pressure rising with every pulse of my heart. "How'd you like that birthday Leosagna?"

Greer's brows furrow in confusion as he puts the pieces together. "You fucking made me eat him?!" He yells, his voice bouncing off the walls and echoing throughout the large space.

I hold up my hands in defense, "I didn't *make* you do anything. You're a big boy, you make your own choices. You chose to eat a delicious meal that was specially made for you. I'm not seeing the problem here."

Greer shakes his head profusely in anger, "You're lying. You're fucking lying. Tell me where his body is. Right. Fucking. Now."

A laugh bubbles inside of me and when I can't hold it in, it falls off my lips. Greer's face turns an undeniable shade of burnt orange as his patience wears thin. "You've digested him already. He's floating around in a sewer disguised as your shit, Greer."

Rage courses through every one of his veins as they protrude through his skin. His yells fill the room as he flips over chairs and pulls at the strands of his hair.

It's crazy what two minutes can do.

When I walked in here, he was calm, cool, and collected. Now he's losing his shit over eating an asshole that deserved to die. Granted, I guess everyone would like to know when they're eating human meat, but Greer is an asshole too so by simple process of elimination, it was information that I didn't feel the need to disclose.

"We were supposed to leave together, you fucking idiot!" Greer yells as he whips a gun from underneath his belt and points it in my direction.

"What are you talking about, man? I'm not playing some decoder game with you. How do you know Leo and why is his death so important to you? Did he owe you money?" I probe, annoyed that I'm going in circles with Greer of all people.

His face twists as if I asked him the most ridiculous question. "No, he didn't owe me money. Leo was…my boyfriend." Greer admits.

"Your what?" I question, my jaw falls slack because of the absolute wrecking ball he just sent my way.

"No more questions. Enough is enough." His finger squeezes the trigger and a sharp pain radiates throughout my shoulder and along my chest.

Eli's voice sounds through the earpiece. "Grimm, are you okay? Who are you there with? Who's Greer? Do I need to send backup?"

I fall back against the wall for stability. The tapping of Greer's soles against the floor sound throughout the room and get closer, and closer, and closer, until he's at my feet. "I've hated you for such a long time, you know that? Our family would have been perfect if it wasn't for you. Our mom wouldn't have missed out on so much of our lives. You drove her away. You and your deadbeat cunt of a mother." He shoves a finger into the wound on my shoulder. "You took away my mother and you took away the one fucking person I loved."

I'm so fucking confused.

"So that's why you're following us around? Because Leo got what he deserved? I'm not fucking following. Why was he so goddamn important to you?" I question, once again.

"He was going to leave her!" He screams, the echo of his voice booming throughout the room. "He was tired of hiding. Tired of using her as a cover. His anger was taking over him more days than it wasn't.

We just wanted to be happy. We just wanted to be together." The barrel of the gun touches my forehead. "But you fucked it all up by trying to play the hero. He wouldn't have done anything that bad to her. She would have survived with a few scratches and a good story to tell her fucking kids. But it's a life for a life so either you die, or she does."

39

VERENA

IT'S BEEN hours and Grimm hasn't given me any update on Flame.

I hope she's okay. I hope she didn't get into an edible or something. I'd be the worst fucking dog mom if she got into an edible. Grimm would never trust me again. Is that why he hasn't answered? Because something terrible happened and I can't be trusted?

I rush home, my long legs making themselves useful to trek across campus and back to my unit quickly. When I open the front door, I sprint to my room to find both of the dogs laying comfortably on their respective beds. Flame's food and water bowls are empty, a sign that she did in fact eat her food and may be feeling better. I refill her water and give her some pets while I try to get into contact with Grimm. It's not like him to not come through, even for the simplest of favors.

Finding his contact, I dial his number and it rings for a minute before prompting me to leave a voicemail. Repeating the process, I leave him four voicemails before my annoyance turns into worry.

My books fall on my bed and I snatch my purse before bolting out the front door and racing over to the RSB house. When I arrive, I scurry over to the garage door and peak inside the clear window. I notice his blacked out McLaren is missing from the garage. *So if he isn't here or with the dogs, where the fuck would he be?*

Losing my patience, I make my rounds to peak in through various windows before finally giving up and pounding on the front door. A moment later it swings open and Eli stands in its frame. "Oh, perfect! You're here! I need your-"

He cuts me off, "Yeah, doesn't fucking everybody. Get in the car, we'll talk on the way." His shoulder brushes mine and I follow him to the car.

"Hey, minus the attitude. I'm just looking for Grimm." I spit back.

"We have to go save his ass." He retorts.

We? Save? His ass? When the fuck did I transport myself into a Marvel movie?

"What the hell is going on?" I ask as Eli tosses his car keys to me.

"I need you to drive. I'll tell you what I know. But you need to focus, Verena. It's the only way we'll be able to help him." Eli says, and my heart thumps so loudly his voice begins to fade into a soft mumble.

He saved my life, it's only right I try to save his, no matter what demons I have to battle first.

40

VERENA

WE'RE SPEEDING down the highway in Eli's Lamborghini, and he's repeating to me everything he hears in his earpiece. What I've gathered so far is:

1. Grimm's brother, Greer, has been following us around, taking pictures and mailing them to Grimm.

2. Grimm kept this from me because he wanted to handle it on his own — and look how well that's working out for him!

3. Grimm is hurt. *Yes, I am absolutely freaking the fuck out, thanks for asking.*

4. And by far the most craziest part of this whole ordeal, Grimm's brother, Greer, was Leo's secret lover and he was just using our relationship as a coverup.

All of the facts whiz around my brain, exhaustion pulling at me and the real fun hasn't even started yet. We pull up to the address at the same time as a blacked out Escalade settles in a spot right out front.

A handsome man, fully dressed in a suit and loafers, with coiffed hair gets out of the car and I recognize him immediately. "Griffin?" I say out loud.

"You know him? Who is that to you?" Eli pesters.

"To me? No one, really. That's Grimm's older brother. I had dinner with his family a few weeks ago. But he isn't close to his siblings, why would he be here?" I question, a migraine creating a home at the forefront of my mind.

Eli sighs and opens his door, "I guess we'll find out. Here," he opens his glove compartment and hands me a sleek black pistol, "hold onto this. If I tell you to shoot, you shoot. No questions, no hesitations. I don't know what Grimm is involved in, but it's up to us to help him."

I tuck the gun into my belt and ask, "What about Emmett? Jaden?"

"Not here, are they?" Eli snaps then huffs out a breath. "Sorry, Jaden is studying and Emmett wouldn't pick up the damn phone. Since him and Blair returned home, he's been up her ass. I get they went through something huge, but we need him too, and he's not here. We're not the main priority anymore and that's fine. We'll get by without them. Just do as I say, and no more questions."

I open the door and follow Eli around to the back of the house. He swings the door open to find Grimm, leaning on the arm of a chair, supporting himself against a wall. There's a rip in his leather jacket from where I assume he was shot and the bullet went through.

Greer stands over him yelling some nonsensical bullshit. Griffin is nowhere to be seen.

Eli raises his gun and shouts at Greer, "Put the fucking gun down!"

A man comes rushing toward us and Eli guns him down before he's within breathing distance. Two shots to the head and he's done.

"Eli? Verena!" Grimm grumbles. He tries to make his way over to us but the pain in his shoulder holds him in place. "What are you doing here, little monster?"

Greer chuckles, "How cute. Your little monster. You know, Leo was my little sugar daddy. It was his favorite candy, but he also loved to spoil me. Jewelry, trips, cars, and all the other beautiful material things in life were mine. But his heart was mine too, not yours to take, and certainly not hers." He shoots daggers my way and I finally put two-and-two together.

"So you're the reason he treated me like shit?" I say with a laugh. "Yikes, he could've done a lot better. Matter of fact, he did. Some of the women he cheated on me with were bombshells. Fucking supermodels! I hate to break it to you, Greer, but neither of us were his one or his only. We were people he kept around to occupy his time and in my case, to be his punching bag whenever he pleased."

Greer growls and Grimm speaks up, "V, what are you doing?"

"Being fucking honest!" I shout. "All these years I thought Leo had some weird fucking attachment with his mom, but those trips were for you two. His mom was a coverup for everything, just like I was was for him. To aid him in keeping up with appearances. It makes perfect sense knowing his family. I was the scapegoat. I was his armor because he wasn't ready to come out." I pull the gun out from my belt and point it directly at Greer.

"Put the fucking gun down and get the fuck away from him." I order and Greer looks me dead in the eyes and laughs.

We'll see who's laughing after I-

POW! POW! POW!

Three bullets sail through the air. One punctures Greer's stomach, the second, his ribs, and the last, skins his arm. My aim isn't the best, I was aiming for his heart, *or rather his penis.*

Greer cries out in pain from the rounds that pierce his skin. "Fuck! You fucking cunt! It was clear as fucking day why Leo didn't want to be with you. He always complained about your complaining. Whined about your whining. Fussed over your fussing. You were nothing special to him. Expecting princess treatment when you're the byproduct of Lucifer and whatever dark princess you believe in, is fucking diabolical."

POW!

Another shot rings out and I lower my arm slowly. "My fucking dick!" Greer shouts, falling onto the ground and cupping the area. He spews and hurtles insult after insult my way. My legs feel like jello but I place one foot in front of the other and walk over to him.

Our toes touch and I bend down so that we're eye level. "Princess treatment?" I ask softly with a chuckle. " I never asked for princess treatment. I asked to be treated like a human being. Respect, boundaries, bodily autonomy. Pretty basic wants and needs if you ask me. But you don't know me, Greer. You only know whatever lies Leo spewed." My voice changes from its soft cadence, to a deep and visceral tone I've never used.

"Take what he said about me and exaggerate it, make it worse. I'm not a princess, I am not soft. I am not demure, nor am I delicate. I am your worst fucking nightmare, Greer Griswold."

Another door from across the room swings open and Griffin enters the room, "What the fuck is going on in here?"

41

GRIFFIN

I'VE BEEN AWAY for three weeks. My trip to to Catalan was a fucking success but I am drained. All I want is three more weeks of sleep.

When I enter the house, the place is a fucking mess. There's left-over takeout littering my coffee table, my fucking kitchen island has dirty napkins and soda cans along it, and my biggest fucking pet peeve: a full fucking trashcan.

I let Greer crash here sometimes when he's going through shit with his boy-toys and ladies of the night. He's never been able to hold something for himself whether that be a job, school, or even short-term odd jobs. Kid is really a useless vessel of muscle and bones. I've offered him a position within The Pyramid and he's declined multiple times.

Shaking my head, I inhale and exhale my frustrations as I come across more garbage littered behind the couch. I bend over to pick it up when a curdling scream breaks out. My head snaps to the back room, where I believe the sound to be coming from. Immediately, I drop the trash in my hands and storm to the back room.

Swinging it open, I see two of my brothers on the floor bleeding with bullets through them. "What the fuck is going on in here?" I shout.

Everyone turns to face me and their faces don't falter or show any weakness.

"Your twerp of a little brother is one of the biggest douchebags I've ever met. Considering he also fucked another one of the earth's biggest douchebags, that just so happens to be my ex-boyfriend, who I killed and baked into lasagna." The dark haired vixen speaks.

Huh?

"Now he's trying to hurt Grimm over his achy, breaky heart, I am *not* having that shit." Her chest rises and falls, her confidence wavering, but I am in awe of her bravery.

"So my booger of a brother has," I stop to count the amount of bullet holes peppering Greer's body, "four rounds buried into his flesh because he's fucking with your happily ever after?" I ask, the familiar minx.

She crosses her arms over her chest, pushing her breasts together. I'm no better than any other man. Huffing out a breath, she says, "Exactly." Turning back to face Greer, she raises the gun, "Now, where were we?"

Greer holds his junk and groans as he rolls about the floor. Fucking pathetic, we were taught to handle any bullet much better than that. Our grandfather was one of the founder fathers of the Catalan Mafia for crying out loud.

A few feet away, Grimm cradles his shoulder, which is also seeping blood. "So, Grimm, what'd you do this time to piss him off?"

Grimm gazes at me, confused, "What the fuck are you talking about, Griff?"

"What petty bullshit did you do to set off the motherfucker again?" I repeat.

Grimm stands in a fit of annoyance and rage, "Fuck you! For years you've all ganged up on me, shoving my head into toilets, putting cleaning products in my food, planting bugs in my bed, and that's just the tip of the fucking iceberg. What you guys did as a group doesn't compare to what Greer was doing on the sidelines."

He stand and stalks over to Greer, grabs him by the chest, and lifts him up as if he's light as a feather. "A simple death is too fucking easy for you. You're coming with me."

I've never seen this side of Grimm before. We all had our reasons for picking on him, doesn't make them valid but from my collection of sidebar conversations with the rest of my siblings, it was something we regretted doing as dumb kids losing our two-parent household. We were too selfish to think about what he was going through and there were too many of us for our dad to handle on his own, incidents were bound to slip through the cracks.

I walk over to the mini bar, pour myself a drink, and take a seat in the wooden chair. Only then do I notice another lifeless body on my floor, "Do you guys know how long it's going to take to get the blood stains out of these floors?"

Making eye contact with Grimm, I speak, "What did Greer do to you that was so bad?"

Greer groans once again on the floor, "Fucking nothing. He's a lying little shit. Help me, Griffin. My fucking balls are hanging on by a thread and the thread is my fucking pube!"

"Enough!" I yell in Greer's direction. I motion to Grimm that he has the floor and he takes a deep breath before spilling all the dirty secrets he's kept to himself about the abuse he endured from Greer. Some of the stories are too gruesome for me to commit to memory wholeheartedly, but it's clear that Grimm has suffered the most out of all of us. His mother gave him up, left him with six siblings and a step-mother who didn't give two shits about him.

I feel for him. *Which is so fucking unlike me.*

I'm a cold bastard. My ice box is my strength, but something about the look in Grimm's eyes reminds me of that little boy who was pushed into the pool right after the pool ladder was removed. I see the boy who was gasping for air, begging to be saved, begging for his life to be spared. That same little boy is asking for someone to help him now, for someone to choose him the way he has wanted to be chosen his entire life.

"I'll help you." I cave.

Grimm's brows furrow, "The fuck is that supposed to mean?"

Sighing, I come to terms with what has to happen and who I need to support. "Kill him, Grimm. I won't say a word. I'll help you cover it up. But…I think I owe you."

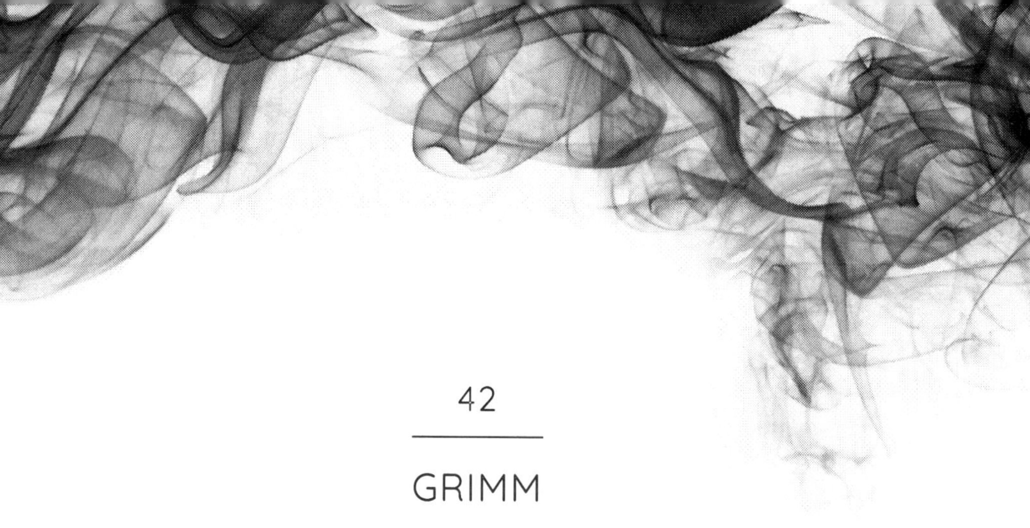

42

GRIMM

DAMN right he fucking owes me.

"Eli, put Greer in the car. Verena, ride back with Eli and make sure he doesn't pull any shit in the backseat. Bring him to the tunnels. We're having some fun tonight." I order.

They leave without another word and Griffin and I are left to discuss what he means by his previous statement. "What do you mean you owe me?" I ask, unsure if this is just another trap to catch me in.

"I'm sorry, little brother. I'm the oldest and it has always been my job to protect you. You were thrown into a den of wolves with no guidance or shelter. It should've been me, but I was drowning too deep in my own shit, I didn't think I could save us both." He confesses.

"Well you did save me that one time," I say with a chuckle.

"Yeah, and I could've done more. I should have. I'm sorry. If you'll forgive me, I've got a high-ranking position on my team for muscle. It's yours if you want it." Griffin offers, and I am taken aback by his politeness, his genuineness, and his apology.

"Thanks, man. I appreciate it. Kind of late by a few years," I joke, "but maybe, in all actuality, you were right on time. I'd love a spot if you'll have me. My current gig is coming to an end and I wasn't too sure about what to do." I admit.

An idea comes to mind, so I milk the opportunity for all that it's worth. "Do you need anyone in the tech department? My friend, the one who left with *my* woman," I put emphasis on the word because I saw how he was ogling her, *again*, "he's a wizard behind the computer. He can hack any camera, shut down any power grid, and get you immediate access into any place of your choosing. If there's a spot for him, I'm in."

A few seconds of silence go by and Griffin sticks out his hand, "You have a deal."

We can't turn back the hands of time, but sometimes a late apology is better than no apology at all.

I bring my hand up to meet his and we shake. Our understanding of each other just multiplied to a magnitude I thought was fucking impossible. But, I'm thankful for the insane turn of events for leading me to greater things, and I'm stoked about taking Eli along for the ride. I know he'd have no problem picking up a job literally anywhere else. With a record as impressive as his, I wouldn't be surprised if he snagged a spot at the White House, but then he'd be way too cool to hang with me and even though I've never told him, and never will tell him out loud, I fucking love that crazy bastard.

TONIGHT, we had a guys night. The first one in a long fucking time. We smoke, drank, finally saw Emmett for more than a fleeting moment, it was great. Eli had the spontaneous idea to get pierced so him and Emmett are rocking pretty new jewelry and Jaden and I have some new ink. I haven't showed Verena yet, but I can't wait to see her reaction.

After all the guys trickled into their rooms, I asked John, the tattoo artist, if he'd stick around and give me a few more pieces. In addition to the *little monster* tattoo across my heart, I've got the letter V on the inside of my ring finger on my left hand, and Verena's eyes on my forearm.

I can't wait to show her, and I will very soon, but tonight, I'm paying Greer a visit.

Greer has been kept down in the tunnels for about two and half weeks, chained to a wall. It felt wrong to let him off with a quick and easy death. I figured it was a fair trade to make him suffer one day, for every year he tormented me.

Seventeen days total.

I hope this has felt like the longest pitstop to Hell. I hope that in death, he doesn't forget this pain.

HE'S BEEN SHACKING up with my old pal, Braxton. Greer fucking hates it and I relish in his suffering. I even asked Emmett for his help to install cameras so I could keep an eye on my little toy whenever I was away.

We've had some good times these last few weeks. On his first night, I gave him a septum piercing with a staple gun. I didn't want to send him into shock and therefore grant him the early death he's wishing for, so I waited for the piercing to heal before I did anything else.

About four days later, I carved a thousand little nicks into his skin. They bled just enough that they itched and burned his skin for days on end as the cuts were healing.

Once they scabbed over, I took one out of Emmett's book and sliced off his skin in a few different sections throughout his body. Layer by layer, inch by inch, he was left behind with raw, pink flesh. I took a bottle of acid to his skin, and his wails for help became desperate.

"Please, Grimm. I'm sorry. We can work this out. It was all just a big misunderstanding." Greer begged.

"No can do, *big bro*, I have this motto. It goes like this, 'You go low, I go to Hell's basement.' It's a simple concept, really. No amount of your charm assaults will get you out of this. You are a dead man. Accept it." I growled.

Tonight, there's nothing planned. Who knows if he'll live to see another day?

I enter the tunnels, backpack of tools hanging off my shoulder, and whistle while I strut down the halls. When I reach the door, I undo the safety locks and drag open the heavy cement. "What the fuck is up, bro? How ya been? Hopefully not sitting around too much." I double over in a laugh.

He's fucking chained to the wall, he's been on his ass for two weeks.

I walk over to him and drop the bag, then sort through its contents. The glint of my butcher knife catches my eye immediately. Gripping the handle with a grin, I pull out the knife and wave it in front of Greer. "Good way to go, eh? Should have made you into an *A Thousand Ways to Die* episode." I lift my hands dramatically as if I'm reciting a title, "We call this one, "The *Oh, Brother!*' It originates from a story of a dimwit who fucked over his innocent kid brother one too many fucking times."

Lifting the knife above my head, I bring it down fast and hard, severing his wrist and causing his limp arm to fall out of the chain. Greer's scream pierce my ears and it'd be painful if it didn't feel so goddamn good.

The butcher knife is above my head and coming down once again in a flash, severing the opposite hand this time. I repeat the process on both of his ankles and finish off by burying the butcher knife into his neck.

His lifeless eyes stare back at me and I feel absolutely nothing. No sympathy. No regrets. Just peace and serenity that my biggest problems on this earth are just floating souls making amends with their lives and their deaths. They aren't my problem anymore.

It feels so good to be free.

43

VERENA

GRIMM IS FULLY HEALED. He's like fucking wolverine. I expected a gun shot wound to the shoulder would take a few months to heal, but within a week, he was back to throwing me around like the rag doll I love to be treated as.

Grimm moved in with me temporarily, for safety purposes.

Or at least that's what we told everyone. "Grimm will stay here because I can cater to him easier if he's with me physically."

It wasn't a total lie, but I need to be so fucking for real. I'm ecstatic that he's here twenty four hours a day and seven days a week. Despite his injuries, we've had the best times.

Sex, snacks, and smoke sessions have become a daily routine and I never want it to end. My gym membership hates me, I haven't been since before I baked Leo into a pasta dish. It was his membership and he required me to go every single day. On the days I didn't have class, twice a day was the stipulation.

But in these last few months, I've gained a few pounds and I have never loved my body more. My muscles haven't lost any definition, though. Grimm and I work out together plenty.

We just finished a quick and steamy workout a few hours ago and Grimm drifted off to sleep peacefully, but I have been up rubbing my thighs together, desperate for any amount of friction. Grimm has shown me a love like no other and my body reacts to it physically. All. The. Time. My pussy is trained to drip when he looks at me, touches me, speaks to me, or breathes around me.

I'm not complaining. I love it. I love him.

Our public displays of affection have grown more common over the last few weeks and I feel like I'm stepping into the skin of the woman I was meant to be.

Confident.

Loved.

Valued.

Happy.

Although it was far from ideal, I wouldn't change my past for the world. What was meant to be, will be and I take pride in knowing that everything that comes to be in my life will be because if there's no rain, there won't be any flowers.

I TOSS and turn in the bed, unable to relax my mind that's currently swirling of thoughts about Grimm on top of me and pounding me into oblivion. I look over at him and he snores peacefully, his angled features look rather angelic when he's not on edge or constantly protecting me.

Reaching over, I softly swipe my hand across his chest. He stirs in his sleep, but ultimately grabs onto my thigh and drags me closer into him. My hand travels down his chest and over his stomach, to the bulge underneath the blanket.

His length in my hands send electric currents straight to my core. It awakens a primitive vixen within me that I can't explain nor control. When she's hungry, there's no stopping her.

I begin stroking Grimm's cock, the feel of his girth already causes my pussy to clench. I continue stroking as I whisper into his ear, "Wake up. Your lady needs to take what belongs to her."

Grimm mumbles and rubs his eyes, then squints before whispering, "Take me, I'm yours. And I'm so fucking thick for you, too."

His words cause my heart rate to accelerate as I press my lips into his neck, slowly descending to his collar bone and then to his chest. I find his nipple and swirl my tongue around his bud. He cups the back of my head gently and moans for me as I suck and pull on his nipple.

Continuing my descension, I stop along the way careful to leave hickeys for him to remember me by. *I love decorating my man.*

I lower myself until I'm eye level with the tip of his penis. I flick my tongue across the crown, collecting the beads of precum that have formed. Grimm groans and his dick twitches against my tongue, his veins rubbing against my muscle, eliciting another moan from him.

Once he gains his composure, Grimm also gains control. He presses me down on my back and flip onto his side so he's facing me. My head lays against one hand while the other snakes its way into the apex of my thighs. His finger swirl around in my wetness, coating them completely, before bringing them to his mouth and sucking them clean.

"The sweetest fucking ambrosia. I cracked the code." He says with a sly, sleepy grin. His raspy voice already has me teetering on the edge of my orgasm, but my gosh, that smile and those dimples set off a reaction in me like no other.

Grimm slips his finger back in between my legs and inserts two fingers into my pussy. He torturously slides them in and out with the pace of a snail, building up the anticipation in my body.

He slips his hand out from behind my head and shifts his weight so he's on top of me. His free hand transforms into a hand necklace decorating my décolletage. The other hand leaves my pussy and focuses on my clit, continuing to swirl his fingers in slow, soft circles. I'm so deep into the moment, that the rasp of his voice catches me off guard, "You want it? Then fucking take it."

Grimm thrusts inside of me until he's fully seated. He picks up the swirling motion to match the rhythm of his strokes and with every motion of his hips, I climb higher and higher to that feeling of pure ecstasy.

He grinds into me, the feeling resembling what I think it's like to be struck by lightening, so dangerous, yet so fucking thrilling.

"Fuck, Grimm, don't stop." I moan.

He shakes his head, reassuring me, "I won't baby. Take everything that you want. Take everything that you need. It's all for you. Every inch. Every drop."

A single tear falls out of my eye, the pleasure building inside of me soars to new heights I've never experience before. My vision dulls from his hold on my windpipe, and my orgasm comes barreling through me, wiping me out completely.

Grimm's hand falls from my neck and it's replaced with soft kisses trailing along my skin. He keeps himself inside of me as we drift off into a peaceful slumber.

TODAY IS THE DAY! It's Grimm's birthday, the first birthday I'm spending with him to be exact. This was the hardest gift-shopping ever. What was I supposed to get the alternative murderous giant? Some prerolls and his favorite cookies would have been just fine, I'm sure, but I wanted to do him one better. Today, I'll have him fill up the other vial necklace so I can wear it around my neck.

I find him in the bedroom rolling up a few joints and flash him a wide smile.

"What's up, beautiful?" He greets me with a gorgeous smile of his own.

"I want to give you your birthday gift. I figured now was the best time, so that we'd be able to match at dinner." I say, shyly.

"Alright, I'm ready. Should I close my eyes?"

I giggle, "Sure."

His eyes flutter close and I instruct him hold out his hands. I place the necklace and a razor in his palms and tell him to open his eyes.

At first, he look at the two objects with confusion, but then it clicks. "Is this a necklace for you? Do you want me to fill it up?" He asks, his eye gleaming with pride and appreciation.

I nod, "Yes, indeed. Same way you fill me up, to the brim." I wink and he bites his lip, nodding.

"Yes, ma'am. Coming right up." He stands and goes to the bathroom. Five minutes later, he emerges with a full vial of his dark red blood and my heart races at the sight. His hand is bandaged and the blood is already seeping through, but Grimm shows no sign of pain or discomfort.

"Turn around, let me put it on you." I do as he says, and he clips the necklace into place. The vial rests just above my heart, touching my bare skin. His warmth emanates from the vial and fills me with so much pride, I squeal.

Grimm's dimples make another appearance and we share a passionate kiss that may or may not have turned into something more.

After our needs are satisfied, we head to Greg's house for Grimm's birthday dinner. I noticed immediately that all the tension had disappeared without Greer's presence. Grimm got along decently well with the rest of his siblings now that there wasn't a Greer-sized blockade stopping that from happening.

No one spoke about Greer's absence, for everyone was secretly grateful for it.

But the one thing I am the most grateful for Is Grimm.

The things we've been through together have made us stronger, brought us closer, and because of it all, we shine brighter, we love harder.

I'd go the distance for him both in this lifetime and the next. It will always be him. It will always be us.

44

GRIMM

MY BIRTHDAY WENT off without a hitch and Verena gifted me the most amazing birthday gift I could ask for. We are forever bonded with one another.

Later that evening, I fucked her senseless as we both wore nothing but our vials of blood around our necks. We loved each other passionately for hours on end, never wanting the moment to end.

A few weeks after my birthday came graduation. After graduation, things were different. The original four were growing. Emmett ran off to New York with Blair, Verena and I got a small starter place together just off campus, Eli and I started working with Griffin, and Jaden, well, I'll save Jaden's story for another day.

This year has been the most exhausting, draining, and emotionally taxing year, but also the most rewarding and bittersweet. It's the end of an era. For the guys and myself, our college life is over, but the real world is just welcoming us in.

Let's fuck some shit up!

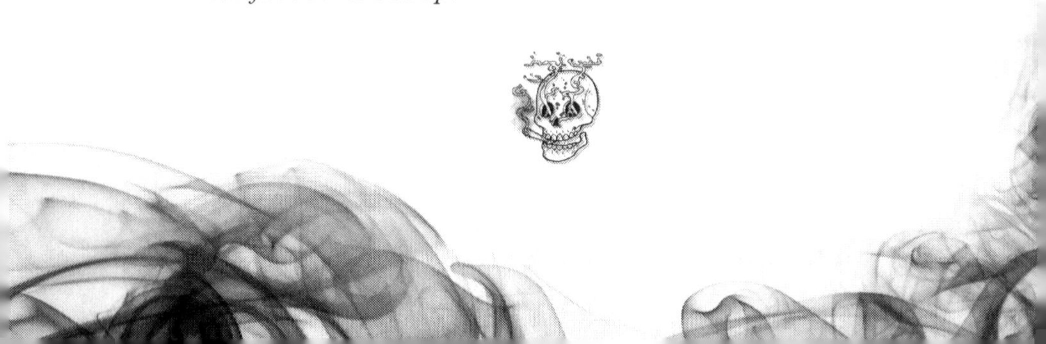

SOON AFTER GRADUATION, The Red Skull Brotherhood disbanded. With Emmett being the successor, he offered to pass it on to me, but there was no way in hell I wanted to be associated with a human trafficking ring. I had one condition, if I'm in charge, the Brotherhood gets shut down, and they come to work for me under Griffin's payroll. I had gathered a shit ton of muscle, brains, and businessmen for Griffin to use as he pleases. Him and his men welcomed us all with open arms.

The pieces of my life are all beginning to click into place seamlessly. After feeling like a pile of broken shards headed to the dumpster for so long, life proved to me that just because it's broken, doesn't mean you can't fix it.

Just because there's a couple of dings in the tool, doesn't deem it useless.

Chipped paint can still be beautiful.

Worn out art is still worthy.

I've learned so much about life, and those close to me in such a short amount of time. I've learned that sometimes these sinful little lies that cling to our backs need to be taken care of and tackled head on, so we're able to live out the life we truly deserve, not just life we think we deserve.

EPILOGUE

Three Years Later - VERENA

I BLOW out a deep breath as I wait behind the double doors of the venue. Greg stands next to me, ready to walk me down the aisle to Grimm, my future husband.

I always thought I'd be doing this with my father by my side, but the truth of the matter is that we don't have that relationship and we never will. It simply wasn't in the cards for us and I need to accept that. However, Greg has taken me in like one of his own. He provides the same treatment to me as he does to Gracie, his precious little girl.

When the wedding planning was set in motion, it was one of the first things we decided. He refused to let me walk down the aisle on my own and it touched my heart. I've felt so distant from my own father for such a long time, being embraced and welcomed into his family felt like coming home.

In true Verena fashion, I went for the more alternative Disney princess route, than actual Disney princess. Where the bouquets typically have shades of whites and yellows, mine is filled with dark purples, grays, and blacks.

My dress isn't white, or cream, or even a soft, subtle pink. Layers of midnight black tulle create the bottom of my gown and a vampiric corset accentuates my bust. The detailing on the corset was customized especially for our wedding and resembled the 'Eternal Lovers' painting I created for Grimm a few years back.

I finished the look with silver jewelry, black pumps with red bottoms, and siren-eye effect on my lids. I feel fucking amazing and I cannot wait to see the look on Grimm's face.

The double doors swing open and my eyes lock with his. He swallows hard before his mouth hangs open. I walk down the aisle, never breaking contact with him. When I reach his side, I whisper, "Close your mouth, you're going to catch flies," with a giggle.

The next ten minutes go by in blurry, exciting whirlwind. We recite our vows to one another and when I scan the crowd briefly, I noticed that everyone is emotional or teary-eyed.

They see our love. They feel it. And if I wasn't already sure, that was the best confirmation I could ever have.

We say 'I do' and share our first kiss as husband and wife, as Mr. and Mrs. Grimm Griswold. Boy, don't I love the sound of that.

Here's to the rest of our fucking lives.

Four years later - GRIMM

The last few years haven't been easy on Verena and I. After our honeymoon, we lived our life, just us and the dogs. But eventually, we found our home to be missing two little feet. We tried for a year to get pregnant but to no avail. Verena went to some specialists and was diagnosed with Endometriosis, therefore she wasn't able to get pregnant.

For now, we are the fun aunt and uncle that every kid prays for and every parent is jealous of because their kids love us.

Verena and I are naturals with kids and we've discussed looking into adoption, surrogacy, and even IVF. We aren't sure of the route we'll take just yet, but we're thankful for the options.

My little monster kick started her career as an artist with Emmett's art program, Painted Pathways. He owns one location here in Devil's Lake that is ran by his mother, and another location in New York that he runs himself. Emmett was looking to offer outreach classes but had trouble coming up with a program. Verena suggested a program where they bring all necessary art tools to the cancer patients in hospitals and provided art therapy. Emmett loved the idea so much, she was bumped up to co-director within two weeks of being employed there.

There's a few kinks we have to work out, like there always will be, but we couldn't be happier.

Here's to the unhinged, the unpredictable, the things that scare us and the ones that bring us comfort. Here's to healing. Here's to the future.

THE END

THANK YOU

Another perfect match in the Blackwood University realm! Did you fall in love with them as easily as I did?

Grimm and Verena have been my favorite characters to write thus far because this book has been made of moments in time from life experience and I've never been more nervous, yet proud of something I'm sharing. Thank you for loving them, supporting me, and taking the time to delve into the Blackwood University world.

I hope you enjoyed your time and plan on coming back soon for more!

ACKNOWLEDGMENTS

To my teams, thank you for your dedication to helping me curate and perfect Grimm and Verena's story.

To Sam and Ellie, another book, another man down! You guys have been here since the very beginning and riding the wave with you by my side has been the most epic and fulfilling ride. I can't thank you enough for the time and energy you dedicate to me and my book babies. I love you endlessly!

To Angel, Paula, Chloé, and Cris, you hype me up like no other. You show endless love and support to me not only as an author, but as my friends. You all have no idea how lucky I feel to have found friendships in each and every one of you. Thank you from the bottom of my heart. I love you bunches.

To my Smutitorian, thank you for being my ultimate muse for Grimm. From the music he loves, to his goofball ways, you helped me create one of my all-time favorite characters just by being you. Thank you for your love, your support, and your…physical contributions. I love you infinity times infinity.

To my readers, you guys have my whole heart. Your posts, your reviews, and the excitement you all show surrounding Blackwood University and the boys is absolutely insane! Never in a million years did I think I'd have my own little corner of the internet to create stories I love that you indulge in and find an escape with. I am eternally grateful to each and every one of you. Thank you for giving me a chance. I hope I don't disappoint.

ABOUT THE AUTHOR

SJ Ryder is a dark romance author from New Jersey. She has written through many periods of her life but since finding dark romance, it has been the number one thing that helped lead her onto her current path. SJ loves writing morally grey characters but also wants to use her writing platform to show all different scenarios, relationships, and backgrounds. Her stories may have you questioning your morals...in a good way, of course.

ALSO BY S.J. RYDER

Blackwood University

Pretty Little Fears

Devil's Night Duet

Eve of Screams

Hell's Hallow

COMING SOON

Eli & Aspen's Story

Jaden & …

Made in the USA
Columbia, SC
09 June 2025

59157982R00148